Storm Clouds Over Broombank

Sunday Times bestselling author Freda Lightfoot was born in Lancashire. She always dreamed of becoming a writer but this was considered a rather exotic ambition. She has been a teacher, bookseller in the Lake District, then a smallholder and began her writing career by publishing over forty short stories and articles before finding her vocation as a novelist. She has since written over forty-eight novels, mostly sagas and historical fiction. She now spends warm winters living in Spain, and the rainy summers in Britain.

D1514424

Also by Freda Lightfoot

A Salford Saga

Ruby McBride
The Favourite Child
The Castlefield Collector
Dancing on Deansgate

A Champion Street Market Saga

Putting on the Style
Fools Fall in Love
That'll be the Day
Candy Kisses
Who's Sorry Now
Lonely Teardrops

Lakeland Sagas

Lakeland Lily
The Bobbin Girls
Kitty Little
Gracie's Sin
Daisy's Secret

Luckpenny Land

Luckpenny Land
Storm Clouds Over Broombank
Wishing Water
Larkrigg Fell

Freda LIGHTFOOT
Storm Clouds Over Broombank

1①CANELO

First published in the United Kingdom in 1995 by Coronet Books

This edition published in the United Kingdom in 2023 by

Canelo
Unit 9, 5th Floor
Cargo Works, 1–2 Hatfields
London SE1 9PG
United Kingdom

Print ISBN 978 1 80436 353 9
Ebook ISBN 978 1 80436 114 6

Cover design by Rose Cooper

Cover images © Arcangel @ Unsplash

Look for more great books at www.canelo.co

Printed and bound in Great Britain by Clays Ltd, Elcograf S.p.A.

1

1940

Chapter 1

Kath Ellis licked the envelope flap, slipped the letter into its appointed place, then quietly closed the door and turned the key. 'Why do you bother?' her friend, Bella, asked. 'Either send the dratted thing or stop wasting time writing them.'

Hardly a week went by without her writing to someone back home. Her father, mother, Meg, even Jack, for all she had no wish to ever see him again. The letters were all there, neatly tied into bundles in her locker, stampless envelopes stuck down as if they'd already been seen by the censor. Except that she'd no intention of posting any of them.

Kath smiled. 'They're like a diary. Who knows? One day somebody may be glad to know what I got up to during these years of war. Were I to be no longer around.'

Her daughter perhaps?

Bella took the pen from her fingers. 'Stop that this minute. I won't have you tempt fate with such wild notions. My father thinks women in uniform are the lowest of the low, so let's brave the local hostelry and prove it, shall we? We have two whole hours before the ten thirty curfew, cocoa, and bed.'

Kath laughed. 'Like good girls at school.'

Bella tucked Kath's arm into hers as they clattered past the row of beds and left the Nissen hut. 'You're lucky if you went to that sort of school. No one gave out cocoa at mine, only verses of Old Testament to be endlessly learned, and the cane every Friday.'

Katherine Ellis only laughed. Not quite the glossy beauty she'd once been, her sleek blonde bob was cut short, although starting to grow again, the once perfectly manicured nails bitten to the quick. But there was still that elusive quality about her that spoke of a sheltered background, of a girl who had taken her natural attraction to men rather for granted, although the price she'd paid for that foolishness had been high.

'I can just see you as a schoolgirl, all pigtails and short socks.' Bella grinned. 'I was a terror. Bigger than most of the teachers. Come on, old sport, tonight we celebrate the end of the dreaded training, for tomorrow we face the horrors of carrying our kitbags half across country to the outer wilds of East Anglia.'

Kath had met Bella on Euston Station. Surrounded by more girls than she had ever seen in her life, all chattering twenty to the dozen, the noise had been deafening. Then one black-haired, black-eyed girl of Amazon proportions had turned to her with a wry smile. 'They'll soon shut up when reality sets in.'

It had set in alarmingly early. The moment they saw the train backing into Platform One it came home to them that this was the moment of no return. When they boarded, they'd be on their way to becoming a member of the Women's Auxiliary Air Force. They'd be a WAAF.

To Kath it had seemed the only answer after Meg rescued her from Greenlawns, the Home for Wayward Girls where she'd given birth to Jack's baby and feared she might be incarcerated forever. When the pair of them had reached Liverpool's Lime Street Station, Kath had pushed

Meg on to the train and thrust Melissa into her arms, not even noticing the irony of relinquishing her daughter to the woman she'd betrayed, her one-time best friend. Kath had known only that she wasn't fit to be anyone's mother, that she had no love to give.

She'd boarded the next train and come straight to London on the money the home had given her, not knowing what she intended, nor caring very much. On reaching the Capital she'd tried a series of temporary jobs – waitress, barmaid, shop assistant – boring, mindless tasks, and always with the problem of where to lay her head. She used the underground if she could get away with it, though it wasn't, strictly speaking, allowed. The government had decided it would be bad for morale to hide like rats in a hole. Or a women's hostel if she could find one, a park bench if necessary.

But then she'd seen the poster and the answer seemed suddenly obvious. In the WAAF she would be provided with food, clothing, a bed to sleep in, work with pay at the end of it, and no questions asked. One of hundreds of girls her indiscretions could be safely buried, if not forgotten. Worn out and feeling far from clean, she'd gladly signed up.

She hadn't minded the weeks of hard training that followed. Nor had it troubled her in the least to stand for hours in the freezing cold, run up and down on the spot or do a half-day route march. She'd been forced to do far worse in the yards of Greenlawns. And it was a blessed improvement upon working in the laundry.

Kath hadn't objected to the school-type lectures on mathematics, geography and morse code. She'd written her letters during some of the more boring ones, meaning at first to keep in touch. In the end her courage had failed her and the letters had stayed in her bag, then been consigned to the locker. For the moment.

'So long as they don't give us any more of those damned inoculations,' said Bella. 'I can take anything they throw at me, but those.'

Bella had been ill with fever and the shakes after the typhoid, tetanus and smallpox injections. Kath was thankful to be able to prove she'd already had them.

'And no more of those unspeakably awful FFI examinations,' Kath laughed. 'Cavorting about knickerless is not my idea of fun.'

Hadn't it been proved already, at the home, that she was free from infection? And no WAAF Officer could make a worse job of it than Miss Blake. Not that she admitted to anyone that she'd suffered the dreaded test once already.

Bella looked at her in open admiration. 'Bloomin' hell, I'll never forget the way you walked in to that room. Cool as a cucumber you were. Everyone else was white-faced and trembling, or giggling and weeping from nerves, and you strip off your pink regulation panties as if it were common place. That isn't what you were, is it, in real life? A stripper?'

Kath giggled. 'No, but maybe I should have tried it. It might have paid better than a waitress job at the UCP.' The best of it was that Bella would have accepted her just the same if she had been.

'Undoubtedly, and with better tips. Only snag would be all those men gawping at you. Give me the shivers, that would. I'm off them myself.'

Kath grinned. 'Right now I'm inclined to agree with you.'

Bella cast her new friend a sideways glance as she handed over a half pint glass of cider. 'Got your fingers burned, did you?'

'You might say so.'

'Well, that's another thing we have in common. No romantic story of partings and promises to wait for me either. My old man put five bob on the table, told me he was off to join the Army and ta ta. That was the last I heard of him. No letters, no pay cheque every month, not even a telegram. I can only assume that he's alive and well and keeping out of my way, which is fine by me. Not a marriage made in heaven, I can tell you, more like in Epping Forest.'

'Any children?'

'Nope. Nor do I ever intend having any, smelly, demanding creatures that they are. My mother had one a year for fourteen years then dropped dead. That ain't for me.'

A vision of a small crumpled face came into Kath's mind and she took a quick draught of her cider.

'Steady on, it's stronger than it looks.'

'When do you think we'll get our uniform?' Kath asked. 'When we get to our new posting?'

'Let's hope so. You look like you might be off to Ascot in that posh suit. Not to mention that fancy tan hat. Have you nothing else to wear?'

'I lost all my luggage,' Kath lied.

'Poor sod. Well, at least take off the hat in here or they'll double the price of the drinks.'

'Sorry, I didn't think.' Kath realised the outfit spoke of money and class but Aunt Ruby never had sent on her other clothes and this was all she possessed in the world.

Even if she'd been dressed in rags, her background would still have shown. It was all there in the way she held her head, the swing of her walk. If she was unaware how her instinctive style, her air of self-confidence, were all signals that Katherine Ellis was sure of her place in society, it also showed how little she cared.

But it would be a misinterpretation, a travesty of the truth to assume she was that same socialising, careless Katherine of long ago. Were anyone to take the trouble to look closer they might find some surprising contradictions. A few calluses and blisters in unexpected places for one thing, as well as the hard-bitten nails. But the almost insolent arrogance hid her fears well, for she didn't intend anyone to probe too deeply.

Let them look and see me as I really am, she thought. A woman who has been to the bottom and is clawing her way back out of the pit. Let them see courage, guts, and a warning to stand clear and not dare to bully me or I'll blast their socks off! Greenlawns had introduced her to physical pain but had failed to destroy the intrinsic strength she held inside. Not so reckless as she once was, nor so restless, but a whole lot tougher.

So let the WAAF do its worst.

—

It was a dull, cloudy day in the early summer of 1940 when Kath and Bella arrived at Bledlow, together still thanks to some crafty swopping of postings on their part. A light drizzle had started and a thick mist was blowing in from the sea.

Italy had declared war on Britain and France. Housewives were stripping their kitchens of pans to make aeroplanes. Churchill was talking of Britain's finest hour, but depression was rife and the forces were pulling in new recruits as fast as they could, even women.

'You would think they'd be glad to see us, wouldn't you? Instead of leaving us hanging around,' Bella said as they staggered off the bus with their kit bags to stand uncertain and abandoned on the cinder path, wondering where they should go next.

'At least we look like WAAF girls now.'

'This tie is strangling me already.'

They'd been issued with a basic uniform at last and for all it was either five sizes too big or fitted where it touched, most of them, particularly Kath, had been glad to get it. It made them seem more professional.

There'd been much complaining, of course, and desperate swops made to try to find a near match in size. But the blue jacket and skirt for all its coarse newness, even the stiff-collared shirt that chafed her neck, seemed an infinite improvement upon the shapeless overall of Greenlawns.

A voice loud enough to lift the dome off St Paul's sounded across the parade ground. 'You two WAAFs! Cut along and get signed in and stop standing about like dummies. There's a war on, you know.' They fled through the first door ahead of them. Unfortunately it was the wrong one. A sea of blue uniforms met their eyes all right, but there were men inside them and not women. And some of the bodies didn't have uniforms of any sort on them.

'Oh, dear lordy, let's get out of here.'

'Hey, look who's come calling, chaps. Two new little darlings. Lost your way, have you? Come over here. We'll explain the drill to you.' A riot of whistles and cat calls

9

greeted this remark, and as one the girls turned and fled, giggling madly, straight into the WAAF Officer. 'Checking out stores already?'

Kath choked. 'Sorry, we – um – made a mistake.'

'Ma'am.'

'Ma'am.'

'And you salute an officer, WAAF, every time you see one. Didn't they teach you that at training?'

'Yes, ma'am.' Kath dropped her bag and attempted a salute. She wasn't very good at it, and Bella was even worse, looking very like a lamp post gone wrong.

'I hope the Airforce hasn't made a bigger mistake in taking you two on. If you'd care to follow me you might give us the benefit of your name and number while I have the pleasure of directing you to your quarters.'

Kath trusted the officer's soft tones even less than her official one. Dragging her kit bag behind her, Kath gabbled out rank and number and followed Bella along the cinder path.

The WAAF Officer stopped. 'Do you have a problem with your kit, Airwoman?'

Kath shook her head, glancing beseechingly at Bella. Whenever she tried to swing it up on to her shoulder she very nearly decapitated herself or else flung herself off her feet. When there was no wall to prop it on first, Bella gave her a hand to lift it.

'I didn't quite catch your reply.'

'No, I don't have a problem.'

'I think you do. *Ma'am*'

'Oh, sorry, ma'am.' And to Kath's great mortification, the WAAF Officer stood and smilingly waited while Kath manoeuvred, with considerable difficulty, the long heavy bag into place.

'You look in need of more training to me, Airwoman.'

'It's my narrow shoulders. The thing keeps slipping off. Ma'am.' Kath attempted to explain but saw by the frosty expression she was wasting her time.

At the Guard Room they booked in and were directed to their billet. With thoughts of hot tea and a soft bed to lay their tired bodies they reached it at a smart pace.

Yet another Nissen hut lined with beds and heated, if that was the word, by an ancient coke stove that no doubt belched out more smoke, dust and fumes than warmth. Kath dropped her bag with a weary sigh. Fortunately this was summer so that was a pleasure in store for later.

WAAF Officer Mullin, or Mule as she came to be known, attempted to show a more human side to her nature. 'Get yourself unpacked. There's hot water for a bath if you're quick. Be in the Mess Hall by six.'

'Oh, blimey, this is good,' said Bella, falling prone on to her bed. The springs creaked ominously, the mattress was as hard as the iron bedstead, but she didn't care. 'Utter bliss.'

'Don't get too comfortable,' Kath warned, her own eyes half closed in almost instant sleep. 'We have to be quick, remember?'

But before the delectable promise of hot water and food dragged them from their beds, an air raid warning sounded and then they did move very quickly, blindly rushing out to follow a trickling mass of people who seemed far from pleased at being interrupted, and confusingly not all going in the same direction.

'Blooming Hitler. I'd just got my head down.'

'Where's the shelter?' Kath asked one passing WAAF.

'Shelter? Ditch more like. We call it a slit trench. Most people only bother when it's really necessary, and if it's dry, for obvious reasons. New, are you? I'm Liz Parry.'

'Ellis. And this is Kendrick.' Kath felt quite pleased with herself for picking up the correct style. 'Does it show very much that we're new?'

'Your tie is all wrong for a start. It'll work loose that way. And you'll need to spend every evening polishing those buttons to get a lovely mellow shine. Then you might not look such complete rookies.'

'This tie's near choking me.'

The girl called Parry laughed and her serious face lit up. She was pretty, Kath decided, with her golden curly hair and neat figure. Reminded her a bit of Meg.

The sound of the siren was overwhelming coupled with the awesome roar of aircraft overhead which would, Kath was sure, at any moment blast them out of existence. It was the nearest she had come to danger and she was not to know they were Stirlings taking off, rather than German bombers coming in. She flung herself into the trench and landed in a huge crop of nettles. Her shouts of agony brought forth no sympathy from anyone, only laughter and ribald offers to rub her down all over with Calamine.

The All Clear sounded and nobody took any notice of that, either. She and Bella seemed to be the only two in the entire camp who had shown any concern.

During an almost sleepless night of itching, despite Bella's ministrations with the said lotion, and the fear of a bomb being accidentally dropped by the noisy aircraft that seemed to be taking off every five minutes right over their hut, Kath spent the time worrying over how ill prepared she was. She thought of the lectures she hadn't properly listened to, the drills she'd skipped. Had she missed anything really vital? What could one do to make a good life for oneself in the WAAF and avoid being ridiculed by the Mules of this world?

Someone gave her a mug of tea sometime before dawn because she happened to be still awake.

'Thanks.' Kath sipped gratefully at it then set it on the shelf above her bed while she started on yet another letter describing her arrival. It was about then that she fell asleep, to be awakened by something hard smacking her forehead and a trickle of warm liquid running down her face.

'Dear God, I've been hit.'

'Where, where?' Bella was by her side in an instant.

'My face. Oh no, my face. I can feel blood all over it.'

A torch was brought and shone into her face. A moment's startled silence then laughter, pure and true, from a whole gaggle of interested girls.

'You're covered in tea,' giggled Bella. 'Decorated by a splendid pattern of tea leaves.'

'It's the vibration from the returning aircraft. Sometimes nearly shakes this place to bits,' chuckled Liz Parry. 'Oh, but the expression on your face! It's the funniest thing I've seen in weeks.'

It was the final humiliation.

Kath decided she didn't much care for being new. It made her feel gauche and uncomfortable and could clearly have disastrous consequences. Nor did she care to be laughed at. Whatever she needed to learn, she would learn it. Fast.

On their way to the Mess Hall, dreaming of hot tea and bacon butties, they came again upon WAAF Officer Mullin.

'Ah, Ellis and Kendrick, sleep well on your first night, did we?' Beguiled by the officer's smile Kath answered quite naturally. 'Yes, thanks. Bit noisy but could have been worse I suppose.'

'Oh dear, oh dear. I must have a word with the pilots and try to get them to turn the engines down. Can't have them disturbing your beauty sleep.'

Kath flushed deeply, most unlike herself.

'You weren't the little WAAF who imagined herself shot with a pot of tea, were you?' And when the flush deepened, the officer smiled with pure delight. 'What a prize you are, Ellis. How did we amuse ourselves before you came?'

Kath ground her teeth together and said nothing. She had learned patience in a hard school, so if this dreadful woman expected, or wanted her to retaliate and humiliate herself further, she'd mistaken her mark.

Bella was ordered to report to Signals after breakfast. 'Ellis, you can take yourself off to the drivers' unit.'

'But I was to be on the switchboard.'

Mullin looked at Kath as if she were something unpleasant the cat had deposited upon the drawing room carpet. 'Not questioning the service are you, Airwoman?'

'No, ma'am. It's only that I understood we could choose our own trades.'

'So you can, as a rule.' The mild tone was dangerously sweet. 'It happens that we find ourselves short of drivers at present and you, I see from your form, were one of the fortunate few civilians who could afford a motor. Now isn't that splendid? How useful you are going to be to us, Ellis.'

'Yes, ma'am.' Kath saluted and was at once reprimanded. '*No saluting unless you are wearing a cap.*'

'No, ma'am.' Oh lordy, would she ever get used to this?

Kath wondered, poignantly, how she could have come to mess up her life so thoroughly. She could be at home now, at Larkrigg Hall, helping her mother do something suitable like holding fundraising tea parties for the soldiers, or perhaps a little light volunteer work at the local hospital. Except that her mother had disowned her because of her carelessness in daring to bring an unwanted, unsuitable child into the world.

'Have you done your morning chores?'

'Um,' Kath glanced at Bella despairingly, not knowing quite what chores Mullin referred to. 'Ma'am?'

The officer sighed, looking delighted at finding this new recruit wanting yet again. 'Before you report in, you can sweep out your billet and give the floor a good scrub.'

'What, all of it?'

Mullin smiled. She'd had this type of girl foisted upon her before. A classy little madam who thought she was easing her social conscience by volunteering, then wasting everyone's time by asking too many questions and thinking herself above discipline. She probably didn't know one end of a sweeping brush from the other.

'Yes, Ellis, all of it. Think you can manage that, do you? Concentrates the mind wonderfully, scrubbing, don't you think?'

Kath bit hard upon her lower lip. 'Yes, ma'am.'

'Best get on with it then. A delightful new experience for you to try.'

'Oh, but…'

'But?'

Kath pushed the thought of breakfast regretfully from her mind. 'Yes, ma'am.'

'Certainly, ma'am. At once, ma'am,' cut in Bella smartly.

The two of them returned bleakly to the Nissen hut. Worse, Mullin followed, and while Bella swept, she watched with obvious pleasure as Kath filled a bucket with hot water and added a good handful of soda crystals.

'More, Ellis. We want the floor clean, don't we, not a murky mess?'

Kath added more, a vicious cocktail that would make any fair hand bleed. Except hands like hers, which were hard as leather after the Greenlawns' laundry.

She plunged them into the scalding water without a flinch, lifted out the brush and began to scrub. Her arms and shoulders moved with a long practised rhythm, and using a separate, well-wrung out cloth, Kath swiftly and efficiently mopped up the excess water leaving not a streak upon the polished floor.

It took no more than a moment or two watching this process for Mullin to frown in puzzled surprise. It was all too apparent, to her experienced eye, that Ellis had done this job before. Odd. She would never have thought it.

'Surprised your mama didn't have a housemaid to do this job for you, Ellis.'

Kath hid a smile. 'No, ma'am.'

Irritated, Mullin snapped her fingers. 'Jump to it then. Remember Parade is at 8.45. Prompt. And since you are so skilled at the task, you can scrub out Picquet Post as well. And don't forget the outside lobby. Call me when you're done then I can check it. Jump to it, Airwoman, jump to it.'

'Great,' said Bella with resignation when the Officer had gone. 'Next time you're asked to do something, make a bad job of it, will you? We can kiss goodbye to any breakfast after all this lot.'

'Sorry, I…'

'Don't worry, I'll forgive you. Thousands wouldn't.'

Driving was a doddle after that, Kath decided. She was issued with a staff car and instructed to drive one of the Commanders to another station. The mist had lifted and the sun was shining. Liz Parry managed to sneak her out a bacon buttie, which quite perked her up.

Besides, she was young and filled with optimism at having escaped from Greenlawns, thanks to Meg. A mug of tea would be waiting for her when she got back from this run, which would go down a treat.

Taking everything into account, life wasn't at all bad. Were it not for the awful guilt and loneliness she felt inside at betraying her best friend and abandoning her daughter.

1941

Chapter 2

In a summer with a late spring and an indifferent July, a few days' sunshine to dry up the land and the fleeces on the sheep were all the farmers had needed to set the clipping off. The early-morning mists had lifted like a fair woman's feather hat to reveal sunshine and beauty beneath. Satisfied the dry spell would continue for the two or three days necessary, the Turners of Ashlea, the Davieses and Meg, had gathered, ready to visit each farm in turn to shear the sheep.

The sheep had been brought down from the heaf, a jostling throng, growing ever larger as flocks joined on from neighbouring heafs. Meg had counted every one of hers as they passed through her gate, to make sure they were all safe and well.

'Yan, tyan, tethera, methera, pimp,' she'd chanted, in the traditional way, enjoying the sound of the old Celtic words as she'd sat on the gate, marking off each five on a slate in her hand. As she counted, she felt as if they were bombers bringing Charlie safely home from a raid. Whatever satisfaction it had given her to see how her flock had grown, near two hundred and fifty now, not for a moment did she underestimate her good fortune. While London had been battered almost daily in recent months, here on the Westmorland hills the sun shone, the sheep bleated and all seemed to be perfectly normal. No blitz for them.

'You'd never think there was a war on, would you?' said Sally Ann, coming up beside her and uncannily catching her thoughts.

'We realise it when we listen to the drone of bombers in the sky, and hear the vibration deep within the ground as some other poor soul is getting it,' said Will Davies, not pausing in his labours as he started on the next sheep. Sitting astride his special stool, in a row with the other clippers, he turned the ewe belly up, the head tucked beneath his arm while he cut the fleece, not too close and with no pulling of the flesh which might form ridges, till the wriggling sheep was released, looking oddly naked and highly affronted by the indignity of it all.

'Or when we have to queue an hour and a half for a paltry few ounces of margarine, or barter precious eggs for extra sugar to make jam. I can't remember the last time I saw an orange or a tin of fruit,' Sally Ann mourned.

'Trying to get a can of paraffin for the lamp the other day was like asking for gold,' Meg agreed. 'I'd love to try that,' she said, her mind clearly still on the clipping.

'Aye, I dare say you would. The sheep mightn't be too keen,' laughed Will, and Meg conceded that although the farmers accepted her as one of their own, shearing was a skilled task. Their confidence in her had not quite reached that level. Watching Will peel the fleece from the neck down each side, then as the sheep was flipped over, off the back like a banana skin, she didn't wonder at it.

She stood ready with her stick with the rounded end to dab her mark on the back of the clipped sheep. Rust red for Broombank sheep, so that if one ever wandered too far another farmer could check it, together with the ear mark, in his Shepherd's Guide and know to which farm it belonged. Come the autumn meet, wanderers could be returned to their rightful owners.

Sally Ann moved out of the way while Meg deftly brought another ewe to the clipper, who never left his stool. Six or seven minutes for each sheep, though some could manage one in less if it didn't kick about.

'I heard the other day that Miss Shaw has had a telegram about her nephew.' All hands paused as eyes, bleak and questioning, were raised to Sally Ann's flushed face.

'Eeh, no. He was nobbut a lad.'

'Lost at sea. Missing, presumed dead, it said.'

After a long silent moment while hands were stilled and thoughts turned to that bright-faced boy who a few summers ago might have been chided by these same farmers for some youthful misdemeanour, shears started to clip again, long breaths exhaled. Life moved on.

A chill ran through Meg and she rubbed her hands together, sore from holding and turning the sheep, and greasy with the lanolin from the wool. Think positive, that was the secret. Charlie said so.

'On Charlie's last leave he was like a dog with two tails. Talk, talk, talk about his dratted aeroplanes and how he'd been promoted to navigator. I told him that I wished they'd promote him safely home again. Call the whole war off as a terrible mistake.'

An impossible dream. It was just that she couldn't bear to think of her young brother in those terrible raids over Germany and France, and prayed each night as she added a few lines to the regular letters she sent him, that he would survive the next, and the next.

And where was Jack? She hadn't heard from him in an age. His letters were becoming more and more rare.

'The war will run its course,' Will said, with a farmer's natural pragmatism. 'Nothing you can do will alter that. Work hard and keep faith.'

'I try to,' Meg agreed. It was easier to do the former than the latter. Charlie was no longer a boy and Tam often told her she worried too much over him.

But then she too was a different Meg to the young girl of four summers ago. This Meg, the one who had lost the man she loved to her best friend, was tougher, quieter and more thoughtful. If she didn't laugh or feel ready to give her love quite so recklessly as that other girl had done, then she at least felt more sure of herself, more certain of where she was going. At least now she had control over her own destiny, her own future. She had Broombank and her sheep. She had Effie, Tam, Sally Ann and her family about her. She was happy in her work, doing her bit to produce good food for a war-torn country. This was the nearest she would probably ever get to peace of mind.

Meg wished that everyone could be so blessed.

Seeing the suspicion of tears in her eyes, Sally Ann stepped closer. 'You look tired. I'll do that for a while.' She took the marker stick from Meg's hand. 'Go and rest. Effie says she's put the kettle on.'

Meg eased her back. 'I won't say no.'

'I reckon Will wouldn't mind a break either, would you, Will?'

'I'll do a few more, then your Dan can take over for a bit.'

Meg smiled at Sally Ann. 'You want me to watch the children at the same time?'

'No, you don't have to worry about them. Hetty has them all in hand. At least as far as they will allow her to.

For such small bairns they're as wick as fleas. They run rings round her sometimes.'

Will laughed. 'And doesn't she just love it?'

Sally Ann's gaze drifted lovingly over to the far meadow where her two children sat with the kindly Mrs Davies in the long grass, a small group of curious cows nosing around them. Young Daniel, the baby, was lying on a blanket, kicking at the delicious joy and freedom of having sun on his chubby legs. Nicholas was curbing his more natural, boundless energy to studiously attempt to thread a daisy stem through the slit Hetty had made with her thumb nail, to form a daisy chain. At thirteen months old, he was a sturdy, well-formed little boy, round-faced and bright-eyed, golden hair shining in the sun. Sally Ann loved him so much in that moment, her heart ached.

Beside him, quieter and far more serious than her companions, Lissa attempted to do the same. Three months older than Nick, yet she copied his every action.

'Sometimes I worry over that child, she's too quiet by half.' Sally Ann spoke before she'd thought to guard her words.

Meg frowned, her eyes resting quietly on Melissa, pretty as a picture in the flower meadow. 'I hadn't really thought about it. I just take it for granted that she's not a chatterbox like your Nick, nor half so naughty. She's so small and delicate, like a little fairy, and no trouble at all.'

'Perhaps a bit too good, don't you think?'

Meg laughed. 'What would you have me do? Tell her to be noisy and rough?'

'I suppose it does sound a bit silly, but somehow it isn't quite natural for a child to be so – so obliging, so mature. I'm sure she understands every word I say. She's far more intelligent than our Nick.' Sally Ann laughed. 'Not that that would be difficult.'

It was a conversation that came to mind that evening as Meg asked Effie to put the child to bed.

'Will you see to her? I can't spare the time from the shearing,' she casually remarked, eating a sandwich on the hoof to keep her going. There would be food for all later, though not eaten in the barn as they would have done before the war, with a fiddle and the lamps all burning.

Instead, all the workers would crowd into the kitchen, everyone having contributed something, due to the difficulties of rationing. Chicken soup thickened with potato flour, stewed apples sweetened with dried figs. But they were lucky here on the farm, having their own butter and eggs. And Ashlea had provided some ham.

Meg bent down and dropped a quick kiss on the child's soft curls. 'Sorry, but Meg is busy tonight.' A shaft of guilt pierced her heart. How often had she said those words? Too often, perhaps, in recent months.

Lissa said nothing. She merely wrapped her arms about Meg's leg for a moment till she had won another kiss, then went, happily enough, Meg was sure of it, with Effie, up to bed.

She watched a moment longer as the child climbed the stairs on all fours, one step at a time. Deep down Meg knew that she did love her, for all she'd fought against it. How could she not when the child was there, a living presence in their midst, and in her heart. Sometimes it was hard to appreciate that Lissa wasn't hers at all. In all these long months, more than a year now, there had been no word from Kath. But Meg still remembered that day, in every tiny detail. The appalling sight of what months in that home had done to her once beautiful friend, and the horror she'd felt when she'd realised whose child this was.

There had been times when Meg had thought the pain would never go away.

For months afterwards she'd been in a sort of panic, as if she wanted to run from the truth except that there was nowhere to run. Jack had cheated on her, with her best friend. So she'd turned her face away from the child who provided, all too clearly, the evidence of that betrayal. She had seen that Lissa was fed and well cared for, by Effie, and Hetty Davies, while Meg continued to torture her mind with questions. What had she done wrong? Why hadn't she been enough for him? Hadn't he loved her? Questions to which there were no answers.

At one time she'd thought she might never get over it, but then she hadn't reckoned on her dear friends, on Effie and Tam. Tam O'Cleary, the Irishman who'd walked into her farm one day looking for Kath, the girl he'd met quite by chance in Southport and who for no reason had gone missing. Curious and concerned he'd followed the only lead he knew, back to her old friend Meg. Why he stayed Meg couldn't rightly say, or explain why it was so important to her that he did. Then there was the unstoppable Rust, her beloved dog who, despite a vicious injury caused by her stupid brother Dan, absolutely refused to give up and retire. With their help Meg had painstakingly put her life back together again.

But deep inside, largely unacknowledged, there still burned a resentment, and a fear. She still held herself back a little from Lissa, rarely touching her, scarcely speaking to the child at times, afraid to show the love she secretly felt in case one day Kath should return, and she lost her. Where would she be then with no one to love at all?

Tam came in, interrupting her thoughts for which she was thankful.

Meg busied herself scribbling on a sheet of paper at the table.

'Not writing him another letter?' There was a mocking tone to his voice that made her hackles rise.

'If you mean Jack, yes, I am as a matter of fact.' She tilted her chin at him in defiance, eyes flashing the message that it was none of his business what she did.

Tam snorted and went to pour himself tea. 'Must be months since he replied to any. Why do you bother?'

It had seemed too cruel to continue to hate Jack for some youthful misdemeanour carried out one hot, lazy summer when they had all been silly and young. Meg had done her best not to condemn, and certainly couldn't bring herself to call off their engagement, not when he might lose his life any day in the war. She'd waited for Christmas by which time the war would be over, before she told him. But the festive season had come and gone, Jack had been sent overseas without ever coming home, so she'd said nothing. Meg continued to write to him every week, telling about the farm, Effie learning to read, Dan getting to be quite full of himself as a contented married man and working for the Government War Committee. Always happy things. 'A man deserves cheerful letters when he's fighting a war. This is not the time for recriminations, or sending him a Dear John letter.'

'Why you still feel this loyalty towards that eejit, I can't work out.'

'Well, there it is, I do.' What other option did she have? The three of them had vowed a friendship for life and, foolish or not, Meg wasn't going to be the one to break it. Whether Jack knew it or not, he was still Lissa's father. Their lives were still inextricably linked.

Tam quietly sipped his tea while he gazed at her with steady eyes, reading her thoughts with uncanny precision. From above came the sounds of a child's voice, objecting to being put to bed. 'Did you ever tell him about Lissa?'

'Nope.'

'You don't think he has a right? What if he were to be killed, or captured. He'd never know then, would he?'

Meg swallowed the hard lump of guilt that came to her throat. 'It's Kath's job to tell him, not mine.'

'But Kath isn't here. We've no notion where she is. And the child needs a parent. Isn't it a bit hard on her, not to be knowing who they are?'

'She has us. She's too young to understand.' Kath could take Lissa back when the war was over. She would have the right to do that, if she so wished. Kath was the child's mother after all. Meg's stomach clenched, as it always did, at this thought. How would she cope with losing Lissa? How did you prepare yourself for fresh pain? However much she tried to avoid it she knew it would be there. Work was her release, her protection, and she must keep her mind firmly upon her plans for Broombank.

She wanted to go to her now, soothe the tears away. Better not. Leave Lissa to Effie.

She set the letter behind the clock on the dresser. She would finish it later. 'I have to get back to the sheep.'

'Can't you hear her crying?'

It was always Tam, if Effie was busy or failing to cope, as now, who comforted Lissa and put her to bed. He'd seemed happy enough about that as he missed his own large family back in America. Now he was frowning, almost glaring at her, sounding fierce and uncharacteristically tough. 'She wants *you*!'

Meg took no notice. 'Be quick with that tea,' she said. 'You know we can't work after dark with the black-out.'

The child's piercing cries caused her to flinch but she set her mouth firm as she pulled open the door and went back to the sheep, her heart beating twenty to the dozen. Lissa was not her child.

Kath decided quite early on that Parade was a horror she could live without. In those first few weeks at Bledlow, she soon discovered that you were excused Parade if on duty. After that she usually managed to avoid it by being hard at work polishing her vehicle so early that she was often picked out to drive the top brass somewhere or other.

Kath found that she loved her job and was almost grateful to WAAF Officer Mullin for denying her the opportunity to become a telephonist. Driving about the countryside was much more fun.

She and Bella became great friends, often cycling into Bledlow itself for a drink at the pub, or visiting the Flicks, as they called the local cinema. Then there were regular dances at the station with no shortage of partners.

There were days when no one could manage to be cheerful, when yet another crew of smiling faces had vanished, or a plane had crashed on landing. Or, as once happened, a whole ground crew were blown to smithereens while trying to unload unused bombs.

But one way or another, despite the awfulness of the war, the weeks and months slipped by.

Mule continued to watch Kath, as stubbornly determined as her name to find fault.

'What have I done to offend that woman?' Kath asked Bella. 'She never misses an opportunity to put me down.'

'That's what should have happened to her, when she was a pup,' grinned Bella. 'Aw, take no notice. It's all jealousy because you're eye-catching and come from a comfortable home. She certainly can't lay claim to the former and possibly not the latter either.'

'Not everything is as it appears,' Kath said, a touch of asperity in her voice.

Bella's eyebrows lifted slightly but she said nothing. Aware that her new friend never spoke about her personal affairs, she had asked no questions, seen no reason to pry. 'Chin up. Don't let her get to you.'

Kath's diligence became a habit and after a while she got promoted to Aircraftwoman 1st Class. She bought the drinks that night. 'Even Mule can't stop me now. Maybe I'll be giving her orders one day.' Kath had a determination never to be in a vulnerable state again. It was a new experience for her not to be in charge of her own destiny. But ever since she had left Larkrigg, that's the way her life had been. She meant one day to change it.

'Don't tempt fate,' Bella warned, being overly superstitious.

Then one morning Kath's efforts came to be noticed by a newcomer to the station – one keen-eyed Canadian, Ewan Wadeson, Wade to his friends, of whom there were many for he was known for his ready wit and generosity. He had groaned when first learning there were WAAFs on this, his latest posting, but having seen the line up of drivers, was beginning to change his mind.

It was Kath's swinging walk that first attracted him. A certain swivel to the hip which he found most interesting.

And when she hitched up her skirt to get into the driving seat, his blood pressure almost peaked.

'Boy, oh boy, what legs.'

Fraternising, or fratting as it was called, with other ranks was of course quite out of order. A hanging offence, almost. But Wade had always been one to take chances. The secret was not to get caught. He meant to get to know this new little sweetheart or his name wasn't Ewan Maximillian Wadeson III.

He made a point of being at the depot by eight o'clock prompt the following morning.

'Driver? Are you taken?'

Kath glanced up to find herself appraised by the most outrageously sensual blue eyes she had ever encountered. Several pips decorating the impressively broad shoulders brought her to attention. And her salute proved the value of hours of practice.

'I need a driver today. Got several meetings to attend.' It wasn't strictly true, but in the Airforce, he'd discovered, you could walk around all day with a clipboard in your hand and no one would bother you.

He climbed into the back seat of the car.

'Where to, sir?' Kath enquired when they had been checked out of the station and were bowling down the road.

Wing Commander Ewan Wadeson was engrossed with trying to decide the colour of her eyes through the driving mirror. Green? Brown? Or somewhere in between.

He cleared his throat. His day was largely free since he was not on duty till the evening. But if anyone ever discovered that he had pinched a staff car, complete with WAAF driver for his pleasure for the day he'd really be up for the high jump. Best to make it look genuine to stop any loose talk.

'Take me to Remlington-on-Sea. I have to speak to my opposite number there.'

Kath did so, and to the next airfield after that. She drove, in fact, from airfield to airfield all morning and well into the afternoon, getting in and out of the car so many times she was quite dizzy with it all, and light-headed from want of food. While Ewan Maximillian Wadeson had a smashing view of those lovely legs each and every time.

'I'll be about a half hour,' he told her on one occasion. Taking a chance, as soon as he had disappeared from view she locked up the car and went in search of food.

She was nibbling her way through a limp sandwich when she decided to step onto a weighing machine. It stood at the door of an amusement arcade and was the kind that told your fortune as well as your weight. Might as well know what she was in for. But before she had time to open her purse a hand had slipped a coin into the slot and a voice spoke in her ear.

'Ain't nothing wrong with your figure, ACW Ellis.' Kath jumped, dropping the unfinished sandwich.

'Aw, gee, now see what I've made you do. Were you hungry? I didn't realise. Look, why don't I go and get us some real food? Er, you'd best wait in the car.'

'No, no, I'm fine. Are you done now? Do you want me to take you back, sir?' Kath knew only too well what trouble they'd both be in if anyone saw them talking like this.

'You go to the car, Ellis. I'll be along shortly.'

'Yes, sir.' She didn't need telling again.

Kath had parked the car, as instructed, on a headland looking out to sea. Wing Commander Ewan Wadeson was sitting beside her in the front seat and the pair of them were eating fish and chips out of newspaper. Sinful, but nothing had ever tasted so good in all her life.

'Do you mind if I ask you a question, sir?' He seemed the approachable sort. Not like some of the stuffed shirts around here. Probably because he was a Canadian, Kath decided.

'Sure, fire away.'

'If one wanted to find out what had happened to someone, a friend say, how would one go about it?'

'One would write to the Red Cross,' he teased, mimicking her accent. 'Sweetheart, is it? Missing in action?' The tone had turned sympathetic and Kath warmed to him. He was also, she hadn't failed to notice, a very attractive man.

'N–no, not exactly. So far as I'm aware he isn't even missing. He's in the navy but I don't know where he's stationed.'

Wade moved closer. She had offered him just the loop-hole he needed to get to know her better. Never miss an opportunity, that was old Wade's motto.

'Not got a boy friend then?'

Kath hid a smile. 'Not at the moment, no. And you?' she ventured, with a flash of her old recklessness.

Straight-faced he replied. 'Nope, I haven't got a boy friend either.'

Kath rolled her eyes. 'You know what I mean.'

He chuckled. 'The answer's still no. Tell me his name, this guy you're interested in. I'll find out for you.'

'You're very kind.' Kath rewarded him with the full warmth of her hazel eyes. The gaze held overlong as chemistry crackled between them, and after a stunned moment, Wade smiled an acknowledgement of it.

'You're some woman. You know that?'

She knew the dangers. She knew he was an officer. Out of bounds. Against King's Regulations. As were most things, Kath decided, that were anything like fun. But to Katherine Ellis he was just a man, a rather fine-looking man: light brown hair, blue eyes, good teeth and a smile to melt your heart. But she was finished with men, wasn't she?

'Some might disagree with you,' she said, very gravely.

'Then they must be blind. This guy, I hate him already, what is he to you?' Wade slipped one arm along the back of the car seat. Drat this war and the rules it created.

'I told you, he's just a friend. Well, engaged to my best friend, in point of fact. Or was.'

'You sound doubtful. Is she about to chuck him?' He longed suddenly to stretch out his fingers and caress the bare neck just inches away. This WAAF's hairstyle might be as short as any man's, but she was all female, no doubt about that.

Kath was staring out to sea, wishing she'd never started this dangerous conversation. 'I'm not sure. It's all a bit confusing. He's called Jack Lawson, from Broombank in Westmorland. I'd be grateful for any information about him.' She turned her beautiful eyes back upon Wade. 'For the sake of my friend.'

'Sure,' he said, heart starting to thump with an excitement he hadn't felt in a long time. 'I'll look into it.'

A small silence fell between them while each seemed to study the other, assessing, considering, liking what they saw. 'I suppose we'd best be getting back,' Kath managed at last.

'I suppose.'

'I'll deal with these. Wouldn't do for your image to be seen with chip papers.'

'It would do my image wonders to be seen with you.'

Kath's breath caught in her throat. 'You don't mess about, do you?'

'Not as a rule, no.'

'It would get me lynched.'

'I know. Me too. That's the pity of it. Damn war.'

Kath stared out to sea again. 'Best not to think of it then.'

'Reckon you're right.' His voice sounded far from convinced. 'Wouldn't do for folks to start thinking things.'

'No, sir.' Kath could feel the warmth and weight of his arm across her shoulder. It was pleasant. She'd forgotten how good a man could make you feel.

'You know it's as if I've known you for an age, not just one day. Tell me your first name, ACW Ellis.'

'Katherine. My friends call me Kath.'

'Aw, I like Katherine best. That's a beautiful name. May I call you Katherine?'

'My mother calls me that.'

'Would it bother you?' He saw the shadow cross her face, fleeting but not imagined, he was sure of it. 'Okay, Kath it is.'

'Thanks. Are you ready to go back to camp now, sir?'

'Don't be so formal, okay?' Wade climbed reluctantly out of the car and got into the back seat. He adjusted his hat. 'Back to camp, Airwoman.'

When Kath dropped him at the Officers' Mess he nodded briskly to her, the smile gone from his eyes, completely professional. 'I'll be in touch about that matter, Airwoman.' And he walked briskly away.

Kath stood holding the car door, at her very best salute. 'Yes, sir. Thank you, sir.'

–

'You drove who?' Bella's eyes were popping. 'Wow. He's a real dreamboat. Aren't you the lucky one. And here's me with my ears glued to signals all day. I'm ferociously jealous.'

Kath laughed. 'Don't be. He's an officer. A very grand officer, therefore untouchable. What are we doing tonight?'

Bella wrinkled her nose. 'Cedric has suggested a foursome.'

'You mean Jimmy is all mine?'

Bella grinned. 'Thought you'd be pleased.'

'I suppose it's better than staying in.'

'Won't argue with that.'

They huddled over the tiny mirror to get ready, fluffing out hair, sharing out what bits of makeup they possessed. Certain items were becoming hard to find, lipstick for one.

'I'm sick of this uniform,' Kath said. 'Somehow it seems worse in summer.' Her eyes met Bella's enquiring gaze.

'So?'

Flagrantly breaking rules, they slipped summer frocks on under their skirts and jackets, and with non-issue shoes tucked in to their greatcoat pockets Kath and Bella set off for an evening out.

They walked to the local hostelry since none of the four possessed the transport to try out distant, more exciting places, despite the obvious risks involved. But Kath soon decided that dressing up had been a bad mistake for she spent the entire evening fending off Jimmy in a corner.

It grew hot in the pub and she suggested they all go outside. Which proved to be a yet worse mistake, she soon realised.

'Good evening, Katherine.'

Kath froze, turning slowly to find Wing Commander Ewan Wadeson gazing at her with open speculation. 'It sure is a hot night,' he said, eyes running over her figure in its silky dress, right down her bare tanned legs to her pretty summer shoes. 'Wouldn't you say?'

She was aware of the others standing fearfully behind her. If this man chose to, he could march them straight to the Guard House, forthwith, on a charge. 'Yes,' she said, smiling warmly, deliberately avoiding the use of the word 'sir'.

His smile tilted the wide mouth to a sensuous curl and Kath responded similarly. He wasn't going to report them, she could see it in his eyes. But he might want paying for the favour, later.

Chapter 3

When they came off Parade Bella nudged Kath rather painfully in the ribs. 'There he is. Glamour Boy is waiting for you already. He'll complain about your being late. I can see why Jimmy doesn't come up to scratch these days.'

'If you want to survive this war, today even, you'd best watch your tongue, Bella Kendrick,' said Kath sweetly.

Bella grinned. 'He sounds pretty smitten to me. Why else would he have you drive him all over the countryside for no apparent reason?'

'Perhaps it's some sort of secret ops he's on, or a survey or something? Not my job to question why.'

'Only to do or die, I know.' Bella strode off, laughing.

Later that day when Bella came off shift, she went straight from the Signals Room to the vehicle depot to find Kath changing a wheel. Maintenance, Kath had discovered, was an essential part of the job if you weren't to spend your life begging favours from the sparks, armourers and ground crew.

'Kath, Kath!' Bella bent down and yanked her friend out from under the car. 'Listen to this. Mule fancies your officer.'

'What?'

'Old Mule. She's got the hots for Wing Commander Wadeson. I heard them talking in the Ops Room. She was telling him that she had two tickets for a symphony in Cambridge and was he fond of music?'

Kath groaned, knowing she shouldn't ask but did anyway. 'And is he?'

Bella's grin stretched from ear to ear. 'I was pretending to be engrossed taking signals but really I was listening like mad. "It was a kind thought," he says. "But really it would be wasted on me. I'm deaf as a post where classical music is concerned. Jazz is more my scene. Besides which my schedule's pretty full at the moment. Thanks for thinking of me." And smiling charmingly at her, he touched his cap and walked off. Boy, was she mad! She went turkey red.'

For no reason that she wished to examine, Kath felt suddenly light-hearted and anxious all at the same time. 'It's probably true, his schedule will be pretty full.'

'Not so full he hasn't time for women.'

Kath concentrated on tightening the wheel nuts. 'Admittedly, there isn't a soul on this camp who wouldn't grab a date with him. But he's not my officer, so I'd appreciate it if you didn't say as much to anyone else.'

'Wouldn't dream of it, old sport. But I'd watch her if I were you, at least if I had any passing interest at all in the gentleman.' Bella stood up. 'Fortunately, as you say, you've given men up so it doesn't matter. See you later.'

–

Kath laid out her kit on the bed, ready for inspection. Next to Parade it was her pet hate to have her gear prodded and peered at. She felt that by nature she was not meant to be a tidy person, especially if she'd been up late the night before driving the top brass back from some meeting or other. Life was too short to waste in polishing and cleaning.

Nevertheless it was a boring but essential part of the daily routine. The Waafery was rigorously guarded and inspected by WAAF Officer Mullin, General Duties, who loved to stalk the length of the Nissen hut, mule face grinning with ecstatic anticipation of discovering some minor misdemeanour.

Mullin insisted that quarters must be kept immaculately tidy at all times. Even shift workers sleeping during the day were frowned upon and liable to have their beds remade while they were still in them.

'Is this your clutter, Ellis?' she would ask, and Kath would smile and attempt to explain about being late which meant that she hadn't had a moment to clean her shoes or buttons or do a thing.

'That is no excuse,' was nearly always the reply.

For some reason she was never afterwards able to justify, this morning Kath decided to answer back. 'I had to drive the Wing Commander out to dinner last night. It was near two when I got in. How could I possibly clean my kit in time?'

The lips thinned dangerously. 'You must *make* the time. I suggest you miss breakfast for the rest of this week in order to rectify these deficiencies.'

'But, ma'am…'

'You wish to say something, Airwoman?'

'No, ma'am.' Drat her runaway tongue.

Against King's Regulations or not, Wing Commander Wadeson had taken every opportunity to deepen their friendship over these last weeks by constantly employing Kath's services as a driver. Their regular weekly jaunts into the countryside had become an important part of her life. He no longer made any pretext of visiting other stations. Instead she would be instructed to drive straight to the headland, or they'd walk by the dyke or drive to the woods and talk.

He was there, as usual on this his morning off, grin on his face, hat not quite at regulation angle.

'Hi.'

'Good morning, sir.' Kath saluted. She never risked slipping from formality while in camp. 'May I be of service?'

Ewan Wadeson rolled his eyes. 'Aw, don't tempt me, honey. I'm sure we can find somewhere I ought to be for all I'm off duty.' Then just as he was about to climb into the back of the car, WAAF Officer Mullin came up.

'Ah, I'm so glad I caught you, Wing Commander.' She half glanced at Kath, saluting like mad as she stood holding open the car door for her passenger. Mule drew Wadeson some distance away while Kath kept her eyes firmly fixed on the distant hangars where the ground crew were busy at work checking over Stirlings in readiness for the next night's op. But she longed to know what was being said. She also couldn't help wondering if it would likewise be out of bounds for a WAAF Officer and a Wing Commander to get too friendly. She didn't know, told herself she shouldn't care. And realised that she cared rather a lot.

'Okay, let's go.' He was beside her again, and with a start Kath saluted and closed the door neatly behind him before briskly going round to climb into the driving seat. WAAF Officer Mullin watched her drive away.

'You can take a car whenever you like, sir?' she asked as they drove towards the coast. The question was very near to impertinent. Kath heard him chuckle.

'Damn right, I can.' He leaned his elbows on the back of her seat. 'You know, if things were normal, I'd ask you out on a date, maybe take you to a movie.'

She caught his eyes in the driving mirror and for a moment became disorientated before forcing her attention back to the road. 'But things are far from normal. Sir.'

'Lot of old gossips round this camp, just love to massacre a guy. Your WAAF Officer, for one, seems concerned about my keeping you out too late. Seems to think I should spread my charms a bit more. Use other drivers.'

Kath's face remained impassive. 'The fault was mine, sir. I used the late night as an excuse, when really I'd simply forgotten to clean my kit.' She flickered her eyelashes outrageously at him. It was worth a try. This man could cause her a lot of trouble if he wished. 'I'm sorry, sir. It won't happen again.' He stared at her for a long moment then put back his head and roared with laughter.

'I bet you gals lead her a merry dance.'

'I'm sure that's true,' Kath agreed, with false demureness. She caught a glimpse of his eyes sparkling at her, challenging, and unable to help herself Kath found her own lips curving into a smile.

'That's better. I hate it when you look too serious. There's a sadness to your face, do you know that, Katherine? And there shouldn't be for it sure looks cute when you smile.'

Later, as they walked in a quiet spot of woodland, he told her that he had news of Jack.

'That friend of yours. She should write to Portsmouth. Jack Lawson is on *HMS Bramton*. Reckon it will be leaving port soon so she shouldn't waste too much time about it.'

'Oh, thank you. That was kind of you, sir.' Kath's eyes were stinging, though whether from pleasure or pain, she wasn't too sure.

'You're looking sad again.'

'Sorry.' She hadn't decided quite why she must contact Jack, or what she would say to him when she did, but was grateful for the opportunity. 'I do appreciate your help.'

He picked up her hand and kissed the finger tips. 'You're a real fine gal. I wouldn't mind getting to know you a whole lot better.'

Kath removed her hand and clasped it behind her back. 'What part of Canada do you come from, Wade?' Formality had no place when they were alone.

'My folks live in Montreal. What about yours? You've told me so little about yourself.'

'There's little to tell. My father is a retired doctor. Mummy looks after him when she can spare time from her garden and her good works.' There was a certain edge to her voice which Wade was not fool enough to miss.

'How does your family feel about your being in uniform, Katherine? Not prejudiced against it, I hope.'

She smiled. Not knowing how best to answer she decided not to. Best to keep the conversation away from herself. 'What did you do in civvy street? Before the war.'

'Would you believe a lawyer? My father has his own practice in Montreal. I went in with him. It was expected, you know?'

Kath nodded sympathetically. 'I can imagine.'

'But what I'd really like is to be a farmer, or a rancher. That would be great.'

'A farmer?' Kath laughed, a short, rather bitter laugh that this time Wade didn't pay proper attention to.

'I know. It's a crazy idea. But I just love the countryside. I like physical things, being outside. I'd just love it.'

'Farming is hard work, long hours and badly paid. Stick to the law.'

'You sound like you know something about it.'

'A little. We have a few acres of our own which are more trouble than they are worth. And many of my friends are farmers.' She wrinkled her nose. 'Don't do it, Wade.'

He was watching her keenly. 'I know what I want to do right now.'

'Oh?' He took her by the elbow and drew her to him. 'Oh, I see. Um, look, I don't think this is a good idea, do you?'

'Best one I've had in a long while. I've held off pretty well, don't you think? I really like you, Katherine – Kath. You're a lovely gal. I'd love to see you again. Properly, I mean, not driving this damn car.'

She relaxed slightly as she saw that he wasn't about to ravish her in the undergrowth. Ewan Wadeson was a gentleman, a real old-fashioned sort. But in a more comfortable setting it might be a different story. Then where would she be?

'That would have been good, if, as you say, things had been normal.'

His eyes were burning into hers and one thumb was smoothing the inside of her elbow. The sensation of it, even through her jacket sleeve was euphoric, making her feel slightly giddy. 'No one need know. What the eye don't see, the heart don't bleed over. Ain't that one of your sayings?'

'I believe it is.'

'I can't keep hijacking you this way, but we could sneak off some place. If we're clever. It's done all the time. I really like you, Katherine, you're my sort of girl.'

'And if we got caught?' In more ways than one, she thought bleakly.

His arms were right about her now, caressing her spine, her hips, pressing her close to him, the hard strength of him intoxicating. He was very tempting. 'The secret is, not to,' he said. His lips came down gently to claim hers and Kath made no protest. One kiss surely didn't matter. Lifting her arms about his neck, she gave herself up to the ecstasy of it.

—

Kath stood at the dock gates, a letter in her hands. She'd been due a few days' leave and had written to Jack to tell him she was coming over to see him.

He'd replied at once, a cheerful Jack type letter saying he'd be delighted to see her. Now she was actually here, she was riddled with a thousand doubts. What should she say to him? She hadn't even devised any plan of action. Should she mention Melissa?

There was also the all important question of what she would feel when she saw him again.

Jack Lawson had been a good friend and great fun, though not to be taken too seriously. But Kath had to admit that there had been a time when, if he'd asked her, she'd have married him like a shot. To hell with Meg and the obvious disapproval of her parents. And not just for the sake of the baby either. Jack Lawson had that certain something to attract any girl, call it charisma, sex appeal, whatever, but Kath was curious to know if he still had it, and if it would still affect her. Would Jack be the answer to her long term problems?

'Kath, there you are, I didn't recognise you in uniform. Hey, you look great.'

A sailor stood before her, tall, bronzed, handsome, hair shorter than she remembered but the same violet eyes wickedly teasing, the same tilt to the wide mouth she'd once been so eager to kiss. Hands were stretched towards her and she grasped them. The next moment she was in his arms, laughing, crying, the smell and feel of him bringing a rush of sweet memories.

'How tall you are. Have you grown?' she laughed.

'It's the cut my tailor gives this outfit. Smart, don't you think?'

'Wonderful. Who presses those creases in all the wrong way?'

'Me, who else?'

He hugged her close. He smelled salty, and as if he spent a lot of time polishing and scrubbing. 'It's so good to see someone from home, you wouldn't believe how homesick I was at first. Stupid when you think how we longed to get away to new adventures, both of us. We were just kids though, eh?'

Kath laughed, feeling oddly numb inside. Her mind racing, wondering what she should say, how much she should tell. He was a man now, not a boy, and so much more sure of himself. 'We did escape in the end though.' He had walked away, she had run.

They started to walk now, arms linked, along the dock road. 'You're not homesick now, I hope?' she asked.

'Hell, no. Been overseas once, and we're off to foreign parts again soon. All a bit hush hush but the word is it's Italy. Looking forward to it as a matter of fact. I prefer life

47

at sea. Come on, I'll buy you a G and T, or whatever your tipple is these days.'

'A half of cider will do fine.'

'A half it is then.'

Tucked into a corner of the local pub, Kath returned to the subject close to her heart. 'Will you get leave, before you go?'

'Probably.'

'Will you go home, do you think?'

He met her gaze. 'To see Meg, you mean?'

'I suppose I do.'

Jack frowned. 'I ought to but — well, it's a long way, Westmorland, just for a few days.'

A shaft of irritation pierced her. 'You're as selfish as ever, you rotten bastard!'

He jumped, startled by her choice of language, as well he might be. The old Katherine would not have used such a word. But then the old Katherine was gone.

'What's that supposed to mean?'

'Meg loves you, and all you care about is yourself. Does she even know you're back in port? I thought not. You don't deserve her, you really don't.'

Dark eyebrows lowered but he didn't deny it. After a moment Jack shrugged. 'Meg is lovely and great fun. She writes screeds of chatty letters all about the farm and what everyone's doing there. A real nice girl.'

Kath winced. 'That sounds rather damning.'

'I don't mean it that way. She means a lot to me, don't mistake that. It's a good feeling, to know she's there, you know? Waiting for me till the end of the war.'

'She loves you and apparently still believes, though God knows why, that you feel the same way about her.'

'I do, I do.' He shifted in his seat, looking uncomfortable. 'What the hell, I suppose I can tell you, Kath. I've been out with other girls. It's a year since I saw her, that's a long time. I would have liked to get home more but, as I say, it's a long way, trains are terrible and I'm always short of funds.'

'Surprise, surprise,' she said dryly.

'Anyway, I'm not ready for all of that…' He downed most of his pint in one gulp and rubbed the froth from his lip with the back of his hand. '…All that marriage and babies and stuff. Want another?'

'Er…' Kath glanced at her scarcely touched glass. She felt empty inside, as drained suddenly as his glass. Yet what had she expected? 'No thanks, I'm fine. You help yourself.'

Jack went off to do just that. There was a bounce to his step now, Kath noticed, as she watched him go up to the bar then return with a fresh, brimming glass. A real sailor's roll, chock full of arrogance. And as totally selfish as ever. What a fool she'd been.

'We get special rations of rum and brandy on board ship. One of the perks of the job.'

'What do you do? What's your job?'

'Just another bloody sailor.' He laughed.

'Following the tradition of a girl in every port?' She wanted, very badly, to smack the self-satisfied smirk from the too handsome face.

'Let's say I'm working on it. Now have you seen the landlord's daughter?' And he burst out laughing.

She did not laugh with him. An awkwardness fell between them and she let it lie, sipping at her drink, wondering why she had come. Wanting suddenly, desperately, to be gone from this place and never to set eyes on him again. She stood up.

49

'I've got to go,' she lied. 'I only have a short pass.'

'Right. I'll walk you to the station.' Jack winked at her as he stood on the platform. 'We had some fun, eh? You and me, once?' Another notch on his belt, she thought.

Kath's heart sank with shame at every word he spoke. She couldn't wait to get away. Had she really found this man exciting? Had her pulses truly raced with liquid fire whenever he touched her? How young and foolish she must have been. But the Katherine Ellis of those youthful adventures had had no one to compare Jack Lawson with. He was the best they'd got because he was all they'd got. Men were thin on the ground on the Westmorland fells.

She smiled briefly, coolly, before climbing onto her train. 'I suppose we did,' she said brightly, leaning out the window, trying not to look at him.

'I'll always remember that, you know. You were special to me, Kath. Always will be.'

'You sound as if you aren't going to see me ever again?' There was a sudden tightening in her breast as she looked into his face, regarding him more keenly.

Beneath the brazen banter, despite the swagger of his walk, there was a sudden panic in the violet eyes.

'Got to go and put Mussolini's lot in their place first,' he said, his tone cocky as if he meant to do it all by himself. 'Time enough to get serious about women and take on responsibility when the show's over, eh?'

She nodded, unable to speak, quite unable to tell him that it was already too late, his responsibilities had begun. Perhaps she'd be best to put it in a letter. Some time. Later. When he got safely back perhaps.

Nothing could bring her to swallow her pride now and tell him, face to face, that she had borne him a child.

Train doors banged, a whistle blew, and Kath sighed with relief. It was over, she had seen him, and with that visit a ghost had been laid. He meant nothing to her. Not a thing. It'd all been just sex, as she'd thought at the time. No more, no less.

When the train drew out of the station she did not look back. Whatever memories she had of that sun-kissed time before the war, Kath knew for certain now that it was over. She had a daughter to think about one day, once she had her life in order again, but for now at least life was shaping up pretty well at Bledlow.

She would enjoy her leave, take a few days' rest in the country somewhere, but not too long.

Waiting for her back in camp was someone she was very much looking forward to seeing again.

–

'Hi, I've missed you,' were his first words to her. They were sitting in a cinema in Cambridge, in the dark, far from the station, having come in separately hoping like mad that no one had seen them.

He took her hand in his. Kath's heart was thumping crazily. All thoughts of celibacy were quite gone from her head. She wanted this man, and, if he still wanted her, as far as she was concerned, he could have her.

Ewan Maximillian Wadeson III, however, was a gentleman, and liked to do things properly.

He kissed her, deep and lingering. 'You realise it is prejudicial to good order for me to be seen with you, as another rank?' Kath ran her lips lightly over his jawline, such a lovely strong jaw. 'No one can see us in the dark, so that's all right.'

'Why don't you marry me?'

'What?' She couldn't see his face in the smoke-wreathed darkness but she could feel his smile. 'Very funny.'

He put his arm around her, pressed his lips close to her ear. 'I mean it, honey. You know how I feel about you. A quiet little ceremony, just you, me and a witness. Our little secret.'

Kath couldn't believe what he was saying. Yet a part of her was not against the idea, she realised. 'Are you quite serious?'

'Never more so. I want you. I've never felt this way about a woman before. We'd be good for each other, Katherine.'

Her heart was racing. A million thoughts teemed through her head. On screen, Deanna Durbin was singing her heart out, and nothing seemed quite real. It would be too, too easy to get carried away on a tide of romance, and look where that got you.

Outside, after the show, reality struck with the cool night breeze and rain-polished pavements.

'Hurry now, before anyone sees you,' she told him as he lingered, holding her hand. 'My bus is over here.'

'Let me give you a lift.'

'Who is your driver?'

'I drove myself here this evening. So you can take me back. Pretend you're on duty.'

'How very clever of you.' Laughing, and against her better judgement, Kath agreed.

All the way back to camp he tried to persuade her. 'Don't rush me, Wade. It's too easy to make a mistake.'

They stopped on a quiet road so he could stroke her face, her throat, her thigh. 'Don't you want me?'

'That's not a good reason for getting married,' Kath protested, returning his kisses with an eagerness she could scarce control.

'It is in wartime. You know damn well we could both be dead next week.'

It was a sobering thought. Still she hesitated. 'You know nothing about me.' Like for instance that I have a daughter, she wanted to say, but the words wouldn't come.

'I know enough.'

'Best to leave things as they are for a while. See how it goes.'

'You're not offended, are you?' Anxiety in his voice, in his face. 'I wouldn't hurt you for the world, Katherine. I hope you realise that.'

Her heart was filled with a rush of compassion for him and she put her lips to his softly. Desire flared like a torch between them and his mouth caught hers, deepening the kiss to something far more dangerous. Did she love him? She didn't know. How could she tell? But he was all male, and she was a healthy, normal woman. He had her jacket unfastened and was reaching for her tie when he broke away with an abruptness that hurt.

'Hellfire, I can't keep this up for much longer! I'm too old to play footsie in a car. Promise me you'll think about it? I'll buy us a lovely home in Canada after the war, anything you like. Just say yes, honey, and I'll buy you the world in gold paper.'

Somewhere inside, her heart melted. Kath could hardly drag open her eyes, so drugged was she with wanting, with loving. But was what she felt enough? Would it last? She had felt this terrible longing for Jack once, and look where that had got her.

But Wade wasn't like Jack. Surely he would keep his promises. What they felt for each other was different. Or was it?

How would Wade react if she told him about Melissa? Would he still want her, with an illegitimate daughter? She certainly couldn't marry him without telling him. 'I'll think about it, I promise,' was all she said.

When she garaged the staff car and walked across to her hut she saw Mule, checking quarters at the end of her shift.

'Late in again. Airwoman?'

Kath glanced at her wristwatch. It said ten fifteen. 'No, ma'am. Still fifteen minutes to go.'

'Driving Wing Commander Wadeson to yet another meeting?' Kath half turned, glancing back over her shoulder as if expecting to see him standing there. Then she realised that since she'd dropped Wade by the gate, the woman couldn't possibly have known for certain she'd been out with him. It had been a guess, but by Kath's own guilty reaction, one that had been proved accurate.

'Just doing my duty, ma'am.'

'I've been told you were at the Ship the other night.'

Kath schooled herself not to overreact. 'That was on our night off and we were back by ten, ma'am.' Worn out by Laddo Octopus, she thought.

'I believe Wing Commander was there too. What a coincidence.'

'Yes. Wasn't it? If you'll excuse me, ma'am. I'll check in.' Kath saluted smartly and started to walk away. Mule kept pace.

'A little bird also tells me you were seen wearing civvies.' Kath's heart jumped with shock. Surely not

Wade? Would he tell on her? No, it could have been anyone.

'I'm afraid I don't understand,' Kath said, with blithe innocence.

'You understand me perfectly, ACW Ellis.'

'Couldn't say, ma'am, whether there were any WAAFs in civvies or not. We would certainly never step off the station without uniform, as you well know.' It was not quite a lie for they had left in uniform, and changed in the Ladies at the pub, so Kath was able to meet Mule's gaze unflinchingly.

A long, silent appraisal. 'There's something not quite right about you, Ellis. You are not entirely what you seem.'

Kath raised enquiring brows. 'I'm a simple WAAF, doing my job. What more could I be?'

'Not quite so simple. Where did someone of your evident class acquire such skills with a scrubbing brush? And such rough hands to go with them. Why had you only one set of civvies? And why do we know no more about you than we did the day you arrived? You say nothing about your family, your background, your upbringing. Why is that, I wonder?'

'Didn't realise you were so interested. Ma'am.'

'Your remarks are close to insolence, Airwoman.'

Kath ground her teeth together and apologised. 'Is this a serious interrogation, ma'am?'

'Quite the mystery woman, aren't you?'

Kath had reached the door of her Nissen hut and turned to face her interrogator. 'I do my job as good as I can. Mind my own business. I expect everyone else to do the same. May I go now, ma'am?' She'd pushed it too far. Kath could tell by the furious expression on Mule's face.

'Let me see you at Parade once in a while, Ellis.'

'Ma'am.'

Smiling to herself, Kath went in to Bella and the waiting cocoa. Nosy old troublemaker, she thought.

Three weeks later the smile was wiped from her face when Kath discovered that a new posting had come through for her. She'd been given her movement orders to go to another section of Group Command, far away from Wing Commander Ewan Wadeson. Mule, it seemed, had won.

Chapter 4

Joe Turner enjoyed his ill temper as some people relish poor health. But then, as he so often told himself, he had a right to be upset. Nothing was going right at the moment.

By heck though, if he were in the government he'd stand no nonsense from this Hitler chap. And he was right glad they'd got that Hesse fellow locked up in the tower. Proper place for him an' all. Keep him out of mischief for the rest of the war, that would. Oh, aye, he made a point of keeping abreast of the news, and offering the wisdom of his opinion upon it. He'd followed with increasing dismay the German advancement on Malta, on Yugoslavia even, for all it'd proved a tricky country to take, and then Greece and Crete. Whatever way you looked at it, things were not good. Now they were after the Ruskies. By, but the Huns would find them a tougher meat to tackle, for all they'd taken Kiev, cheeky as you please.

'What we need is Lloyd George to take this lot on,' he announced, not for the first time to Sally Ann who patiently read him snippets from the newspaper each morning and tuned in the crackling nine o'clock news for him at night on the battery wireless.

'Don't talk soft, Dad. Lloyd George isn't running the country now, Churchill is.'

'Aye, well, Lloyd George'd do better.'

Sally Ann sighed and spooned cereal into little Daniel's mouth. 'You live in the past, that's your trouble. Dad. You'll have to come into the twentieth century one of these days so best start getting used to the idea.'

'You sound like our Meg.'

Sally Ann laughed. 'Sometimes I understand exactly how she feels about you, you old misery boots! Pour me out another cup of tea, my hands are full.'

Joe did as she asked. He was not displeased with this new daughter-in-law of his. She could cook, was easy to live with, and kept a smiling face about the place. And she had given him two grandsons. 'Meg's alius wanting summat she can't have.'

Sally Ann wiped the baby's mouth and lifted him against her shoulder, rubbing his back gently. 'I know you miss Annie. It was sad she was taken so soon, but you can't expect Meg to step into her shoes.'

Joe glared into the fire. 'You can't turn back the clock, that's for sure, though there's things I'd put right if I could.'

'We all feel that way when we've lost someone,' Sally Ann said softly. 'Don't blame Meg for not being more like her mother. She's like you. She wants what it is perfectly reasonable for her to have, a farm. She's your daughter, all right.'

'She's nowt like me.'

Sally Ann actually laughed out loud at that. 'Isn't she just? More than either you or she realises, I reckon. She's tough as old boots, and soft as good leather. Just like you. Only difference is you won't show it. You'd go to any lengths to keep your feelings hidden, and Meg has been behaving exactly the same way with little Lissa.' Sally Ann frowned. 'It worries me, it does really.'

'That one maintains that child isn't hers.'

'No more it is, in my opinion,' said Sally Ann quietly. 'Though I don't lay claim to having the answer, I have my own idea on the subject.' She caught the gleam in Joe's eye and laughed again. 'No, I'm not going to tell you what it is, you old goat.'

'She should get herself wed and stop messing about with things she knows nowt about. Sheep farming is man's work. Bairns are for women. I've said so afore…'

'…And you'll go on saying it, I know. Now, if you've nothing better to do than gossip, you can fold those nappies for me.'

Without demur, Joe pulled the nappies one by one from the rack and folded them into a soft white pile, not realising the incongruity of the task after his last words. He found he didn't mind having childer, as he called them, about the place. They kept a man feeling alive. Pity Meg didn't bring her youngster to visit him more often, though a girl was not to his taste. A man needed sons to follow him on. One day Joe would like Dan to have the farm, as was only right and proper, for himself and his sons. Though what he'd make of it, God only knew. Mebbe, if Joe played his cards right, Broombank an' all.

But money was tight just now. Things weren't going well at all. Childer took a lot of feeding, wanting clothes and such like. How Ashlea would manage to keep them all he didn't know. Now if Meg would only stop being so stubborn he and Dan would be right set up. There was plenty of time, though, to get his hands on the land he wanted. He hadn't given up hope yet, not by a long chalk.

But first he had to secure Ashlea.

–

'Haven't you done enough for today?' Tam said to Meg a few days later when she was poring over the accounts one evening by the light of the lamp. 'Don't you know paraffin is in short supply?'

'I know, but I must finish these figures.'

'It's rest you're needing.'

Tam knew everything there was to know about both her and the business. He was always there for her when she needed a friend. Meg knew she was lucky to have him stay on since he was a man who claimed to have no roots, and might decide to leave at any moment. A good reason to keep him at a distance. He was simply an employee after all, and a man. Therefore not to be trusted absolutely.

'I must get these accounts done. I've an appointment to see the bank manager on Friday.'

Tam tightened his lips in that familiar way he had which spoke volumes without his saying a word. He set the kettle on the new range they'd had fitted in the great kitchen inglenook. 'I'll make cocoa and you fetch some of those rice biscuits Effie made today.'

Meg tossed down her pen with a laugh. 'You aren't going to give up, are you?'

'I usually get my own way, in the end.' He looked at her gravely. 'You can have ten more minutes then bed, no matter what you say.'

The shutters were drawn, Effie and Lissa were in bed and there was a reassuring cosiness about being here, with Tam. A feeling that she was very safe, protected from the world outside. Yet there was more to it than that, more than cosiness and homeliness, cocoa and biscuits. She'd had it before, this feeling that couldn't quite be defined and Meg chose to ignore.

The gaze held a moment longer and she smiled in order to break the tension growing between them. It disturbed her yet she couldn't quite say why, not seeing him as he saw her, her mind already turning to the figures and why they wouldn't add up. Tam sighed and the sound said that it was just as well he was a patient man.

As they sat companionably enjoying Effie's biscuits, Tam nodded in the direction of the account books. 'Go on then, I'll listen. Why is it you must see the bank manager? Is it trouble we're in then?'

She liked it when he said 'we'. As if he was a part of the project, and meant to stay.

Meg flushed with excitement and pleasure. 'No, quite the opposite. We were lucky in having a good lambing season this year when for many people it was a disaster. Thanks, in no small part, to you and Effie.'

'Thanks duly accepted.' Tam regally bowed his head.

'Which means that our stock has increased, even accounting for some losses. Which is good, don't you think?'

'Splendid.' Tam reached for another biscuit. 'Perhaps then Effie could afford a bit more sugar in these?' He held one up, puckering his lips.

'Sugar? You'll be lucky. Be grateful you have biscuits at all, you oaf.'

Tam chuckled. 'Go on. What's your plan? I can see that you have one by the twinkle in your eye.'

Meg wrinkled her nose at him. 'You are far too knowing, Thomas O'Cleary.'

'Where you are concerned, maybe I am. Don't you know how transparent you are?' The biscuit airily instructed her to continue and Meg, feeling suddenly shy, did so. Her plans felt oddly precious, hard to share. She took a deep breath.

'I mean to buy a tractor.'

'Ah. A tractor now, is it? Hence your decision to see the bank manager.'

Meg's eyes glowed. 'Yes. Look.' She laid out the pages showing her reckoning on the table before them. 'I've paid what I owe to Will Davies for the cows and tups, and Lanky's debts are all settled. We've bought in two Tamworth pigs which are fattening up nicely. The ducks and turkeys are doing well. But these are largely ways of feeding ourselves, and of surviving from day to day. We should start looking to the future. We need to expand but more sheep means more land, more work, and more time needed to attend to them. The War Committee are asking for still more land to be ploughed up. Mechanisation is the way forward. Don't you agree?'

Listening, chin in hand, to the excitement in her voice, watching the lamplight dance over the high cheek bones, Tam O'Cleary would have agreed if she'd said the moon was made of green cheese. Not that she recognised this in him for he had the sense to keep his feelings well hidden. A man had his pride, after all.

He'd loved Meg Turner from the moment he'd first set eyes on her, the night he'd arrived and she'd stumbled into this kitchen all wet and muddy shouting for rope and a sack. They'd spent hours together out on the fells rescuing Rust. The dog had been taken to the Veterinary and, against all odds, had healed well in the end. But his mistress was still smarting from Jack's betrayal, and still loyally standing by him.

Tam struggled to focus on what she was saying. 'You say you intend to get more land and more sheep?'

'The land idea will have to wait, but I mean to buy more Swaledales.'

'Why Swaledales when you've got a growing flock of Herdwicks?'

'Herdwicks are fine strong sheep, their meat is sweet, but the wool is only really suitable for carpets, and heavy army blankets. The days of hodden grey are long gone. Swaledales make bigger lambs and I can sell them on to be crossed with other sheep such as Leicesters to make better apparel wool. I might make more out of that than the meat. I can even cross them myself with a Herdwick tup to keep them hardy if I want. They're much more economic, do you see, so why not?'

'How will you do it?'

'By selling half of my Herdwicks this backend and starting to buy in Swaledales.' She closed the book with a flourish, nearly knocking over the untouched mug of cocoa in her enthusiasm.

'For goodness' sake, drink it. You get so involved with your damn sheep you almost forget to eat sometimes.'

Tam's fingers closed hers about the still warm mug and Meg felt herself jerk, as if something had moved inside her. They were such comforting, strong, reliable hands. That was all it was. No more than that. Safe. Tam was good to her. What would she do without him?

'Do you think it's a good idea?' It mattered, somehow, that he did.

Tam chuckled. 'Would you not carry out this wonderful plan if I disagreed?'

She pretended to consider. 'Nope. I'd still do it.'

'Will you have enough money to buy in your new Swaledales, pay your quarterly rent, and instalments on a tractor?'

Meg flushed. She hadn't quite got that far yet, but she was optimistic, broadly speaking. 'I don't see why not, if we work hard. But I need you to be with me on this.'

Tam gave a half laugh, almost at himself. 'I told you once before, I'm with you all the way.'

Meg finished the cocoa swiftly and set the mug on the sink. 'Good. I'm off to bed then. See you in the morning.'

'Goodnight to you.'

Tam sat staring into the empty grate long after she had climbed the stairs. Was he a fool to stay, to want her so much? He couldn't quite make up his mind.

—

On Friday morning, Meg stood before the mirror, adjusting her small blue hat, her spirits high.

A small hand tugged at her skirt. 'Lissa come too.'

Meg did not glance down. 'No, darling. Meg has to go out alone today. See, I've got my best setting-out suit on. You stay here with Tam and Effie.'

Lissa stamped a foot. 'No. Want to come.'

Meg bent down with a sigh. 'Don't do this, Lissa, not today. I have an important meeting.' She picked up her bag and a brown paper packet in which were her carefully worked-out figures and plans. The small hands gripped the skirt, preventing her from taking one step.

'Effie,' Meg called.

'What is it?' Effie gazed at the child clinging to her skirts. 'You should take her out more. She needs you.'

Meg's eyes were pleading. 'Not today. I can't today. This is important, for all of us. Take her, Effie, please.'

Effie heaved an exaggerated sigh and reached for Lissa. The child at once stiffened her body, refusing to be picked up. 'Don't be naughty, there's a good girl,' Effie pleaded, prising the curled fingers from the blue fabric. 'By heck, she's wilful.'

'I hope her hands were clean,' Meg mourned. 'I can't go into the bank manager's office looking crumpled and covered with sticky finger marks.'

Effie was panting for breath. 'I wish you'd help a bit more with her, Meg. She's getting to be a right handful.' But Meg had taken her chance and slipped out of the door. With a cheery wave to Tam who was striding off up the fell, she hurried down the lane to the bus stop. A bright future beckoned, far more important at the moment than a wilful child.

–

It was the bank manager who brought Meg down to earth. 'Perhaps you are trying to run before you can walk, Miss Turner? Changing to Swaledales seems to be a sound proposition, but a tractor?' What do you know about tractors? his expression seemed to ask. Nasty, smelly, unreliable things.

Meg explained her belief in the future, the need for mechanisation. But she could tell by the bland politeness in the bank manager's eyes that he was not convinced.

'Farming is going to become far more competitive,' she persisted. 'And efficiency is essential. So much time, and land, is wasted by trying to do it all by hand.'

'The War Committee would do your ploughing and harvesting for you.'

Meg sighed. He simply wasn't listening to a word she was saying. Patiently she continued with her explanation. 'I know they will. My own brother works for them.

They've given me grants to drain my low-lying land and helped me with the work. But I get two pound an acre for doing the ploughing myself and the War Committee will not always be with us, nor will the war, praise God.

'In farming you have to think long term and plan ahead. I now have a dozen more acres of well-drained, good land to deal with. Because of the war most of it must be ploughed but later it will make winter pasture for my sheep. Even land that isn't to be ploughed needs tending, cleaning and harrowing. Feed has to be carried to those sheep that need it. Sick animals carried back. A tractor would more than pay its way in time alone.'

'Yes, but you are a woman, Miss Turner.'

'So?'

'So, when the war is over,' his lips curved into a condescending smile, 'you will no doubt be wishing to marry, have children?' She wanted to tell him that she had a child already, which fact didn't at all prevent her from working. Common sense stopped her. There were those in the community who still believed that Lissa was her own daughter, she could see it in their eyes. Joe for one. There was little to gain by involving the bank in the mess.

'It doesn't mean to say, even if I were to marry, that I wouldn't still need a sound business behind me. On the contrary.'

'Oh, quite, quite,' he agreed, clearly not meaning it. 'But then you would have a husband to attend to such matters for you.'

'I have never found any prejudice in the farming community,' said Meg, very firmly. 'I have been accepted from the beginning, the moment they realised I was serious about making a go of the farm.'

'I do not doubt your determination. But taking on a loan, Miss Turner, demands a different kind of commitment.'

'You are afraid I won't be able to pay it back?'

The bank manager tutted. 'These are difficult times, Miss Turner. Money is in short supply. Do you have a guarantor for the loan? Your father perhaps?'

Meg knew then that she had lost. She picked up her portfolio of accounts and plans from the bank manager's desk. 'Thank you for listening to me. Will you tell me just one thing? I can see that I would have had no difficulty at all in getting the loan had I been a man. Will the same rules apply when I come to you for a mortgage?'

'Mortgage?'

'To buy Broombank. I have three years left, according to Lanky's will, to find the deposit. If I make a go of the farm in the meantime, will you look more favourably upon me?'

Fingers tapped thoughtfully together, the same bland smile. 'We shall have to see. Time, as they say, will tell.' Which meant no. Disappointment was keen in her as she walked away. But she wasn't defeated, oh dear me no. It would take more than one bank manager to stop Meg Turner, once she had her mind set on something. There were other banks, after all.

Not a speck of cloud marred the blue heavens on this perfect, late September day as Effie dragged her bike out of the lean-to and clattered it over the slate slabs of the farmyard, startling a family of sleek-coated weasels as they squabbled over a heap of chaff by the barn door. She was setting out early for school this morning since she wanted to post her latest letter to Mam. Effie was proud to be able to write a letter every week to her family, not that her mother could read it, of course, but she would take it to the parson and he would read it for her.

Effie liked to tell her what she was learning at school. Lissa's latest naughty tricks. Her happy life at Broombank and all about Meg and Tam, Sally Ann and the children. Her mam liked to hear about the children.

There had been times, recently, when she'd been able to send her a postal order, if Meg had sold enough milk or eggs. That made Effie feel proud, to be able to contribute a bit towards her younger brothers and sisters' care. And every now and again, when he had time, there would be a note back from the parson, to say how they all were.

All in all, Effie was very pleased with life. Except that this morning, Meg had been in another of her 'moods'. There'd been a few of those recently, most unlike her usual cheerful self she was. All to do with banks and money and being a woman. Effie didn't understand one bit of it, but oh, even when Meg was at her most irritable, Effie would rather be here than anywhere else in the world.

If the thought wasn't so wicked, she'd wish for the war to go on forever. What she really meant, of course, was that she wanted to stay here at Broombank for ever and ever, with Meg and Tam and her lovely Lissa. She wouldn't ever take to the cows but she'd come to terms with the crags and towering mountains.

She was twelve now, or so she supposed, and almost a woman. Clean, healthy and well fed, and though she'd never make a scholar, doing well enough at her lessons to get by. The thought of returning to the Manchester slums made her want to throw up. This was her place now, as it was Meg's. She felt safe here, and exquisitely happy.

Effie was pedalling furiously, as she usually did, half her mind on the day ahead: helping Miss Shaw with the younger ones, doing a bit of work on her own account, though not too much. The other half was on the potato and onion patties she would fry up for their tea. Maybe she'd open a tin of that Spam she'd managed to get the other week. Meg needed a bit of cheering up.

She was getting up a good speed, pretending she was riding a horse, not a rusty old bicycle that squeaked because it was in need of oiling. Galloping across country on a fiery steed with the wind in her hair.

The best bit was when she reached the crest of Copper-gill Pass. If she went really fast along the flat part of the hill, she could zoom down to Slater's Bottom with her feet stuck out at the sides and the pedals whirling free. It was almost worth the climb up for the exhilaration of that descent.

This morning when she reached the top of the hill she heard the sound. A great droning noise filling the heavens, frightening the birds into silence. The noise grew louder and when she half turned to see what it was, she almost fell off her bike with shock.

It was an aeroplane, flying alongside the hill. It was right over the dale and heading straight for Ashlea.

–

Sally Ann heard the plane just as she was pegging out the washing. She saw it bank once as it zoomed over the house, shaking all the windows with the vibration of its engines. She ran, frantic with fear, back into the house, desperate to find Nicky who, as usual, was not where he was supposed to be. Heart pounding, her screams frightening the little boy into hiding all the more securely she finally located him under the sideboard. By the time she had snatched up little Daniel from his crib, and got them safely out in the yard the plane was again overhead and she flung the children down beneath an old hawthorn bush with herself on top of them.

The plane rose up over the house, banked, tipped its wings in an impertinent salute and flew on. But it wasn't done, even then, for Sally Ann saw it turn and start to come back towards her.

Breathless with fear, mouth hanging open, Effie watched it swoop across the blue sky, trailing vapour behind it. 'Bloody 'ell, it's coming again.'

She jumped on her bike and started to pedal furiously, as fast – faster, than any horse could gallop. The plane came level with her and for a crazy instant it seemed that she and the aeroplane were travelling each at the same speed as the other, and Effie was in the unique position, from so high on the fell, of looking right down into the cockpit, at two faces grinning at her through the window.

The shock was too much. The bike went flying and Effie with it. If this was the end, dear God, let it come quick. Don't let it hit the house and Sally Ann and the children. She didn't think much of Joe, or Dan, so their safety did not cross her mind. She flung her hands around her head and waited for the explosion.

When nothing happened, only the continuation of the terrible droning noise, Effie dared to peep through her fingers.

There it was again, coming round for a fourth time.

'He's teasing me,' she cried. This time she saw something fall. No bomb doors had opened, nor was it a bomb that drifted down on the morning breeze to land on the bottom field behind Ashlea. But whatever it was, Effie meant to find it.

With all thought of school gone from her mind, Effie pedalled back down the lane, flung herself through the gate and started to search the grass. It took some time as the bag lay in a clump of nettles.

Oh, very clever, she thought, getting stung for her trouble. But the moment she had examined her find, she was on her bike again, pedalling with the wind behind her, back to Broombank.

Effie ran into the house, panting for breath, her hand shaking as she gave the paper to Meg.

'Look! Look what I've got.'

Meg took it, frowning her puzzlement. 'What is it?'

The paper carried a few words, in bold black pen. 'Got married on Saturday. Letter and photo to follow. Love, Charlie.'

Meg gave a shout of laughter. 'Where did you find this?'

'The plane dropped it. From the sky. The plane...' Effie's knees finally buckled and she collapsed on to a chair, clutching her sides in agony.

It was some moments, and several glasses of water later, before the whole story came out.

'The mad crazy fool!' cried Meg, admiring her brother's guts all the same.

'He must have been miles off course,' Tam pointed out. 'Good job he didn't meet with any problems. Who would have known where to look for him?'

'Don't even think of it.' But Meg hugged the paper to her breast, thankful just to know that Charlie was safe and well, if cheekily flying where he shouldn't.

'And married. Goodness, I have a new sister-in-law. I wonder what she's like? I do hope we get on.'

'She'd be a fool, to be sure, if she didn't get on with you, Meg Turner.'

'Oh stop your blarney, it won't wash with me,' she laughed.

'I know,' said Tam mournfully. 'That's the trouble.'

–

What was going on? Sally Ann crawled out from beneath the hawthorn bush with her two children, scratched and dishevelled but surprised to find herself still alive.

She got to her feet, cradling the weeping Daniel on one hip while trying to keep hold of the squirming Nicky with the other hand. Were her eyes deceiving her or was that Effie pedalling like fury down the lane? Watching the tail of the plane disappear, Sally Ann realised now that it was one of theirs, a Lancaster. So what was it doing playing games over Ashlea? She'd go up to Broombank later, when she had the children settled for their afternoon nap. Joe could take care of them for once and she and Meg would catch up on a bit of gossip. Perhaps she would understand. It would be good to go up anyway. Must be a week or more since she'd seen Meg. Right now though, she'd have a cup of tea. She felt in dire need of one.

–

'Married? I don't believe it. The sly boots. Oh, and we've missed out on all the fun.'

'That's war, isn't it? I don't blame him for doing the deed so quickly, though I would have loved to be there,' Meg agreed, grey eyes alight with joy as she told Sally Ann the news. 'Let's just be glad he's well.'

'I wonder if it's the same one? You know,' put in Effie, 'the one he danced with in the Tower ballroom that time.'

'Heavens, I've no idea. The letter doesn't say.'

Meg clicked her tongue with disgust. 'Isn't that just like him? Tells us he's married, but doesn't say who to. Not that it matters. I'm sure she'll be lovely. We'll have to wait for his letter, if it ever comes.'

'I still think it's a pity,' Sally Ann mourned. 'We could have done with a good wedding to cheer us all up.' She slanted her eyes across at Tam who was sitting in the porch, cleaning tack with saddle soap and linseed oil. 'You weren't thinking of taking the plunge, were you?'

He looked at her, a dry humour in his Irish eyes. 'Would you like me to call on Miss Shaw, and see if she's available?'

Sally Ann giggled. 'She's well past fifty. You can do better than that, I'm sure. There's a dance on Saturday as a matter of fact. Renton Ralph's Blue Rascals are playing at Kendal Town Hall. How about it?'

'Is that an offer?'

'I mean for us all to go. It's in aid of the War Appeal Fund and soldiers' comforts.'

'I can guess what sort of comforts the soldiers would like,' quipped Tam with a wink, earning himself a slapped wrist from Meg.

'A lot of service people will be there and some of the VAD nurses. You never know, Tam, you might strike lucky.'

Meg laughed along with the rest of them as he brought out a comb and started to titivate his mahogany curls, but the thought of him dancing with some pretty little nurse did not greatly amuse her, oddly enough.

Chapter 5

Meg had her head pushed into the side of the cow, working at the teats with such fierce effort she had a wonderful head of froth in her milk bucket. She loved the smell of the warm milk, the sense of seclusion here in the cow shed. It was a good place to escape. 'Meg? Are you in there?'

She heard the door open, felt the draught of cool air flow in. Drat, she'd been discovered. She heard him approach and stand beside her, silently condemning. 'Are you going to be much longer?' She did not pause for a fraction of a second. 'Why?'

'Dan is coming for us in the Ford at seven and Effie is asking if you'll be wanting a bath before we go.'

'No.'

'Why not?'

'I'm not going.'

The silence grew ominous, then he kicked out at a bale of hay. He was cross, even angry, she could tell. Tam wasn't normally aggressive. 'Are you going to tell me why?'

'Someone has to stay with Lissa, and Effie deserves a night out for once.'

'Effie is too young to go to dances. They'll be fine here. It won't hurt them to be alone for once.'

'What if something should happen? I'd never forgive myself.'

'Well, that's easily solved. We'll get Mrs Davies to come and sit with them. Or better still, they can go and sleep at her house. I'm sure she'd be delighted to have them.'

The cow lifted one foot and stamped it in protest as Meg's fingers dug in too hard. She eased off a little. The poor animal was almost dry now but Meg continued to pull on the teats, not wanting to get up and face Tam. Unfortunately, he guessed.

'You'll make her sore if you carry on at that rate. Meg, leave it.' He hunkered down beside her. 'What's the real reason?'

'I don't want to go, that's all. I don't like dancing.'

'Yes, you do.'

She shook her head, turning away, picking up the milk pail as if to use it as a shield between them. At dances people put their arms around you. They took you outside and kissed you. As Jack had once done. She couldn't face that, not again. It would remind her of how stupid and naïve she'd been, taking the attentions he'd paid her far too seriously. No wonder he'd cheated on her and escaped into the arms of her best friend. It had all been her own fault, and she wasn't for making a fool of herself like that with a man ever again. Oh dear me, no.

She heard Tam sigh. It sounded rather like a growl. 'All right then. We won't go. I'll walk down and tell Dan not to bother coming for us.'

Meg was astounded. '*You* must go. I don't mean to stop your pleasure.'

The leanness of his face looked almost boyish, and strangely vulnerable in the dim light of the cow shed. But he wasn't a boy, he was a man. He moved closer and Meg just managed to stop herself flinching away, but all he did was reach down and take the bucket from her. He set it safely on the slate floor. 'It's that damn Jack, isn't it? You're still pining for him.' The words were grated out, mercilessly cruel, and now Meg did flinch, inwardly at least.

'Y-you don't understand.'

'I do. Don't I understand very well? More than you might think.' He took hold of her shoulders and pulled her round to face him when she might have escaped and run from the shed, from his accusations. 'Are you never going to let him go? He's gone from your life, Meg, forget him. He rarely replies to those damn letters you insist on sending him. He has no intention of committing himself to you, ever. He's a lout.'

The words were cruel, intentionally so. Meg opened her mouth to protest but on seeing the implacable expression on the face so close to hers, she thought better of it and merely gave her a head a sad little shake.

'It's time you stopped mourning for him and started living again.'

'I'm not mourning. I'm too busy with the farm to mourn.'

'Ah, yes, the farm. Broombank, which you guiltily feel should still be his by right. Why? Jack wasn't interested in farming so his father chose to leave it to you. Stop looking backwards all the time, comparing, analysing, feeling guilty. And you hardly acknowledge Lissa's presence.' He half shook her in his irritation. 'You are only half a woman, do you know that? Your mind is so fully occupied with making plans for the future of your precious farm, that nowhere in those plans is there time for any personal happiness.'

Meg wriggled furiously but his grip was unrelenting. 'I'll please myself what I do.'

'Maybe you will. But don't tell me that you don't want to spoil *my* pleasure. Because I'll have you know that you spoil it all the time! You don't give a thought to what *I* want, whether I might like to take you to this dratted jive. Just by living and breathing you ruin my life. Did you know that, Miss Turner?'

He kissed her then. Long and hard. Holding her fast in his arms so there was no hope of her escaping, or even breathing. But judging by the cataclysmic sensations surging through her body, she was still very much alive.

When he had done he gathered her up in his arms and sat her, very firmly, in the cold water trough in the yard. 'Take your bath here then, in your precious farmyard. And when you've done, get dressed in your prettiest frock. You are going to a dance, Meg Turner. With me.'

—

Effie was giggling as she helped Meg button up her best dress. It was a blue print crêpe with a slightly bloused bodice, padded shoulders and soft pleats falling to just below her knee.

'For a soft–hearted Irishman, he can make his wishes felt when he has a mind to.'

'It's simply the wickedness of an eccentric sense of humour,' said Meg, somewhat huffily. 'I could have caught double pneumonia.'

'Instead of which you just lost a bit of your pride.'

'I'm still going to this dratted dance under protest.'

'You'll have a lovely time.' Effie hugged her. 'And no trouble at all keeping him away from the VAD nurses.'

Meg opened her eyes wide in surprise. 'As if I shall try! He can dance with them all night, for all I care.'

Effie giggled again. 'If I had the chance to dance with an attractive Irishman, I'd not complain.'

'Oh, Effie.' Meg clung to her young friend in a sudden gesture of affection and fear, as she might have done to her mother, or Kath, had they been here. 'I daren't go. I simply daren't.' The tremor in her voice was lifting it to something very close to panic. 'I do like Tam, I do. He's good and friendly and he makes me laugh. But you know he doesn't intend to stay for ever, don't you? One morning I'll wake up and find him gone, I know it.'

Effie smiled and tucked back a stray curl of Meg's hair. 'I wouldn't be too sure about that. Go on now, off you go and have a good time. We can't disappoint Hetty, now can we? You know how she enjoys having Lissa. She's even getting me into the bargain tonight. So be off with you and not another word.'

'Oh, Effie, I do love you.' Meg hugged the girl close, no longer a child but still much too thin, as she always would be, no doubt. 'I'm so glad you came to us.'

'Me too.' They held each other for a moment, as they had so often done, sharing their strength. Then Rust came and pushed his nose between them, giving a whimper of jealousy at this show of affection which did not include him. They both laughed, hugging him close and tickling his ears till he rolled over and waved his legs in the air with pleasure.

There was the sound of the van in the yard and Tam's voice, calling to her. 'Will you be coming, girl, if we're ever to get to this dratted dance!'

Meg dabbed at her eyes, quickly powdered her nose and grinned at Effie. 'I'm coming,' she called. 'I'm ready now.'

Meg had a wonderful time at the dance. They all did. It had been crowded, packed with uniforms as well as hard-working civilians wanting to forget the war and their worries over loved ones for a few hours. On the way back they sang 'Green Eyes' and 'Chattanooga Choo-Choo', sitting on blankets in the back of the old van. Dan proved to have quite a good baritone and their praise brought a flush to the tips of his ears, making them all laugh.

Broombank was in darkness when Meg and Tam stumbled out, slightly the worse for the several glasses of beer they had drunk. They waved, giggling, as the old Ford bumped off back down the lane.

'It seems odd with the children not here,' said Meg into the sudden silence. 'As if the world were empty of everything but us. It always surprises me how big the sky is here, how wide and lonely the fells.'

With the same thought they turned to gaze at the fiery glow that flickered in the sky over the distant coast where the Royal Navy base was situated at Barrow-in-Furness. It brought a sick feeling to the pit of Meg's stomach to see this fire of death from their green and quiet world.

'It's hard to imagine that elsewhere homes are being destroyed, lives torn apart. Puts things into perspective, doesn't it?' Tam said. 'At least our plane was only a message from Charlie, not a package from Germany. What do bank managers matter?'

Meg nodded. 'I'm lucky, I know that. I have Effie, and Lissa, and Sally Ann. Even Dan speaks to me in a half-civilised way these days.'

'And there's always yours truly, don't forget,' said Tam softly.

She turned her face up to his. 'How could I? Where would I be without you, Tam?'

'Without my Irish brawn, you mean?'

'No, I don't. I could never have managed Broombank this well without you.'

'Ah, yes, the land. But what of *me*? Have I been of any use, for myself perhaps?'

'I hope that we are friends.'

Tam was silent, wanting to say that no, they were not friends. He could never think of her as simply a friend, but Meg was again talking of Barrow and how she could feel, rather than hear, a humming vibration through her feet.

'How do the German bombers know where they are? They might miss and drop their bombs in the wrong place.'

'I suspect even the Germans can find the sea,' said Tam, in his usual jokey fashion.

'Yes, but how can they *see* where to drop them? I mean. I've heard that our pilots eat carrots, to improve their sight in the dark. Do you think the Germans do too?'

Tam, obviously straining against laughter, considered her suggestion gravely. 'If carrots are so useful, perhaps you should become a vegetable farmer.'

She slapped at him, catching his mood. 'I'm serious. If it's cloudy and dark, how can they know where the target is? How do we know they won't make a mistake?'

'We don't. That's the problem with war. It's often the innocent who suffer.'

Meg stared at him with such earnestness in her expression he was hard put not to kiss her there and then and hang the consequences. 'I pray every day that Charlie will be safe.'

'You know that he is. He's proved it. Spectacularly so.'

'Yes. It's a good feeling.'

'You must tell him to eat more carrots.'

Meg started in astonishment and then burst out laughing. 'You're wicked.' Tam grinned.

'You've got the black dog on your shoulders, that's all. Just because of that stupid bank manager. Stop worrying. Charlie is fine and you're doing your bit here, quietly, without heroics. Just plain hard work, but growing food is important. Never forget that.'

He wiped a tear from her cheek, his fingers lingering over the silk of her cheek bones, wondering how she would react if he kissed it away instead.

Meg looked up into his eyes for a long moment then brushed past him to walk into the kitchen and light the lamp. 'I'll put the kettle on. Tea or cocoa?' She was trembling, he could hear it in her voice.

Tam sat in the rocking chair by the fire, saying nothing, watching with a smile in his eyes as Meg busied herself with the kettle. She said not a word while she waited for it to boil.

The tantalising aroma of tea filled her nostrils and she risked a half glance at him. The light from the Tilly lamp highlighted the planes of his face and set a gloss on the mahogany curls but Meg could not see his eyes which were in deep shadow. She would have given a good deal, right then, to read their expression. She set a mug by his hand upon the table. He did not move to pick it up.

When his voice came to break the silence, Meg started as if she'd been stung.

'You don't seriously expect for one minute that I am going to sit here meekly and drink tea with you in an empty house?'

Her own mug half raised to her lips, she found her fingers setting it down again, quite of their own volition. 'Wh–what do you mean?'

'Do you know how lovely you look in that pretty frock? Like a bluebell in spring, you are.'

Meg got to her feet. 'I think you're drunk.' Tam caught at her hand as she would have passed him and held her still. He leaned forward slightly and she could see his eyes now. The expression in them set a pulse beating deep in her stomach. 'I think I might be, Meg Turner, but not with beer. Do you know what I want to do?'

When she didn't answer, not because she didn't want to, but because she couldn't, he pulled her down on to his lap. His arms came about her so firm and warm and hard with his desire that a spiral of shock, mingled with delicious pleasure, surged through her. She could have touched his face now had she wanted to, it was so close. Quite unable to prevent herself, she did so, with the softest brush of her lips.

'Why didn't you tell me?' she softly asked. She felt as if her insides were burning and her head was somewhere close to the ceiling.

'Tell you what?' The voice was oddly gruff.

'How you felt.'

'Would you have believed me? Would you have listened, or even cared?'

'I'm listening now.' He considered her for such a long time that the ache inside threatened to devour her. Then slowly, desperately slowly, he lowered his mouth to hers and she drank in the sweetness of his lips as a thirsty woman might take her first drink after a lifetime in a desert.

Why hadn't she realised how much she wanted him?

Why could she never see what was right in front of her?

His hold upon her tightened and she felt him shudder against her.

'It's not a child I am, Meg Turner, to be content with kisses. Don't kiss me back like that if you don't want more.'

'Oh, I want more. Much more.'

His face was quiet and intensely serious as his eyes moved lovingly over her face, as if memorising it for all time. 'Let us be absolutely clear about this. I want to take you to bed and take off all your clothes and make love to you as you have never been loved in your life before.' The lips curved upwards into a crooked smile and the lamplight glinted upon the whiteness of his teeth. 'Would you have any objection to that, I wonder, Miss Meg Turner?'

'Oh, no. No objection at all, Thomas O'Cleary. Except…' She dipped her head in a moment's embarrassment. 'I'd want you to keep me safe.'

'You will be.'

'Isn't it wicked?'

His lips touched her brow, her nose. 'No, not wicked. Doesn't everyone think we've been doing this for months already? So why not? If you want me, that is.'

A gurgle of happiness bubbled up inside, setting light to the excitement. Oh, she wanted him all right. How she wanted him.

—

The loving was every bit as wonderful as he had promised. He took off her garments with exquisite care as if he was afraid to startle her, afraid she was a fragile bird who might fly away if he moved too quickly. He laid her on the bed and traced the line of her breasts with the tips of his fingers, exploring, learning her till she was pulsating with need of him, crying out for him to take her.

But just to make sure he had the picture right in his head, he followed along with his lips. Meg clutched at him, pulling him closer, offering herself to him, a willing, joyous partner in this loving. 'Tam?'

'I won't hurt you, my lovely.'

Nor did he, making sure she was moist and ready before taking her with a love and passion that made her cry out with joy in her climax. Their lovemaking was fierce, and all too short. Later, when he took her again, it was slower, more sensual, their first flush of passion sated so that he was able to pleasure her till every nerve throbbed.

Afterwards Meg lay with her face a rosy glow from their loving, an after-love lethargy making her limbs heavy as they lay still entwined with his. They talked softly, punctuating the words with frequent kisses, as lovers do.

'To think you were here, all the time, and I never noticed.'

'A year or more wasted. We've some time to make up.'

Meg burst out laughing. 'You are a wicked Irishman, Tam O'Cleary, and...'

His eyes teased her in the shaft of moonlight that traced its ghostly light over their naked bodies. 'And?'

Meg was glad he could not see her blushes. She had very nearly said it. Nearly said that she loved him. Yet that would never do. She'd made that mistake before. It was too soon. Even if she could ever allow herself to risk such a thing again, love was dangerous, painful. No, she would take a leaf out of Kath's book, and stick with sex. That was fun, and far less complicated. Safe from pain.

'Stop your teasing, you dreadful man. Do you know that in all this time you've been at Broombank, you've told me nothing about yourself.'

'There's nothing at all to tell.'

Meg snuggled down into the curve of his side. 'Nevertheless, I want to know everything about you.'

Tam drew in a long breath and told his life story swiftly, being far more interested in studying the line of her shoulder blades and the small hollows in between.

'How many brothers and sisters have you?'

'Seven. At the last count.'

'No wonder you are so good with Lissa.'

'Families are important.'

'Then why are you here, in England, if they are in America? Sorry, I shouldn't ask.' What she really wanted to ask was, how long are you staying? But she didn't.

'Didn't I want to see the world? I've worked and lived in as many places as I could find. I'll go home and see them all one day. For now I am here.'

For now, she thought, repeating his comment in her head.

His hand was looped about her thigh, stroking the soft inner flesh with the heel of his thumb, and Meg began to lose track of her thoughts. 'What was that you said about making up for lost time?'

'You are insatiable, Miss Turner.'

'Yes, Thomas O'Cleary, I am.' She moved to kiss him, rubbing herself enticingly against him while holding his hands away so that he was frustrated in his efforts to touch her. His breathing quickened and Meg felt her own resolution to hold him back rapidly slip away. 'Perhaps you don't want me, is that it?' she asked, her voice thick with need.

'Since you are my employer and I have no wish to find myself out of a job by morning, I dare say I'd best obey. Not that I want you for my own sake, you understand?'

'I understand perfectly.'

His words were coming out jagged and raw with his efforts to keep control. 'Shall I be about what you ask of me then, Meg Turner?'

'If you think you're up to the job, Thomas O'Cleary.'

'Dear God in heaven, will you listen to the woman? I should have known better than to have got myself a woman boss. 'Tis time you learned that in bed the man is master.' Thrusting aside her staying hands he spread her beneath him, pinning her down with his own body. Meg laughed softly and arched herself to him, winding her legs about his thighs. 'It's shameless you are, woman.'

'Whatever you say, oh, master. Only make it quick, for God's sake, Tam. I need you.'

–

'Did you enjoy the dance?' Effie stared at the two untouched mugs of tea, still sitting on the kitchen table the next morning, then removed them quietly to the sink. Meg, avoiding Effie's gaze as she considered her answer, did not notice.

'Yes. It was fun. The band was excellent and there were loads of people there. I think it did me good to get out.'

She was busy mixing Lissa's breakfast cereal very carefully with milk in her teddy bear bowl as she talked. Then she set it down upon the kitchen floor for Rust to eat.

'I can see that it did,' Effie replied, very seriously, staring at the bowl.

The child gurgled and laughed delightedly as Rust swiftly devoured the luscious treat. Meg rolled her eyes in self-disgust. 'Would you look at that? What must I be thinking of?'

'What indeed?' said Effie dryly, and got on with the washing up.

–

Meg was in a fever of excitement all day, just longing for the evening when the children would be in bed and she and Tam could be on their own. She had to admit, even to herself, that she had known nothing like this feeling in her entire life before.

Losing her virginity to Jack in the barn had been a painful, clumsy affair by comparison. She could see now that only Jack had gained pleasure from it. With Tam she felt needed, cared for, nurtured, as if she mattered to him more than any pleasure he might get from their loving. It was a wonderful feeling.

She supposed he was her lover. Even the word sent shivers down her spine. She had a lover.

Changes would have to be made. Though they each had their own bed, Effie was still a physical presence in Meg's big, high-ceilinged bedroom. How could she explain the situation to her? Was it fair to think of carrying on such a relationship with a child in the house? All day she agonised over how she was to approach the subject.

'I was thinking,' Effie said, as she served Meg soup at dinner time, 'that maybe I should move in with Lissa, or take the room next door. What do you think? Would you mind very much, Meg, being on your own?' She waited for her answer, wide-eyed and mildly enquiring.

Dear, darling Effie, so sensitive to other people's needs. Right from those early days when she had helped Meg over Lanky's death, her one concern had been to think of others and not be a bother. As if she ever could be. Meg heard Tam smother a spurt of laughter. She cleared her throat and smiled at her friend. 'I think that would be an excellent idea. It's time you had a room all of your own. And Lissa would enjoy having you near, wouldn't you, darling?'

'Yes, yes. Want Effie next to me,' cried Lissa excitedly, and Meg refused to catch Tam's glance.

It was a simple matter to dust out the bedroom next to Lissa's, set up the bed and make it up with clean sheets. Meg set a lamp on the chest of drawers and a nightlight by the bed.

'There you are, Effie. Leave the candle lit till you sleep, if you like. Just make sure the shutters are closed and no light shows out the window.'

'I will.' Effie put her arms about Meg's waist and laid her cheek against hers. 'Didn't I say it would be all right? I'm so happy for you.' Meg very nearly protested innocence of her meaning but then thought, no, this is Effie, my dear friend, so she hugged her close and didn't pretend.

'Yes, I am happy.'

Then it was Effie's turn to look anxious. 'You won't be wanting me to leave, will you?'

'Leave? Heavens no, why should we? We love you.'

'And Tam loves you,' Effie said quietly. 'I've known for ages but you were too blind to see.'

'As always.' And then with some curiosity, 'What made you think so?'

Effie laughed. 'Oh, it was in his face every time he looked at you. In the way he moved close to you whenever you passed by. And once I saw him capture the scent of you from your scarf by holding it against his lips. Then he brought it out to you in the yard as if it were a plain old thing, of no account.'

Meg was stunned by these disclosures, afraid suddenly of what she had unleashed. 'I can't love him. I mustn't love him.'

'Whyever not?'

'I just can't, that's all. It's too soon. How will I know if I can ever trust him?' There was the hint of a sob in her voice and Meg quickly swallowed it. 'See how weak I'm getting already? It won't do.' She snatched up the pillow. 'Maybe it's a mistake to move you. Come back.'

'No.' Effie took the pillow and placed it on the bed. 'It's time I grew up and slept alone. It's time for us all to grow up. I know you loved Jack, and he let you down. So what? It happens. Now he's gone, you have his home and you feel guilty. Well, I say you've nothing to feel guilty about. It was him who did the dirty on you. Him and that so-called friend of yours. When I meet that little madam…'

'Kath is still my friend. If she came here in trouble, I would still welcome her.'

'Maybe you would, because that's the way you are, Meg. But what you have to ask yourself is, would she do the same for you? Would Jack, if he were here?'

'I really can't say.'

'Yes, you can, you know very well, neither one of them would give you a second thought. No, perhaps that's a bit hard on them. They'd think about you right enough, and probably be nice as pie to your face, but they'd still reckon that their own needs and wishes were of greater importance.' Meg gazed at Effie, transfixed. There was an awful logic in her words. How was it some children were born with wisdom? And others, herself included, remained vulnerable and naïve, seemingly throughout life?

'I thought I was getting stronger, a tough woman running a farm practically single-handed.'

'So you are. But that doesn't mean you don't have a heart. Let it love, Meg Turner. Let it love.'

Chapter 6

'It crossed my mind,' said Joe, 'that you might I not be averse to letting me buy me own land off you. Well, what I think of as me own land.'

Jeffrey Ellis frowned. 'I didn't realise owning land was so important to you.'

'Well, I have sons to think of, and grandsons now. I happen to have some money saved and, begging your pardon, since I'd heard you weren't too well, I thought you wouldn't mind being rid of the worry of it, like.' Cheap, he meant.

Jeffrey Ellis thought he didn't care one way or the other about land. The income from the rental that Joe Turner paid for Ashlea was useful but the capital, properly invested, would do almost as well. But he was surprised by the offer. 'I thought money was tight. Things haven't been good in farming these last years.'

'Aye, well. We make do. Just.'

'I had hoped, one day, to leave it to my daughter.'

Joe shuffled his feet. 'If you want my opinion on that score, women shouldn't be trusted, not when it comes to land. They can't cope with it. It's a living thing is land and needs a man's hand to control it.'

'Your own daughter seems to be managing well enough.'

'She isn't on her own though, is she?' Joe blustered. 'She's got that great Irish lout staying with her.'

Jeffrey Ellis smiled. 'But the responsibility and the decisions are hers.'

'Happen.'

'It's funny how we fathers never take to the men our daughters choose.' Not that I know whether Katherine has a man, he thought bleakly, or where she is or why she left. If he knew she was well and happy, he'd have some reason to get up in a morning. He could fight off any illness then. As it was...

'You've not heard where she's at?' Joe, as ever, was blunt.

Mr Ellis turned away to fiddle unnecessarily with papers upon his desk. 'Not recently, no.' Not at all, in fact. 'But I'm sure we will hear soon.'

'Aye, aye. They come round in the end. Alius do.' Joe cleared his throat. This conversation was wandering a bit far off track for his liking. Nevertheless he sympathised with this man. Jeffrey Ellis had been a good landlord, leaving Ashlea very much to Joe's care, not like some who were always poking and prying where they'd no business to. 'We all have our troubles with family,' Joe confided, thinking it would do no harm to butter him up a bit. 'Our Meg took it upon herself to fetch a child home, says it's an orphan from Liverpool.'

Jeffrey Ellis listened with half his attention. 'Yes, I'd heard something of the case. Must be plenty about at this time. That was kind of her.'

'There's some as say it isn't an orphan at all but her own brat.'

'Do you think it is?'

'Don't know what to think. She tells me nowt. I'm only her father, aren't I? But I can put two and two together and it looks very like that lad of Lanky's.'

'Jack?'

'Aye, that's him. Black curly hair just the same it has. And blue eyes you wouldn't believe.' Joe's tone had softened slightly. 'Not that it's any fault of the child's, but if Meg was going to have a bairn, better if it'd been a son to follow on.'

Jeffrey Ellis laughed. 'You have to take what you're given and be thankful where babies are concerned.'

'Aye, mebbe. But now she has this other chap living with her. No morals that girl. I'm ashamed to call her me own daughter.'

'How old is this child?'

'Oh, eighteen months or so by now. Born last March after that hard winter.'

Jeffrey Ellis was looking oddly thoughtful. 'I saw Meg once or twice around that time. She didn't say she was having a baby, nor look it. Certainly didn't mention it or ask for my advice. How surprising.' It would be easy enough to check. The local midwife would know.

'You never can tell what daughters are at, can you?' Joe was regretting ever mentioning the subject, impatient as he was to get back to the question of his land. As a sitting tenant he might get Ashlea for a few hundred and save himself the rent every quarter. He was of the opinion that land would rise in price, after the war. Things always seemed to, and then he'd never get it.

'I knew she and Jack were very friendly. Katherine too,' Jeffrey was saying. 'The three of them went everywhere together, like peas in a pod.' He lapsed into silence, seeming to forget for a moment that Joe was there.

94

Joe gave a polite cough just to remind him. 'So then, about Ashlea. Would you consider selling it to me, as sitting tenant? At a reduced price like.'

Jeffrey Ellis studied Joe with new interest. He didn't like the man, but he'd always paid his rent each quarter, never a day late. Katherine probably wouldn't be interested in Ashlea, anyway. She'd get his savings and investments and Larkrigg of course, which should be enough for anyone. All the same, he didn't want to give it away. He was a careful man and Jeffrey felt surprisingly optimistic all of a sudden, after talking to Joe Turner. If what he suspected was correct, he might find another purpose for Ashlea.

'I'll speak to my lawyers about it, first thing in the morning,' he said, and named a price that made Joe blench.

'Here! I weren't thinking in those terms at all.'

'Ashlea is a fine farm.'

'Aye, because I've made it so.'

'We'll see what my lawyers have to say, shall we?' Joe was forced to doff his cap with unusual deference and leave Jeffrey Ellis to his thoughts.

—

Nobody would have known, looking at Meg beside Tam in the saleroom, that she was nervous. Dressed in a soft green tweed jacket and cord slacks, she looked relaxed and confident, a woman who knew what she was about.

They had walked her flock of Herdwicks the nine miles or so from Broombank down into Kendal, a long cold trek with all three dogs working hard the length of it. She'd seen each and every one of them booked in and penned. It had taken hours of effort and she felt tired and flustered and very far from confident.

'What if nobody wants to buy them?' she whispered, and felt Tam's body shift beside her as if he were smiling, though she dare not, for the life of her, look up into his face. 'What if I don't get a good price?'

His hand closed very briefly but firmly over hers. Held it by his side long enough to reassure, his firm grip telling her to stop worrying and have faith. Meg drew in a great gulp of air, not that it was particularly fresh in the confines of the auction ring but it got her lungs working again. 'I'll leave you to it then,' he said briskly, turning away, and she instantly panicked, almost snatching at his sleeve till she realised people were looking at her, smiling and nodding. She thrust her hands in her pockets, and smiled and nodded back.

'Why? Where are you going?' she hissed. She was appalled. She needed to know he was there, feel him beside her.

Tam's eyebrows raised very slightly. 'I suppose a man might enjoy his day off without interrogation from his boss?'

'Don't play games with me, Tam O'Cleary. You said you would be here with me. Morning, Will.' She nodded at Will Davies as he took his place by the ring.

'And so I am. But you don't need me to hang around all morning and hold your hand, now do you? You're the farmer.'

Doubts beset her. 'Do you think I'm doing the right thing? It's not too late to withdraw them. Even if I do get a good price that isn't the end of our worries. There's always the danger that the new flock won't settle. They might simply walk away. It has been known for sheep to walk forty miles or more, with lambs at foot, back to the heaf where they were born.'

'Then we'll just have to make them feel at home, won't we? You have other Swaledales, that'll surely help. You mean to buy them in young, don't you?'

'Yes. Gimmers, first-year sheep.'

'So there shouldn't be too much of a problem. As soon as they have lambed in their turn, the new stock will know no other place.'

But she wasn't to be reassured. 'Then again, with no natural immunity to the bugs on my land, they might sicken and die. Then I'll be bankrupt, finished, and have to go home, tail between my legs, and listen to my father gloat over how a woman can never make a farmer.'

Tam leaned back to consider her rump carefully. 'Then I'd say your father must have docked your tail when you were young. I can't see one for you to bring home, and I'm sure I would have noticed. It's a very nice rear.'

'Oh, Tam. Stop joking with me,' she hissed in a fierce whisper, even as the corners of her mouth twitched into a smile.

'Then stop fussing, woman. I'm just the hired help, remember? You've bought and sold sheep before and managed perfectly well enough on your own.'

'But not almost my entire flock.'

'Don't exaggerate.' Tam winked at her with his usual outrageously wicked grin. 'It's no more than half of it, and it's no fainting female that you are, Meg Turner, so don't pretend otherwise. Not with me who knows you so well. Haven't I told you that I like my women strong?' Then hands in pockets, he strolled away, whistling.

Damn him!

Meg gazed in desperation at the first lot of sheep already jostling into the ring. How long would she have to wait before her own came up? Every moment would seem a lifetime, more than enough to wonder at her own sanity in taking this risk.

If she didn't get a good price for her Herdwicks, then all her plans would fall flat. There was admittedly no hurry for the tractor, but she needed to buy in enough Swaledales to start her off well. She also needed to leave some money over to put in the bank towards the deposit she was saving for Broombank. She had some saved already, but nowhere near enough. And then there was next quarter's rent. She groaned. What had she done? Today's sale was vital.

At last Meg went to join her flock in an agony of suspense. She was doing all right with the Herdwicks. Why was she never satisfied? Why make changes?

They came into the ring at last, dark and lively, their hoar frost faces looking faintly bewildered, white ears perked. As Tam had rightly pointed out, there was no room for sentiment in farming, nevertheless she was woman enough to hope they went to a good farm where they would be well cared for.

'A handsome crew we have here,' said the auctioneer. 'Good stock. Miss Turner tells me she is only parting with these splendid animals because she is making some changes at Broombank. Now, who'll give me the first bid?'

Silence for a moment while a hundred faces turned upon her. Pipes were sucked, eyes of every hue considered her but not a soul moved. Meg strove to keep her face impassive. It wouldn't do for them to think her weak or anxious. Not that she was, Meg told herself, stubborn to the last.

These were good sheep, fit and healthy stock, animals to be proud of, and here she was in the ring with them to prove it. Sometimes you had to take a risk in life, in order to make progress. Her land was clean, her plan sound. She lifted her chin with fresh resolve and waited. All she needed was a good price to get her started.

—

'I did it, I did it!' Meg was almost bouncing with delight as she met up with Tam for a quick bite of lunch at the Duke of Cumberland. There was a fire in the inn's hearth for which she was grateful as there was a bite to the air this autumn day. 'They've gone to Blencary, a good farm in the Langdales. Perfect spot for them. Didn't I do well?'

'Yes,' said Tam, quietly. 'You did.'

'I mean we. *We* did well. I couldn't have got this far without you.' She hugged his arm close and smiled up at him, finally getting a like response. 'So now you can buy in your new stock.'

'Yes. I've been thinking about that. I shall buy half now, and half later. Perhaps next spring, just before they lamb. Then I can keep an eye on them easier. I'll need to gather the new sheep in every day, shepherd them well to make sure they stay. Once they've had lambs the progeny won't know any other heaf so it will get easier. I can do it, I know I can.'

'Whatever you say.'

'Then in a year or two I can sell on the progeny that I don't need. Probably make me more money than selling for meat.'

'You seem to have it all worked out.'

She glanced up at him, eyes shining. 'Oh, I have, I have. Everything is going right at last. The tractor will have to wait, but never mind. You can't have everything.' She took a sip of her beer then frowned at him. 'What is it? Why are you looking at me like that?'

'I'm pleased for you, that's all.'

She glanced at him again, finding herself catching the excitement that seemed to emanate from him. 'Tell me. Is it something I've said?'

Tam shook his head. 'Not that I'm aware of. Eat your sandwich. Then I'll show you what I've been up to this morning. I've a surprise of me own.'

It was a pony and trap. The fell pony stood, its grey coat already developing a winter fluffiness, patiently waiting in the yard behind the inn.

Meg could hardly believe her eyes. She walked up to it, then reached out to rub its nose with tentative fingers, constantly glancing at Tam.

'Is this ours?'

'If we can't afford a tractor we'll have to stick with the old ways for a bit longer. Petrol's hard to come by anyway. But I thought it was time Broombank had its own transport. We can't keep relying on other people.'

'But how did you find the money?'

'Don't worry about the money, I got it cheap from a bloke I know, complete with the old trap. It should make life easier. Now horses I do know about. She's a grand mare, don't you think? We can get her covered and sell on the foals. Make a bit that way.'

Meg's eyes were shining. 'Oh, Tam, you are clever.' She hugged him. He was so thoughtful and kind and strong, a gentle, quiet man, just like this grand horse. Maybe she would let herself love him, just a little, though nothing in any way serious. 'What progress we're making. Come on, let's go home then I can really thank you.'

'We can go home in style today. Climb aboard, ma'am.'

They rode the long miles back up to Broombank with no trouble at all. Which was a relief, since it was all uphill with the wind in their faces, and Meg was far too excited to find her breath.

—

The mare was called Carrie, which seemed appropriate as she did a good deal of that. Winter was coming on and the ground was iron hard. Meg and Tam were collecting the last harvest of the year. Together they scythed the tawny bracken, packing it on to the sled which Carrie would pull down to the farm so they could use the fronds as winter bedding for the cows. The late sun was warm on her bare head and Meg could hear the drone of bees, busy with their own harvest in the heather blossom. It made her think of another harvest, another time when she had lain in the bracken with Jack and he had given her a ring.

The tiny sapphire and diamond ring was now tucked away in a dressing table drawer. She supposed she should write to Connie about it one day, for it had belonged to her mother. Make sure she got it back. But she couldn't do that until she'd spoken to Jack. It wouldn't be right.

Why should she think of him now, when she had her lovely Tam and things were going so well? She lay with her lover nightly in the great bed and never thought of Jack then.

She wondered sometimes if she still held some love in her heart for him, or whether it was simply nostalgia and the tug of old loyalties.

Jack Lawson had been so much a part of her life for so long it was hard to put him from her mind. If there hadn't been the war it would have been easier to hate him for what he'd done to her. It was hard to be angry with a man far away, who might die at any moment.

Where was he? Was he still overseas? Why had he never come home on leave? Had he been captured perhaps? Made a prisoner-of-war?

If he had come home, as promised, they could have talked things over, as old friends perhaps. They could have discussed in reasonable fashion what was best for Lissa, and whether Jack objected to Meg's still planning to buy Broombank. They could have come to terms and agreed to go their separate ways. Instead, her life and future was left undecided with nothing settled between them.

'Penny for them?' Tam was easing his back, resting from the arduous task of scything, and Meg went to him at once, slipping her hands about his waist, pressing her cheek against the strength of his body.

'They're worth much more and I've no intention of flattering you by revealing what they are,' she said, crossing her fingers against the white lie.

He turned and crunched her in his arms, making her squeal, then kissed her till she was beating him with her fists, appealing for him to let her draw breath, just a little.

'Then I can start over again?'

'Hm, please.'

He handed her the scythe. 'Back to work, shameless hussy. The days are too short to waste in play.'

And so they were, all too short. The swallows had left already for warmer climes though Meg could still hear the chack-chack of fieldfares and the clear throated tones of the robin to cheer her days.

Close by her feet, harvest mice and voles gobbled up the insects disturbed by the scything, filling their stomachs with as much food as they could find in readiness for the long hard winter ahead. Not for them the endless queuing.

Watching them, taking care not to disturb a vole's lunch, Meg prayed this winter would be kinder than the last. Never had she known such hard winters as they had experienced since the onset of the war. It was as if the weather wished to echo everyone's gloom.

'I think I'd better go and round up the new Swaledales.' Rust was at her feet in a second, understanding every word. 'Come on, Tess, Ben.'

'Right,' Tam agreed, frowning slightly but accepting her sudden need to be alone.

'I won't be long. You know I have to do it regularly.'

'I know.'

Meg thankfully set down her scythe and strode off, up to the heaf. Would the new sheep stay? Would they thrive? Or would they up and leave her as Jack had done, and Kath? As Tam might do, one day.

High up on the fells could be heard the deeper-throated carrion crow, and the funereal black raven. These birds brought a shiver to any farmer for the damage they could do to stock trapped or injured on a crag. Nothing of the sort must happen to her new flock.

She reached down a hand, feeling the wetness of Rust's nose nudge against it. At least her lovely dog stayed with her always, for all his three-legged gait. Even horrific injury had not kept him from her side. He'd been saved from the crows and from her brother's jealousy. Dan had learned his lesson and not bothered her since. She hadn't given in to his bullying then, nor would she.

As she looked over her land and gathered her sheep, finding only one or two had strayed and would need fetching back from their old heaf, Meg knew she was as ambitious as ever, if not more so. Life might be hard with the worry of the war, the grinding work, bad weather, little ready money and a whole list of shortages, not to mention her anxieties over Charlie and Kath, but despite all of that, her world was about as perfect as it could be.

Lanky had wanted her to have Broombank, not his son. She should remember and honour his belief in her. Her new sheep were doing well. She had Effie and Tam. She had her Luckpenny still, didn't she? Everyone was happy. So what could go wrong?

–

As she sat at supper that evening, almost too exhausted to eat, it seemed Meg had made her judgement too soon. One person was not happy. Upstairs in her cot, handmade from finest birch-wood by Tam, Lissa began to cry.

'Go to her, Effie, will you?' Meg asked, pulling the string from her hair with a tired hand, and shaking out her curls.

'I've been up six times already,' Effie complained. 'The little madam's playing me up something shocking. I love the bones of her, but she won't do anything I say these days.'

Meg sighed. 'Well, what's wrong with her? Is she hungry?'

'No, course she ain't hungry.' Effie was affronted. 'Would I send a child hungry to bed?'

'What is it then?'

'Don't you realise that Lissa has needs too? She's crying for you,' Tam said, not looking up from his mutton hot pot. More potato than mutton in it, but it tasted good after a hard day's work all the same.

'I can hear she's crying.' Meg's own appetite had quite deserted her. Why did she fail to make Lissa happy? The child was well fed and nurtured. What was wrong? Even Effie was implying that the fault was hers.

'Then go to her.'

Meg glanced up in surprise at the tone of Tam's voice, but still she did not move. She could feel a headache starting and all she wanted was to fall into bed and sleep. 'Scything bracken is a hell of a job. And I have to do this extra shepherding every day. I'm tired.'

'Damn you, woman, can't you think of someone else besides those sheep? Lissa *needs you*.'

She turned on him then, furious as a spitting cat, ready to scratch his eyes out. 'Don't you tell me what to do! Or imply that I don't care, because it's not true. I do care, I do!'

'Then prove it.' Tossing down his fork he caught her flailing hand in his own. Sensual lips curled into a harsh line upon the disturbingly handsome face. 'Show it.'

Meg longed to smack that face, hard, but this was their first real argument and it terrified her.

Then the soft, Irish tones melted her anger to butter. 'Don't take it out on me, Meg, or that child, for the damage Jack did to you. Lissa needs your *love*. It's unworthy of you to deny it.' The words cut deep into the heart of her and when he gently let her hand go, Meg hesitated for a long moment, then pushed back her chair and went upstairs.

–

She stood and gazed upon Lissa. The child sat in her cot, fat tears rolling down her chubby cheeks, small hiccuping sobs filling the room with heartbreaking sadness.

She looked so desperately unhappy. Kath's child? Or her own now?

'What is it, sweetheart?' Unable to prevent herself, Meg reached over and picked up Jack's child, of her own accord, for the very first time.

Lissa's sobs quieted instantly and violet-blue eyes swimming with tears gazed up into Meg's in a silent plea for loving. As small arms curled, warm and damp, about her neck, Meg closed her eyes against the agony of it, unaware of Tam and Effie watching with smiles on their faces from the door.

Soft fingers curled about her ear, baby lips pressed against her cheek and a tiny, snuffling sigh was expelled on a hiccup of relief. Only then did her own tears come. Whether she was crying for the baby's father, whose silence seemed deafening in this dreadful war, or washing away the last of the pain for a man she had once loved, Meg did not rightly know or care. The relief was wondrous.

Only then did she realise that self-pity and bitterness was destructive, not only to herself but to those about her. It was true that Lissa was too often watchful and silent, as if she were not entirely sure if she were a part of things and was trying to work it all out. As if she felt she did not quite belong. Meg hugged her closer, breathing in the sweet baby scent of her.

'If only Kath had written,' she said now, looking at her two friends with pleading in her eyes, begging them to understand. 'I was so afraid. Still am. If I only knew what the future holds. If I knew I could keep her.'

Tam came and put his arms about them both. 'We can none of us know that. Life is a risk for us all.'

'What will I tell Lissa, when she asks?' A day Meg dreaded. 'I can only explain that she was sent to the

Liverpool orphanage because her mother wasn't allowed to keep her at Greenlawns, and so never – never bonded with her.'

'Then that is what you must say. But if she must accept that her mother didn't love her, it does no good for her to think you don't love her either.'

'Oh, but I do, I do!' Meg cradled the child close, tears bursting out afresh. The tiny eyelids fluttered closed, grew heavy. As translucent as porcelain, blue-veined and beautiful. A small contented sigh banished the last of the heartbreaking sobs.

Though it troubled Meg that Lissa might not be told the full story, what else could she do, in the circumstances?

'Once, I told my father that I would never put the land before those I loved. Yet look at me, I've done exactly that.

'When Kath needed me, where was I? Did I hurry to get her out of that dreadful place? No. I stayed home to see to the lambing. Have I given any time or thought to Lissa's needs? No. I've left her to you, Effie, and Tam. Yet it is people who are really important, not land. We can only borrow land, for the length of our lifetime. After that it belongs to someone else. But people live on in your heart even after death, don't they?'

Tan smiled. 'It's never too late to learn a lesson.' Meg dried her eyes. 'Do you truly think so? Will she ever forgive me?'

Effie, anxious as always to be a part of the scene, came into the room. 'Course she will. Lissa loves you. She always has.'

Meg smiled down at the now sleeping child curled contentedly in her arms, belonging at last. 'I understand. I'm all right now. You go and finish your supper, the pair of you. I'll sit with Lissa for a while, make sure she's all right too.'

She laid the baby down in the cot and drew the covers up to her chin. So much time she had wasted. Yet if she hadn't worked hard, where would they all be now? But she must always remember that however important her farm and her sheep, Lissa was more so. As were Effie and Tam. She must remember that.

Never must she make this mistake again.

Chapter 7

Charlie came that autumn, seeming bigger and more mature than the young boy of memory who'd liked to avoid chores and play with cigarette cards. With him came his new bride, a shy and smiling fair-haired girl whom he called Sue with such affection in his voice, and so rarely released her hand, that Meg felt quite choked with emotion just watching them together.

They stayed for three days and it was such fun, just like old times with Charlie eating them out of house and home, and talking twenty to the dozen about his plans for the future.

'I'll have finished my thirty missions as navigator soon. Then I could do a second tour or go on and learn more about engineering. Once the war is over that will be the way forward, I'm sure of it.'

'Meg wants to know if you eat carrots,' Tam said, and as they all laughed, a blushing Meg was forced to explain.

'Actually, many pilots did at first, thinking it might help. But now we have pathfinders. They drop markers so we know where to drop the bomb. Makes it much easier and there's less likelihood of hitting civilian targets by mistake.'

Meg shivered. 'Does it bother you, dropping bombs?'

Charlie's jaw tightened and she knew she'd asked the wrong question. 'I've nothing against the German people.

Many of them want rid of Hitler just as much as we do. So I'd rather not hit them.'

'Of course. I didn't think. I'm sorry. But you'll be glad of a quiet job for a change.'

'Maybe. But all jobs are important. We'd be nothing without the ground crew. Anyway, I might change my mind. I might do another tour.'

He looked like a flyer. He had about him that casual, devil-may-care appearance that all flyers had. It declared him a veteran of many missions and promised he would win this war, no matter what.

Tam, noticing that the new young bride was looking less than happy at this talk of a second tour, changed the subject and they talked about farming for a while, telling how Meg had tried and failed to buy a tractor.

'Are you anywhere near buying Broombank?' asked Charlie, and she shook her head.

'Not yet. Not till I raise the money.' The bank manager would give you anything, she thought. A man, so young and handsome, and with such an air of determination about him. But not me, a mere woman.

'I have absolute faith in you, Meg. Whatever you make up your mind to do, you'll do it. You're right, mechanisation is the way to go. You never know, you might even get electricity up on these fells one day. Never say die.'

Never say die. No, thought Meg. Nor you either, my lovely boy. She was forced to flee to the kitchen and fuss over the huge pie she'd baked to hide her sudden flood of emotion. It was cooked to perfection, crust lightly browned with a bubble of gravy coming from the steaming hole in its centre. It consisted chiefly of vegetables but with just a flavour of rabbit. And the pastry was good, made with their own pork dripping. It would go down a treat.

But as she set out the warmed plates and called for everyone to come and eat, she couldn't help but think how unfair it was, that their youth and love should be threatened by this awful war. Would it never end? Did she have the courage to see it through?

–

It was late on a November afternoon when Jeffrey Ellis finally plucked up the courage to call and see Meg. He had walked all the way from Larkrigg, glad of the exercise, smiling at the thrushes feasting on the bright rowanberries. He hoped the thick flush of scarlet berries did not betoken a harsh winter ahead. He was tired, as the whole country was. Beginning to realise that they were in for a long haul and there would be no quick solution to Hitler's threat.

He found Meg busily engaged in layering a hedge. The energy and skill she displayed in the task gave the lie to her slender youthful frame. It made him feel ashamed of his own inactive lifestyle.

'You look busy. I hope I'm not interrupting?'

'Not at all. I'll just finish this bit.' She'd cut a long slit down the side of the slender trunk, now she bent it over and wove the pliant frond into position with the others to form a living windbreak against which the sheep could shelter but not escape. Then she set down the small billhook she was using in a safe place, pulled off her leather mitts, and wiped her brow. 'I'm glad of the excuse to stop, to be honest. Tea? I was just about to have one.'

They sat at the big deal table in the kitchen, enjoying the scalding tea, weak though it was, not speaking for some time. Meg could almost hear him thinking.

From the bedroom upstairs came the sounds of Lissa playing with her dolls. Effie had made them for her out of clothes pegs and she loved to line them up and pretend to teach them, as if they were in school. Meg could tell that Mr Ellis had his ears cocked, for every time Lissa's little singsong voice rose in pitch, he half turned his head towards it.

'Would you like to see her?' Meg asked at last, finally finding the courage.

Eager eyes met hers. 'I would.'

She went to the door and called up the stairs. 'Lissa, it's time for your cod liver oil and orange juice. Come on down, there's a good girl.' A moan of protest followed by running feet, and Jeffrey Ellis found himself holding his breath. Too late now to wonder if he should have come at all.

A pair of chubby legs appeared on the stairs, followed by the prettiest little girl he had ever seen. At least, since Katherine had been about that age. He was instantly disappointed that Lissa bore little resemblance to that long-ago child. But why should he have expected her to? Yet there was something about her, in the way she walked, the toss of her head. Or else he was a foolish old man with an over-ripe imagination.

He smiled reassuringly as the child hesitated. He couldn't have found his voice if he'd been strung up by the heels.

Meg held out the cod liver oil spoon. 'Come on, Lissa, open wide.'

The child screwed up her nose. 'Don't like it.'

'Cod liver oil is good for you. Isn't that right, Mr Ellis?'

'It must be, that's why it tastes so nasty. Hold your nose, Lissa, then you won't notice. I think I have a mint in my pocket somewhere when you've finished.'

The mixture went in a trice and the mint was accepted with one of Lissa's most entrancing smiles.

'She is a lovely child,' Jeffrey said, eyes never leaving the small figure.

'Yes.'

'Your father thinks she's yours.'

'I know.'

'She isn't though, is she?'

'She is now.'

'I mean…'

'I know what you mean. We ought to be careful, she's like British Gaumont News.'

'I beg your pardon?'

Meg chuckled. 'The eyes and ears of the world.'

'Oh.' Jeffrey Ellis laughed while Meg turned to the watchful violet eyes. 'Go on, you can take your orange juice upstairs, but see that you drink it all.'

'I will, Meg, promise.'

When Lissa had gone, Meg turned to Mr Ellis, damping down the spark of fear that had suddenly kindled deep inside. 'Was there something particular you wanted to say? I don't mean to be rude, only it's rare for you to call. In fact in all the years I have known you, this is the first time.' She smiled to try to soften the impact of her words.

Jeffrey Ellis returned her frank gaze with an equal frankness in his own. 'You're right. I did have a purpose in calling. I'm glad to have found you on your own because it's connected with Lissa. She's Kath's child, isn't she?'

Meg didn't answer immediately, the fear clenching the pit of her stomach. 'What if she was? How would you feel about that?'

Jeffrey Ellis was not an insensitive man, and recognised the panic in her steady gaze. 'It's all right. I wouldn't dream of taking her from you. Seems to me you are doing an excellent job of bringing her up. Besides...' He paused, and took refuge in sipping his tea.

'Mrs Ellis would not approve?'

Jeffrey met her clear-eyed gaze. 'Rosemary means well, but she is bounded by convention. She has lived a sheltered life, too sheltered perhaps. Never had to rough it in the real world as most of us do. It is very important to her that her respectable, rose-tinted life is not besmirched in any way.'

'She pretty well said the same about you, though not quite in such picturesque language.'

Jeffrey set down his cup sharply and some of the tea spilled out. 'She is far too protective for her own good – for my own good, I should say.' He drew in a long steadying breath. 'You know how I longed to find her. Why didn't you tell me that you knew where Kath was?'

'Because I don't. I have no idea where she is.' Meg found herself setting aside pretence, deciding there had been too much secrecy already. 'Oh, I did find her once, by bullying the address out of your wife, if you want to know the truth. But Kath refused to come home with me. She bundled the baby in my arms on Lime Street Station, said I would make a better mother, and disappeared into the crowd. There was nothing I could do but come home without her.'

'I see.' Or did he? It hurt to think that Rosemary had known where their daughter was all along. Why hadn't

Kath written to him direct? 'Where was she when you found her?'

'In a home for unmarried mothers.' Meg did not wish to reveal the stark horror of the place. She could leave him with some illusions at least.

'And the father? Do you know who he is?'

She looked him full in the face, summoning every vestige of courage she possessed. 'Yes, I know who he is.'

'It was Jack then?'

Meg felt choked suddenly, grateful she didn't have to say his name out loud. 'You only have to look at Lissa to know that.'

Jeffrey Ellis nodded, compassion strong in him. 'I guessed as much. You loved Jack, whereas my daughter – bless her careless heart – merely wanted to play with him.'

Meg swallowed the sudden lump that came into her throat and stood up, taking the empty cups to the sink. 'It doesn't matter now. That's all in the past. I have Effie, and Tam, and I have Lissa. I don't need anyone else.' Coming back to the table, she took Mr Ellis's hand. 'But I still miss Kath. I want you to know that I bear her no grudge. She is still, despite everything, my very dear friend. How could she be otherwise when she left me her child to care for?'

He blinked. 'I hope one day she might appreciate that fact. I wish only for her to come home.' After Mr Ellis had gone, accepting gratefully Meg's invitation to call and see Lissa at any time, Meg laid her head upon her hands and cried her heart out.

–

Bad news arrived on the heels of the bitter east wind that scoured the fells before Christmas.

'The Japanese have attacked Pearl Harbour,' Sally Ann read, ashen-faced. 'Even while their special envoy was making peace talks with Washington, Japan's fleets were attacking Hawaii and Manila. Oh, dear God, there were more than two thousand Americans killed.'

'That'll fetch them in,' said Dan, with some satisfaction.

Sally Ann frowned at her husband. 'Don't be so brutal. They'd have come in anyway. What a price to pay. All those young men and women.' Tears ran down her plump cheeks. 'What if they were your sons? How would you feel then?'

Dan looked at his two boys, pride evident in his round face, and pain at such a dreadful prospect. 'We're fighting this war for them. Then they won't ever have to fight another. Mark my words, we'll win it. Right always triumphs in the end.'

'By heck,' said Joe. 'You've learned some long words. Been swallowing a dictionary?'

Sally Ann held her breath, wondering fearfully what Dan would answer. Many secret hours had been spent improving her husband's reading skills, teaching him simple addition and subtraction. She had hoped it might give him the courage to stand up to his father. Was this the moment?

Dan got to his feet, crimson to the tips of his ears. 'It was only an opinion, that's all.'

'You great daft oaf. Thee, have an opinion? In that empty rattle head of thine. Pigs might fly!'

Knocking over his chair, Dan blundered from the room.

Sally Ann was on her feet in an instant, red in the face herself, livid with her father-in-law. 'How can you talk to him like that, your own son? He's working flat out driving tractors for the Government Committee all day, as well as helping to run this place with you.'

'I don't hold with tractors. Nothing better than a good horse.' Joe was in a particularly sour mood this day. His hopes of buying Ashlea had died a death. Jeffrey Ellis's lawyer had increased the price he'd first suggested, not reduced it. Anyone would think Ellis didn't need the money, which couldn't be right. What did he want with Ashlea? Joe hated failure, it made his bitterness against life more acute. He was feeling his age today, full of aches and pains he was, and a cough coming on. Annie would have made him a paper of goose fat for his chest.

'Not to mention working in the Home Guard at night,' Sally Ann was saying. 'Sometimes dangerous work, conducting prisoners to the POW camp, fire fighting, as well as drilling and training in case of invasion or bombing.'

'There are no bombs here. He's safe enough.'

'He doesn't feel safe, or wanted. Can't you ever give him credit for trying, offer a kind word, just once in a while?'

'Kindness makes a man soft.'

'It makes a man feel he's appreciated.' She steadied her breath. It did no good to shout at Joe Turner. That way he was bound to win. 'You were glad enough to see Charlie here, yet you never showed him that you were. Why not?'

'I don't approve of my son's choice of career.'

'He's fighting a war, that's hardly a career.'

'All this talk of engineering when it's over. He should be a farmer.'

'You already have two farmers in the family, Dan and Meg. Isn't that enough?'

'Only one.'

Sally Ann sighed. 'Not that again. Won't you ever acknowledge her efforts?'

'She'll get fed up. Women have no staying power.'

Sally Ann decided not to pursue this fruitless argument. 'Anyway, how do we know what the future will bring for any of us in the years ahead? The war is a long way from over yet. It seems to be getting worse in point of fact. There might not be work for any of us by then, or not here at least. We might not manage to hang on to Ashlea. I know it's a hard enough struggle now to make ends meet.' She reached for his hand. 'Why don't you put Dan properly into the picture? Tell him what state the farm really is in. Perhaps then he'd work on it more. He'd feel wanted.'

Joe got up from the table and flicked on his cap, adjusting the neb to its right position over his eyes. 'There's no danger of us losing Ashlea. I'll see it's there for my grandsons when they need it. You leave the worrying to me. I'll let you know when I can't manage.'

When he had gone Sally Ann sat alone by the fire. There was no getting round Joe's stubbornness. Oh, but he worried her. He really did. He insisted on doing everything himself. Wouldn't share a thing with them, not a thing. She reached for her two boys and pulled them on to her knee. They always soothed her after an argument.

—

'Joe's in a temper. He's been up to something, I can tell.'

Sally Ann was watching Meg split logs. She stood by the old yew chopping block, chips of wood all about her, a fine figure of a woman, there was no denying it. Taller and slimmer than the young girl she had once been, her fair skin tanned by the weather though hair as raggy and unkempt as ever. Its beauty came from its colour, as bright as a polished penny. She was looking more than usually attractive today, Sally Ann had to admit, for all she was dressed in work overalls and a checked shirt that could have belonged to Dan or Charlie.

'So what else is new?' Meg had neither the time nor the inclination to worry over her bad-tempered father. She hummed as she swung the axe, more interested in the satisfaction of seeing a growing pile of logs for the winter evenings ahead.

Sally Ann propped herself against the edge of the saw-horse. 'I think there's something wrong.'

Meg stopped workings pushed back her hair and set down the axe carefully. 'What can be wrong?'

'There isn't much money coming into the house. We've had two bad lambing seasons. Joe and Dan hardly speak, let alone work together. Dan would rather be off working with the tractors than on his own farm. But then he has to. We need the wages he brings in.'

Meg sat on the chopping block and propped her elbows on her knees. 'I'm sure you're worrying unduly. Ashlea will be all right. It's a good farm.'

'It was a good farm.'

'You must make Dan talk to Father. Get everything out into the open.'

'Huh.' Sally Ann gave a bitter little laugh. 'Easier said than done. The tension between them is something terrible. He still wants Broombank, you know. More than ever now Ashlea isn't doing so well.'

Meg smiled and squeezed her sister-in-law's hand. 'Ashlea will do all right. Every farm has its bad years. It'll pull back next season, you'll see. As for Broombank, well, he'll get over that. Let him want.'

'You don't seem too bothered.'

'My father can do his worst for all I care, Sal. We are doing fine, thanks very much. He can't hurt us now. Nothing can.' Brave words, but she believed them to be true.

Sally Ann examined her sister-in-law with new interest. 'You've fallen in love.'

'What?'

'You have. There's a glow about you. I can see it in the way you can hardly stop smiling, and I could hear you singing from right down the lane. You look like a woman in love. Why, you're positively blooming. You're not...'

'No, I'm not.'

Sally Ann laughed. 'It's Tam, isn't it? Oh, I'm so glad. He's a lovely man. When's the happy day?'

Meg tried to look shocked. But deep down she knew that in spite of all her efforts to the contrary, she could not deny it was true. She was falling in love. And she wasn't even sorry. 'Who said anything about a wedding?'

It was Sally Ann's turn now to look disapproving. 'My word, you've changed your time. There was a time when you couldn't wait to get down that aisle. Now you're presumably content to give the gossipmongers a run for their money.'

'Things change. I've changed.'

'Are you saying you don't trust him?' Sally Ann asked quietly.

'I didn't say that.'

'Why don't you marry him then?'

'I don't want to make a mistake, that's all. There's no hurry.'

'There's always a chance Jack might come back, is that it?'

'That's not it at all.'

'I should hope not. Because you'd be a fool if you let some kind of misguided loyalty spoil things for you and Tam. If he were mine, I'd marry him like a shot, before he had time to think twice.'

'I'm not you, Sally Ann. I like to think things through more carefully.' She smiled at her dear friend, to soften the implied criticism.

'You think too much sometimes. Follow your heart, that's what I say.'

'I did that once before and look where it got me. Anyway, he hasn't asked me, so there.'

'Aw, Meg.' Sally Ann's soft heart filled with remorse. 'I'm that sorry. I didn't think.' And she put her arms about her sister-in-law and hugged her. 'Men,' she said, with feeling.

—

Meg pulled on her clean white nightdress and climbed in between the sheets, sighing with contentment as she stretched out, a knot of anticipation in the pit of her stomach as there always was when she waited for Tam to come to her.

I don't need Sally Ann's pity, she told herself. I don't care about marriage. But conviction was hard to find.

They were like a real family already, she and Tam living together with Effie a sister to Meg, and Lissa their own little girl. Except that they were not a married couple, and Lissa was not the child of either of them. It was a game of pretend that could all end at any moment.

Only Effie was really a constant. Meg reminded herself of that fact now. One day she could lose both Tam and Lissa. Kath would come, or Jack, and take Lissa away. Or maybe even Mr Ellis might decide to exercise his right as a grandparent. She had seen the love and longing in his eyes whenever he looked at Lissa.

Tam had never claimed to be anything but rootless, a man who liked to be free to move on whenever he chose. Marriage had not been mentioned by either of them and Meg understood that, for their different reasons, neither of them wanted it. How could she even consider such a thing while she was still engaged to Jack, theoretically at least? She would need to see him and give him back his ring.

How she had changed. Some might say not for the better. Proper little Miss Meg Turner with a lover. She hugged herself with pleasure, determined not to feel guilty. Well, why should she? There was a war on. Things were different.

Count your blessings.

Effie was happily settled in the bedroom next to Lissa's while she and Tam shared this lovely big double bed.

Her new flock of Swaledales, which she checked almost hourly, were well and healthy, standing on all four feet.

And the purchase of the horse must be a good sign. Perhaps Tam meant to stay for a long time. At least until the end of the war. Meg dared think no further than that. She wanted him to stay for ever. So badly, it hurt. Snuggling down between the sheets, her body began to tingle with anticipation.

These were the best times, when they could shut the door on worries over the war and the daily grind of endless chores and lie together between the covers.

He came to her now and she flung back the sheets, opening her arms to welcome him.

'You've got my favourite nightdress on,' he said.

Meg looked surprised, then laughed. 'The one you like to take off, you mean?'

His body sank on to the mattress beside her. 'I enjoy unfastening all the buttons down the front. Naughtily Victorian.'

'It was my mother's, and the warmest I could find. This house is freezing.'

'I expect she was as lovely as you.' He ran his eyes over her face, then followed his gaze with his hands and while he cupped her cheeks he kissed her with a delicate tenderness. Meg nestled her face into the warmth of his palms, the familiar excitement mounting within. It seemed wicked to be here with him, like this, but she couldn't have stopped it, not for the world.

'I want you, Thomas O'Cleary.'

He chuckled. 'And shall I let you have me, I ask myself?'

She loved the touch of his hands upon her naked flesh, the loving warmth of him beside her, the thrust of him inside her. He was her man, and protest how she might, she loved him. What did it matter about the local gossips?

Life, Meg thought as he started the ritual of undoing buttons and kissing each freshly exposed inch of flesh as he did so, was deliciously sweet. She was so lucky, with no room for complaint at all. Despite the rationing and the endless queuing, despite her worries over Charlie which knotted her stomach at night when she heard the drone of faraway aeroplanes, despite even her fears for the future, she was coping. She was happy.

Tam laid her back upon the pillows as he drew the garment from her. 'There, didn't I do that nicely?'

Oh, yes, everything was fine, and there was no reason that she could think of why they shouldn't continue to be so.

–

They had an unexpected visitor in time for Christmas. Everyone was enjoying breakfast when they heard the sound of a vehicle turning in the yard and Meg opened the door to find Connie standing on the doorstep, several ominous looking suitcases about her feet.

'I've left Grange-Over-Sands,' she announced peremptorily. 'Peter's gone and volunteered before he's even been called up and I won't stop there on my own. Anyway, they're using the lovely estuary to fire anti-aircraft guns and I've had enough. Even when there are no enemy aircraft overhead they practise all the time, using old biplanes to tow targets about. It's too much, it really is. I can't stand any more, I simply can't.'

Meg bowed to the inevitable. 'You'd best come in then, Connie. Have you had breakfast?'

'Oh, I couldn't eat a thing.' She surveyed the breakfast table. 'Well, perhaps just a slice of toast, plenty of butter. I dare say you've no shortages here. My word, that porridge smells good, Effie. Perhaps I might manage a spoonful. I've eaten hardly a scrap for days. My nerves, you know. They can take no more.'

Can we take you? Came the uncharitable thought which Meg quickly banished. She felt a wave of sympathy for the absent Peter who would rather face the Germans than stay with his own wife.

Yet how could she turn Connie away? Not only was there a war on, but she was Lanky's daughter and Jack's sister. She was also Lissa's aunt. Oh, it was all so complicated.

'I'm very worried about Jack.'

Meg lowered herself into her chair, at once sensing bad news. 'What is it? What's happened?'

'I don't know. That's the annoying part. He's never been the greatest letter writer in the world, as you know, but he generally sends me one a month. I send him little treats: knitted socks and such like. But I've heard nothing from him for weeks. I'm very concerned.'

Tam pushed back his chair. 'I'll be up mending walls on the Knott if you need me.' Meg could tell by the way he strode from the room that he was not pleased by this new development, or by her reaction to it.

'I'm sure there's nothing to worry about,' Meg consoled the older woman. 'Letters often get delayed. You'll probably get half a dozen all at once.'

Connie dabbed at her nose with a monogrammed handkerchief, but her other hand was already reaching for a fresh slice of bread. 'You're probably right, dear. We'll not start to worry till we hear something definite, shall we?'

Meg excused herself, assured Connie she could stay for a few days, for Christmas, at least, and went in search of Tam.

Chapter 8

Meg had to run to catch up with him, slipping on the rain-slicked stones in her haste as his long legs made short work of the distance, striding over the coarse grass at such a cracking pace he was halfway up the fell and she was out of breath by the time she reached him.

'You ought to go in for fell running with those legs,' she gasped. 'What is it? Why are you angry?'

Tam had reached a tumbled down dry-stone wall and began to sort stones on the ground, rather as Lanky had once done, only in short, jerky movements. 'Who said I was angry?'

'I know you well enough by now. It's in the way you walk, the tilt of your head. What was I supposed to do, tell her no, she couldn't stay here? When she knows we have bedrooms to spare?'

'Finding bedrooms is not the problem.'

'She'll have brought her ration book.'

Tam threw down the stone he had just carefully selected and met Meg's pleading gaze with the closest to fury she had ever seen in him, barring the time he had dropped her in the water trough when she wouldn't go to the dance with him. 'I'm not talking about rations, and you know it. The woman is a bore, but worse than that, she's a trouble-maker.'

'She's Jack's sister. He might be the one in trouble, Tam.' Meg spoke quietly, her skin parchment cold. 'Why does Jack always have to come between us? I feel nothing for him. You surely know that by this time?'

'And there's me thinking that you're still riddled with guilt and some foolish kind of loyalty. Why has she come? If she never came before, not even to visit her own father, this lovely Lanky of yours, why is this the perfect place to come to now?'

'Because it's safe. She's frightened, can't you see? She needs sanctuary for a while, as we all do. She's worried.'

Tam sighed. 'I see that you are a difficult woman to teach a lesson. You see no bad in anyone, do you? Hell's teeth, what am I to do with you?' Meg, sensing a softening in him, a light sparking in the green eyes, moved closer. 'I can think of something.'

'What, here? On a fellside, in December? Do you think I'm made of stone?'

A stiff breeze wrapped itself about them, reminding Meg of reality. 'Perhaps you're right.' She leaned against him, loving the warm closeness, the sense of being cherished. 'Later then?'

He pulled her roughly into his arms and kissed her savagely. When it was over, leaving her gasping, he thrust her from him. 'Didn't I say I wasn't made of stone, you witch?' He gave a playful slap to her bottom. 'Go and see to those fine sheep of yours and give a man some peace.'

Listening to Connie's endless complaints later that day, Meg couldn't help but admit that Tam might have a point.

'I've always liked this house. Were anything to happen to Peter, I might well come back to live here.'

'Come back? How can you come back? I have a lease on the place,' Meg gently reminded her.

'Ah, yes, but only for five years and three of those are very nearly up. Let's face it, Meg, you have little hope of finding the purchase price. Your stay here is only temporary.' Connie folded her hands and her lips, well satisfied with the start of fear she had produced in Meg's grey eyes.

'I'm doing rather well, actually.'

'I'm sure you are, dear,' Connie simpered. 'But it's a fair sum of money to find, and who would give you a mortgage? A woman alone. It isn't likely, is it?'

'Perhaps you should leave me to worry about that.'

No indeed. Life was not going to be easy with Jack's sister around.

—

That night as Meg and Tam lay, untouching, in the great bed, she fiercely regretted their quarrel and ventured to resolve it.

'I think you might be right, about Connie wanting to cause trouble,' Meg admitted at last. 'She's got it into her head that one day she might come back here.'

'Not she,' said the soft voice in the darkness.

'She might, just so's she can sell it for a higher price than I would pay her for it. Is that why you were angry, because you guessed that's what she'd say?'

When he didn't answer, Meg rolled over and nuzzled into his neck. 'Or is this all about Jack?' she whispered. 'That's the real reason why you didn't want Connie here, isn't it? Because she reminds you of Jack.'

'Because she reminds *you* of Jack.'

She smiled. 'You're jealous.'

'Rubbish.'

'You are.' Very gently Meg nibbled his ear lobe with her teeth. 'You think that since I've let Lanky's daughter live here, I might do the same for his son.'

She felt Tam twist round in the bed, then he was on top of her, wrapping her body in his own. She wasn't complaining, but from what she could see of his face he still didn't look too happy. 'Would you?' he asked, very quietly.

'Would I what?'

'Don't play games with me, Meg Turner. Would you let Jack come and live here?'

'Not live exactly.'

'But you'd let him stay?'

'Only for a little while. If necessary. I could hardly throw him out now, could I?' she pleaded, seeing that this was not at all the reply he wanted to hear.

'Why not? I would have thought that was exactly what you should do, after the way he treated you.'

She supposed that he was probably right. 'I find it hard to hate people.'

Tam made a sound of exasperation deep in his throat and flounced away from her to sit on the side of the bed. Meg felt the loss so acutely she was stunned for a moment. Then she crept up behind him and slid her arms about his waist. When he didn't protest, she leaned her cheek against his back. 'I find loving harder though.'

He made as if he wanted to turn round but she held firm, not letting him. 'No, listen to me for a minute. Hating is easy, wanting revenge may seem a good idea at first, but bitterness only makes the hurt worse. I've learned that much.

'Healing the wounds, rubbing away the scars, that's the hard part. Learning to love again. It's not that I don't want to trust you, Tam, or that you've given me any cause not to, it's just that I can't believe you'll ever love me as I love you. I expect any day for you to pack your bag and go off on your travels again, or find someone you like just as much, or better. You'll leave me. As Jack did. As Kath did.'

Tam did move then, to gather her in his arms and hold her close against him. 'How can you think that? I love you, Meg. I'll never leave you, not of my own free will. For as long as you want me, I'm yours. For a day, a year or a lifetime. You must be the one to decide.'

He cupped her face in his hands and his lips were seeking hers while Meg clung to him, loving, wanting. 'Then I shan't ever let you go. Not ever.'

Their lovemaking was the fiercest and most passionate yet. Held fast in the security of Tam's arms Meg felt completely fulfilled. For the first time in her life she really believed herself cherished and loved. What did it matter if he'd made no mention of marriage?

–

On Christmas Eve, Meg and Effie worked a twelve-hour day but sold all their poultry, and such butter and cheese as they were allowed. The streets of Kendal were packed with people seeking bargains at the street stalls run by farmers' wives. But everyone was in good spirits even if some greedy stallholders were forced to lower their prices as the day wore on.

Meg and Effie went home content, if exhausted. They arrived home to find that Connie had done very little towards preparing for the Christmas Day festivities. Restrained they may be, due to the shortages and the war, yet the Turner family meant to celebrate, as was only right and proper.

They exchanged long-suffering glances and set to work stuffing the bird and making mince pies with more than a fair helping of apple, carrot and bread crumbs amongst the dried figs and fruit they'd managed to scrape together. But they'd saved enough dripping to make a delicious pastry. It was Christmas, so what did it matter if they used all their ration?

Connie sat with her feet up on a stool, a damp cloth across her forehead and declared herself, 'Quite worn out from looking after that child all day. What a handful she is. Kept wanting me to play with her.'

Effie giggled and cast a sideways glance at Meg who attempted to remain impassive.

'Endless imaginary tea parties can get a touch trying, I suppose, if you're not used to children. But you should be pleased by her attention, Connie. She doesn't take to everyone.'

Connie looked unimpressed by this piece of flattery. 'The Victorians, in my opinion had the right idea about children.'

It remained a mystery to Meg how it was that Connie could find nothing appealing about Lissa. Nor had she ever remarked upon the child's resemblance to her own brother. Either she was short-sighted, or else blind to Jack's faults. Possibly both. In her eyes, Lissa was Meg's problem and nothing at all to do with Jack or herself. Meg chose not to enlighten her.

'I expect it seems rather dull for you in this remote spot after Grange-over-Sands?' Effie suggested, thrusting her short arm up to the elbow in the huge turkey. Connie took one glance at what she was doing, and shuddered.

'Not at all. Grange will never be quite the same again in my estimation. The young women seem to spend half their time searching for parachute silk to make into under-garments.'

'And the other half showing 'em off?' whispered Effie, earning herself a dig with Meg's elbow for her cheek.

'Perfectly immoral,' finished Connie. 'And most unsafe with all that shooting going on. Who'd have thought it? In Grange-Over-Sands. I am glad to be out of it.'

Meg and Effie exchanged glances again. 'You'll be wanting to return soon though, to see Peter?' Meg suggested.

Connie pinched her lips. 'He seems to be enjoying the army, would you believe? I'm sure he can find me, when he can spare the time to come and look.'

'Probably thinks he's done well to escape the old nag at last,' Effie hissed, and this time Meg smacked her on the wrist, terrified they might both burst into fits of giggles, though it wasn't really a laughing matter. The last thing she wanted was to be stuck with Connie for the duration.

'I'm sure he will,' she said, trying to sound sympathetic. But if the woman intended a long stay, then she'd best learn to make herself useful. 'I wonder, Connie, since we're so busy and you are thinking of returning to country life, if you wouldn't mind going to shut the hens up for me?'

'Oh.'

Meg smiled brightly. 'I'd hate to dirty my hands when I'm making pastry and Effie is still stuffing the bird. We don't want to lose them. The hens, I mean.'

'But it's dark outside.'

'There's a torch in the lean-to, with a hood to shield it. You can use that.'

'You'll know the way anyway, in the dark, won't you?' Effie cheerfully suggested. 'None better. You having been born here.'

'I'll have the kettle on by the time you come back,' Meg promised. 'Now where's my rolling pin?'

With obvious reluctance Connie put on her galoshes and raincoat as if she were travelling a mile instead of half a field. But then it might start raining or she could step into something unspeakable. She added her thick scarf and bonnet for it was sure to be bitterly cold out, and collected the torch.

It was black as coal outside, a blanket of thick cloud obscuring the moon and stars and a brisk wind whining hollowly about the farm buildings.

She had never enjoyed this task, even as a child. Connie had always been quite certain that ghosts and ghoulies lurked behind creaking barn doors, and the black mountains seemed to move in on her. No, indeed, she would talk Meg Turner into giving up her preposterous idea of buying the freehold of Broombank, then it could be sold for a proper price and Connie could enjoy some comfort for a change, once the war was over.

With these pleasant thoughts in mind she stepped out across the yard. Pulling on the string, she released the door and let it drop down over the pop hole. She turned to hurry back indoors, anxious to get out of the cloying darkness that blurred the edges of her narrow torch beam, and have a soothing cup of tea. She had hardly taken two steps when the faint light from her torch caught the reflection of a pair of glinting amber eyes.

'Oh, dear God.' In her terror she dropped the torch and heard it smash as it rolled away. Then the sound of stealthy footsteps and something not quite human brushed against her legs.

Connie screamed, and fell to the ground in hysterics.

Meg and Effie came hurrying to her aid. 'What is it, Connie? What's happened?'

'It's the devil, or a German. They've invaded. Or dear Lord, they've invaded.'

It took several cups of tea, a tot of medicinal brandy, a sound sniff of sal volatile and a soothing hot water bottle in her bed to calm her. But investigation proved it was neither Hitler nor the supernatural which had come to claim her.

By the state of the hen ark next morning it was all too evident that it had been a fox that Connie had disturbed. Not one live hen remained. 'It's my fault,' Meg mourned, desolate at her loss. 'I was so busy with Christmas, I forgot them.'

'No point in worrying,' Tam soothed her. 'We can get some more.'

But it seemed a bad omen somehow, to lose her hens just at Christmas, and Meg spent a great deal of time that evening before going to bed, polishing her Luckpenny and setting it in pride of place on her bedside table.

The day after Boxing Day, Connie took the first train home. Grange-over-Sands was less terrifying than vermin running wild in your back yard.

—

When bedtime came the next night Meg refused Tam's appeal to retire early, despite the silent accusation in his eyes, and sat up for hours with her account books, adding up, making notes, drawing plans and thinking, thinking, thinking.

It seemed more important than ever that she make her future at Broombank secure. She couldn't give it up now, not with success so near. Not to Connie, nor her own father, not to anyone.

Perhaps she should slow down her programme of growth and not buy any more Swaledales in the spring, as she had planned. It would be a disappointment and mean the lamb crop would be less than she'd hoped for. And it would make it worse the next year too. But she could then use the money saved towards the deposit. Could they tighten their belts still further? Could they manage with fewer sheep for the moment?

'Will you come to bed now?' Tam asked, seeing her put down her pen.

'No.'

He said no more. Merely tightened his lips and left her.

Her eyes were pricking for want of sleep but she couldn't bring herself to go to bed, even with Tam waiting for her. Her thoughts were whirling too much.

She'd bought in a couple more cows, neither perfect, but the regular milk cheque from the Coop helped. Small but essential. Their food stocks for the winter were already stored. And they'd done well with the Christmas Eve market.

Only when the figures started doing a jig before her eyes did she crawl off to bed and snuggle up to Tam's broad back to fall instantly asleep. She wasn't much nearer finding a solution but tomorrow she would go in search of a mortgage.

Meg had been awake before it was light. Quickly she milked the cows, apologising for her haste, accepted a cup of tea from Effie but declined anything else.

'You must eat.'

'I'm too nervous. I'm going in to town. I have some business to do.' Tam offered to drive her in the cart, but Meg opted for the bus.

'We can't both afford to take the time off. I'll take the bus.'

'Something special?'

She saw the questions in his eyes but Meg refused to answer, smiling to herself.

'I'll tell you later.'

'Secrets, is it?' He looked almost hurt, like a small boy, and she laughed at him.

'Have patience. You'll find out all in good time.'

'When you're ready to tell me, eh?' He stood up and went to the door. 'Of course, I forgot. I'm only the hired man round here.'

'Tam!' Damn his pride. But he had gone and Meg sighed with exasperation. Never mind. He would forgive her for deserting him when she brought back some good news tonight.

Meg trailed about town all day trying every bank she could find. None was interested.

'You don't have an account with us. Miss Turner.'

'Farming is a risky business.'

'There is a war on.'

'Were you perhaps be considering marriage? Children?'

Meg's patience ran dangerously short but no mortgage was forthcoming.

In the end she was forced to return to her own bank manager who had declined to loan her money even for a tractor. She sat on a hard chair in his wood-panelled office, her knees placed neatly together and her hat on straight. He scarcely looked at her. He shuffled her carefully drawn-out plans on his desk and adopted an anxious expression.

'I don't see how I can help you, Miss Turner.'

'I have raised one hundred pounds towards the purchase price as you can see, Mr Bricknell,' she carefully explained.

'That is a very small deposit.'

'It's the best I can manage at the moment.' She'd put her blood, sweat and tears into raising it. 'I was hoping that you would grant me a mortgage on the balance, at five percent interest.'

'Were you indeed, Miss Turner?'

'That is the usual rate, I believe?'

'For farmers, and for men of good character.' She raised her eyebrows at him. 'I am a farmer. Are you questioning my character, Mr Bricknell?'

The bank manager cleared his throat. 'Hm, well um. May I speak frankly, Miss Turner?'

'If you wish.' She could feel the thump of her heart against her rib cage. Why did people always ask your permission when they meant to insult you?

'You are very young still, I appreciate that. As such you are perhaps not aware of the – um – correct way of going about things.'

'I am ready to learn,' she said, thinking he meant her farming.

He looked at her with a pained expression. 'It has come to my notice that you have a hired man living in.'

'Indeed that is so. As do most farmers.'

The bank manager actually blushed. The red stain started at his neck and spread upwards to his jowly cheeks. Meg was fascinated by it. 'But you are not, if you will forgive me, Miss Turner, quite the same as most farmers. You, my dear, are a woman, and as such it is not proper. Not at all proper. You have a child too, I believe. Tch, tch. Not proper at all. You do see that?'

She was so shocked that for a moment all breath left her body. Then she was standing, her knees knocking so much she felt certain he must hear them. 'No, Mr Bricknell, I do not understand. Lissa is an orphan, if it's any business of yours. A war orphan you might say. Tam is a good worker, and a friend. I have come here today for a mortgage, not comments upon my – my personal life.' She had very nearly said 'my lover', right in the sanctum of the bank, thereby setting proof on the tittle-tattle.

Mr Bricknell flapped a hand at her, waving her to be seated again. 'Pray do not take offence, Miss Turner. You permitted me to speak frankly and there has been talk, you see. Which does you no good, nor your growing business, no good at all, to acquire the reputation of a...' The red stain had passed his moustache now and was heading for his spectacles. He took them off and wiped them on a large handkerchief.

'No need to say the word, Mr Bricknell. Your meaning is perfectly clear.'

The bank manager cleared his throat. 'If you were considering marriage, of course...'

Meg swallowed. 'No, I am not considering marriage, as I think I have already said, until this war is over. I have a fiancé overseas.'

'Of course, of course. But this man, he is Irish, I believe? An itinerant worker, no doubt. Will he be moving on soon, do you think?'

Meg was surprised her voice sounded so calm when all she wanted to do was shout that of course Tam wasn't leaving. He loved her, didn't he? 'I wouldn't know. I hope not. He is a good worker and I trust him. Even if he did, I would still need a man about the place, for the heavy work. So I do not see the problem.'

'Oh, quite so, quite so, but one of respectable character, Miss Turner. A local man, do you see? And he should live in the barn.'

'The barn is falling down, Mr Bricknell. Would you care to give me a loan for the repairs?'

The bank manager laughed as if she had made a joke. It turned into a fit of coughing. 'All in good time, my dear, all in good time.' She wanted to tell him that she was not *his dear*, but she held on to her dignity, what little she had left. 'Do I take all this to mean that you will not consider a mortgage. Ever? Unless you are permitted to vet the people who live in my house?'

The bank manager had the grace to look embarrassed. 'As I think I mentioned once before when you expressed a fancy for a tractor, if you could perhaps persuade your father, in lieu of a husband, to act as guarantor, there would be no difficulty, no difficulty at all.'

Meg ground her teeth together in silent fury, all the while smiling serenely. At all costs, even to her pride, she must get a mortgage. But to allow her father to have any say in her affairs was out of the question. Joe would take control and rob her of Broombank, as he had always intended. Then he would have his revenge against poor Lanky, and against her, for being a girl, and for being so determined to beat him in spite of that. He would give Broombank to Dan and she would have nothing.

A thought occurred to her. 'What about my brother Dan? Would he do?'

The bank manager pondered.

'He is respectable.' She emphasised the word slightly. 'A married man with two children, and a farmer.'

The bank manager stood up and extended a hand.

'Bring your brother in to see me and I will give the matter my serious consideration.'

Meg swallowed her pride and shook the outstretched hand. But at the door she turned and faced him again, her expression resolute. 'I will agree to your request, Mr Bricknell, only because I must. But I assure you my brother will have no say in the running of Broombank, nor will the bank. And whom I employ and have living on the farm is my affair, and mine alone. No matter what problems may come in the future, I will succeed, woman or no. Believe it.'

–

'I'll not do it.' Dan stood stubbornly in the farm yard, a too familiar pugnaciousness to his face.

'Whyever not? It's only your signature I'm asking for, as guarantor. Nothing more. You'll have no say in Broombank, no work, no involvement at all.'

He was far from mollified. 'You think I'm daft? Well, I'm not. A guarantor means that if you can't pay the mortgage, then I would have to, and I've no money. You know damn well that Father pays me a pittance, or nothing, which is more likely the case these days.'

Meg sighed. 'I'm not asking for you to pay anything. There's no danger of my not being able to pay the mortgage.'

'That's easy said but things can go wrong in farming very easy. Disease, a bad winter, and you're up the creek without a paddle. Be content with what you've got for once, Meg. Pay rent and have done with dreams. I'd like to help but I daren't take the risk. Not with Sally Ann and the bairns to think of. You must see that?'

She sighed, conceding that he did have a point. 'Yes, I do understand.'

'Besides which, Sally Ann is expecting again.'

'Oh, Dan, congratulations. I didn't know. When is it to be?'

'Not till the summer,' he said gruffly, sounding pleased for all his previous moans and groans. 'So you see, I daren't take the risk. I don't want her worried about money. She has enough with the children, and Dad.'

'Yes, I can see that. I do understand, about the guarantor business. Forget I asked. I'll think of some other way.'

Then she surprised him by kissing him on the cheek. Never close as she and Charlie were, yet he was her brother and marriage seemed to be softening him. 'Sometimes, you know, you're very nearly human.' And laughed at his blushes.

Perhaps she could find some other solution.

—

Meg marked out the area to be ploughed with sticks. March had come in with a bluster. There was still the bite of winter in the air, a crispness to the soil, and that clarity of light peculiar to the north. A perfect day for the last of the ploughing. A few seagulls whirled overhead, blown in on the bitter winds from the coast, seeking food.

She and Tam were set to work it themselves, taking turns with Carrie, teamed with Will's old horse, Arlott, pulling Lanky's rusty old plough cleaned off and brought back into service. It was back-breaking work but more cost effective than bringing in the War Committee to do it for them. Besides, she needed to prove that she could cope without help from anyone.

Meg flicked at the reins, hoping the two horses wouldn't prove too mettlesome.

'Don't pull too hard on one side,' Tam called after her as she set the pair in motion. 'Keep them well balanced.'

Meg attempted to fix her eyes on the stick planted at the end of the field and drove the horses towards it. The rough fell ponies, taking no notice of the stick, and finding an amateur driver at the end of their reins, started to veer off at an angle to where more tempting vegetation beckoned.

'Damnation.' She could hear Tam's laughter as she struggled to keep them on an even course, without giving them their head and losing control altogether. Not an easy task. What had made her think she could do this?

The draining work had successfully given her more usable land and after decades of rest was proving to be surprisingly fertile. But the War Committee kept on putting up her quota to be ploughed. The wheat and oats she grew would be taken by the government while Broombank would be allowed to keep the kale for the milk cows and some turnips for the sheep.

'An acre a day,' Tam said.

After two agonising hours she judged his reckoning to be out by a half, certainly so far as she was concerned. Her longing for a tractor had never been so strong. But she wouldn't give in, oh no. She'd plough her acres or die in the attempt. She'd show her father and brother, and the bank manager, and everyone else who cared to watch, that a woman could farm.

Meg was nevertheless profoundly thankful when midday came at last and she could let Tam take over for an hour or two.

'Are you all right?'

'My knees feel like jelly and my back and arms will never move again. I'm going to find Effie and some embrocation.' Turning her nose up in the air, refusing to rise to his great guffaws of laughter, she staggered away.

Later Meg lay on the bed, unmoving, flat on her stomach, too exhausted even to think while he rubbed her aching limbs with lavender oil, smiling at her groans which were a combination of agony and ecstasy at his touch.

'Why aren't you in agony too?'

'I've worked with horses most of my life. My muscles are attuned, and it's partly a knack.' He kissed her ear. 'You'll learn, given time.'

Meg groaned. 'When the ploughing is all done, we're still nowhere near the end, are we? Every grain of seed will have to be sown by hand, broadcast in time-honoured fashion.'

'Then chains attached to the horses and the whole lot harrowed in.'

'And every root crop planted by hand?'

Tam nodded, eyes brimming with laughter. 'Regretting the extra land now?'

'I shall die, Tam, I know I shall. This land isn't meant to be ploughed. What has it all to do with sheep?'

He kissed her neck and slid the towel from her, so he could admire her slender back and swelling hips. 'It has to do with feed for sheep, and for cows.' His hand was sliding beneath her now, seeking her breast. 'It has to do with feed for people. With war. With being a farmer.'

'I hope you weren't thinking of making love to me this night? I couldn't move a muscle,' she mourned.

'You don't have to,' he whispered. 'I'll move them for you.'

To her surprise she managed to turn over and respond without any difficulty at all.

The next morning she was back at the plough before eight. By now she was determined to stand no nonsense from the two horses. Gritting her teeth, she drove them straight as a die. She'd show them who was in charge.

1942

Chapter 9

It was a soft spring day with the kind of settled warmth rarely found in Lakeland, the crags looking blacker than ever against the sharp green of new grass. The kind of day a raven might fly upside down for the sheer joy of living. Meg felt a similar joy as she checked her flock. All her efforts seemed to be working for the Swaledales were settling well. Lambing had started and she hoped for a good crop.

She and Effie laughed now when they remembered that first lambing season.

'How green we were,' Effie said. 'I even remember trying to put each hen to bed at night. Didn't realise they all lined up in proper pecking order and did it all by themselves.'

'I made plenty of mistakes too.'

'We did it though, didn't we? We managed to keep the farm, Meg. We succeeded.'

'Yes,' Meg agreed with a smile. 'We did, didn't we? We can thank the Luckpenny for that.'

'And hard work.'

Jeffrey Ellis came striding up the hill towards her and Meg tried to ignore the flutter of fear in her stomach that she always felt when she saw him these days. Foolish, she knew, for though he came once every few weeks under some pretext or other to see Lissa, he never suggested that he should remove her from Meg's care. Nevertheless, she still worried that one day he might. That's what people did. Got up and walked away one day. At least you could rely upon land to stay put.

'Run and put the kettle on, Effie. We'll be down in a minute.'

His conversation was not about Lissa today.

'You know that we have about sixty acres of land with Larkrigg? Pasture for Kath's horse, some woodland, the rest too stony and steep to be of any use for anything but grazing.'

Meg knew Larkrigg land and said so, curious at what this was all about.

'Well, I've sold Bonnie. Gone to a good home, where she'll get the attention she needs.'

Meg was astounded. She didn't know what to say. If he had sold the old pony then he had obviously given up hope of his daughter's ever returning home. It was a bleak moment. She took a hesitant step forward then put her arms about his neck and hugged him.

'I'm so sorry.' Meg felt close to tears. How could Kath be so cruel? Why didn't she at least write to her father?

He patted her shoulder but said nothing more for a long moment. Probably couldn't. Then he became his brisk self again and turned the conversation. 'We ploughed up the two-acre paddock, according to instruction, at the beginning of the war. The rest has great crags and rocks sticking out of it, as you know. Too stony for the plough and too much work for me to deal with. I wondered if you would be interested?

'What I'm suggesting is that you take over responsibility for all my sixty acres and my few sheep. I'm a hobby farmer, always have been. Supposed to be good for my

148

health, once upon a time. Now my own doctor tells me it's too much for me to manage. What do you say?'

Meg dipped her head and blinked hard. She felt choked by emotion at his generosity. 'I don't know what to say.'

'I've depended upon a few POWs. They come every day but need more supervision. Much of the grazing is going to waste for I've hardly any sheep on it these days. A dozen at most. It seems a shame, and we're not supposed to waste anything, are we, these days?' Jeffrey Ellis thrust his hands deep in his pockets, not looking at her. 'We're almost family, in a funny sort of way. I'd like you to make use of it, Meg.'

'What about Rosemary? How does she feel about the idea?'

'Haven't told her yet. But she'd have no objection. She isn't at all interested in the land, only her garden.'

'I'm not sure that I could afford...'

'Oh, there would be no charge. No rent or anything. In fact, quite the opposite. I'd pay you, my dear.'

'Pay me?'

'Oh, yes, I'm sure we could work something out that was beneficial to us both.'

Meg smiled. 'Without my losing face, you mean? Mr Ellis, you are a very kind man, but even if I agreed to work your land, and I'm not saying I could, I certainly would not accept wages for using your grass for my sheep. It wouldn't be right.'

'All right then. Rent-free grazing for your sheep and you keep us provided with lamb or mutton.'

'We are only allowed to kill one lamb or sheep for ourselves each year. The government checks up, you know. The same would apply to you.'

'I see, but if you take over the care of my sheep in lieu of payment for the use of the land, and provide me with some fresh food, whatever you can provide, then I'd be quite happy. Do we have a deal?'

She'd be a fool to refuse. 'It's a deal.'

Jeffrey Ellis grinned. 'I also understand you've been trying to get a mortgage, so you can buy Broombank?'

'I won't borrow the money from you, so please don't offer it.'

'I am aware of your desire for independence and applaud it. I've been having a word with my bank manager. I have told him how much you have achieved here already in such a short time. He sees no reason why he shouldn't be able to offer what you require.'

'Oh, Mr Ellis!'

'You would need to provide a deposit. Can you manage that?'

Her eyes were alight. 'I have it all saved up ready. Oh, but it's in another bank.'

Jeffrey Ellis smiled. 'My manager will be happy to open a new account for you and offer you very favourable terms.'

'I won't need a guarantor?'

'Not at all. You are your own woman. This is a business proposition between you and the bank. You must go and see him, of course, explain your plans for the future, impress him with your ability and creditworthiness, which I feel sure you can do. Is that not so?'

Meg was grinning now. 'Absolutely. Mr Ellis, you must be Santa Claus.' She flung her arms about his neck and kissed him, making him blush scarlet.

'No, Meg. I won't have that,' he protested, embarrassed by this show of affection. 'It's your own hard work that has brought this about. I feel it deserves recognition. I've only offered the right word in the right ear to help you on your way, that's all.'

'I do appreciate it.'

They shook hands. Tea was poured and Lissa was brought down to climb upon Mr Ellis's knee and demand a story that he had promised to tell her, if she was a good girl.

Meg sat and watched them, sipped her tea and listened too, with pleasure and joy in her eyes.

—

A day or two later she was working with Tam out on the fell when suddenly he turned to her with a defiant twist of his body and said, 'I'm going to join up.'

She stared at him, speechless with horror. 'Join up? Why? When?'

'You're going to get your mortgage to buy Broombank. You have Mr Ellis's land as well as your own and you can use POW labour. You can manage without me now.'

'That's a damn fool thing to say and you know it. I don't want you to go. I need you here, with me.'

He looked at her levelly. 'You managed well enough before I came.'

'That was different.'

'How so?'

'I didn't know you then. As I know and need you now. In every sense.' She took a step towards him, laid her hands flat against his chest. He smelled of sunshine and fresh earth and she drew in those scents to be a part of her, for ever. 'You said you didn't ever intend to join up. Didn't need to fight.'

'The Americans are seriously in the war now. Everyone is. I feel I ought to be too.'

'But you are Irish, not American, and Ireland is still a neutral country.'

Tam didn't smile at her, or joke as he once might have done. He gently removed her hands, looking serious. Far too serious. 'I still think I should go.'

Meg became very still. 'Because America is in? Are you saying that when the war is over you'll go back there, to America?' A pain was starting somewhere around the region of her heart. But he shook his head.

'That's up to you. I rather thought I might ask you to marry me. Probably should have asked you already.' He attempted a smile. 'Make an honest woman of you.'

'I did rather wonder.'

'I love you, Meg.'

'And I love you, Tam.'

'So what do you say? We could marry now. Before I go.'

She met his gaze. Open, loving, with anxiety in it as if he were not quite sure of her.

'You want me to marry you and then you intend to go off and fight in the war?'

'I have to.'

She swallowed, but it did nothing to ease the ache in her throat. She had longed for these words, now she hated them. 'I can't.'

The silence was appalling. 'Why can't you?'

'Because.'

'Because of Jack?'

'I still have his ring. I'm still engaged to him. Officially, that is. At least, I've never managed, never had the opportunity, to end it.'

'Perhaps you didn't try hard enough.'

'Don't be bitter, Tam.' She put out a hand, wanting to say she would marry him, wanting to have him gather her in his arms, say he wouldn't go. But he ignored it and the hand fell to her side, untouched.

'He betrayed you. You owe him nothing.'

'It was a youthful madness. It could happen to anyone. But until the war ends he needs me. I can't just abandon him. You know that I was waiting for him to come home on leave. I didn't want to go into all the recriminations by post. I never intended to fall in love again. Only I did. And then I couldn't bring myself to send him a "Dear John" letter.'

'Lots of other people manage it.'

'Well, I'm not other people. I'm me, and I thought it best to wait till I saw him. Only, I never did. He went overseas and disappeared.' As you might do, her heart said, and fear shot through her, hot and piercing. Oh, why did I ever let myself love again? she thought.

'So the answer is still no?'

She licked her lips. 'It would seem so – so cruel for Jack to think he still had a girl at home and come back to find me married. Can't we stay as we are, for now? Once the war is over I can tell him, explain about Lissa, decide what's best for her. Then there's Broombank, which I only accepted because I thought Jack and I...' She ran out of words, a sob on her breath, but Tam was too hurt to respond to it.

'Ah yes, of course, the land. It's fine for me to work it so long as I don't claim any rights to it. I'm just the hired man.'

Meg flushed angrily. 'That's not what I said.'

'Isn't it?'

'No.'

'What's best for the land. What's best for Lissa. What's best for Jack. What about what's best for you? And me? My needs don't count, is that it?'

Meg searched desperately for the right words to explain how she felt. How by rights both Lissa and the land belonged to Jack and how she couldn't bear to part with either of them. But she couldn't say all of that without hurting Tam further. 'I can't do anything about Jack, not yet. Why won't you understand?'

'Suit yourself,' he said and strode away.

Just as she had always feared would one day happen, it was over. He packed his few belongings and that night as they lay in the great bed made no move to touch her until she whispered his name, a painful sob coming from deep in her soul.

Then he reached for her and loved her with such a sweet fierceness it was as if he could not get enough of her, as if it were the last time.

When she woke the next morning, the bed was empty. Tam had gone.

—

'I reckon that Lord Haw Haw chap should be horse-whipped, prating on every night.'

'Yes, Dad. Write to the BBC and suggest it.'

'It's not the BBC who's at fault, you daft woman, it's that Hitler. I'll not have no jumped-up little dictator telling me what's what. "Jairmany calling. Jairmany calling." Makes my blood boil.'

'Why do you listen to him then? Go to bed.'

'No, I want thee to read me that news again. I want to understand what's going on.'

Sally Ann laid down the paper with a weary sigh. 'Sorry, Dad, but I'm licked. Little Daniel will have me awake by five and I can't take any more.'

She came to stand by his chair and rested a gentle hand on his arm. 'Don't sit up too long. You're tired too and it could be a long while before Dan gets home. You know he's often late after a training exercise.' She glanced about the muddled room, children's toys and clothes scattered about. There hardly seemed a spare minute in the day to do all that had to be done. And she didn't feel up to trying. This pregnancy seemed more wearisome than the last two, somehow.

'I need more help,' she said now, surprising herself by the suddenness of her request.

Joe glanced up at her, then at the homely clutter. 'Aye,' he said, after a moment. 'Happen you do, since you're carrying again. I'll find a girl to help you, next time I go down town.'

Impulsively she kissed him on the forehead. He had never returned her signs of affection but she knew they did not displease him. 'I'm lucky to have you to keep me cheerful, do you know that?' she gently teased. 'Meg's on her own again now that Tam has joined up. Apart from little Effie, that is. I feel for her.'

'Perhaps she'll see sense now then, and give up. Get yourself to bed,' he said gruffly. 'Thee needs rest. I'm all right for a bit.'

Smiling, Sally Ann went wearily up the stairs. It had been a good day for her when she'd come to Ashlea to borrow money. She had no complaints, none at all. Dan had proved to be a good husband for all his insecurities and Joe wasn't a bad old stick, once you got used to him. More bark than bite these days.

Down in the kitchen Joe got up and turned off the wireless in disgust. He'd had enough of that propaganda rubbish. But he would wait up for his son and find out just what he was up to. Training exercise indeed! The last time Dan had come home late, there had been the unmistakable smell of beer on his breath, if Joe wasn't mistaken. He meant to check it out tonight. If he was right, he'd have a few words to say on the subject.

Despite his best efforts, Joe's eyes soon began to droop. Jerking awake again, he went to brew a pot of tea to keep himself alert. When Dan crept quietly through the door at half-past midnight, his father was snoring gently by the ashes of a dead fire. Grinning to himself, he made sure not to disturb Joe as he lurched past the old carver chair towards the stairs.

He might have made it too, had it not been for Nicky's pile of wooden bricks. Dan put his foot on one and skidded from one to the other like a cat on marbles.

'Bloody hell,' he yelled, crashing to the ground with such force that not only did he wake his father, but his wife and two sons as well. The baby's screams burst forth like ack–ack fire.

Joe was on his feet in a second. 'I knew it. Drunk! And swearing too. What have we come to?'

Dan groaned in agony. 'I think I've broken my ankle.'

'Get up and don't talk soft. What have thee been up to, eh? No good, I'll be bound.'

Sally Ann came hurrying downstairs, dressing gown pulled hastily about her swollen stomach, eyes blinking with sleep. 'What is it? What's going on?'

'This lout is drunk,' Joe announced. 'Just look at him, great lump that he is.'

'Don't call me a lump.' Dan had had enough of being reviled and criticised. All his life his father had told him how useless he was. Charlie and Meg had been petted by his mother, but nobody had given a toss about him. He'd had enough. Pulling back his arm, he swung his fist with all the power of his awesome muscle.

Had it not been for the several pints he had consumed with his mates earlier that evening, some of it home brewed at Mike Lanyon's house, he might well have done considerable damage. As it was, the very act of swinging the arm sent him clean off balance and before he could stop himself he'd banged his head against the kitchen cupboard, tipped sideways, and landed with one foot in the coal scuttle, a look of comical surprise upon his face.

'Huh,' scoffed Joe, a curl of contempt at the corner of his mouth. 'Can't even get that right. I'm off to bed.'

Dan shook a fist at him, determined to prove his point. 'If I want a drink, I shall have one. I'm near thirty years old and I'll please meself.'

'Thee'll do as I say while you live in my house.'

Flushed with fury, Dan shook off the clinging coal scuttle, fortunately empty of coal since it was so hard to come by, and lurched to his feet. 'You're a flaming bully, that's what you are!'

'Dan, don't.' Sally Ann stepped hastily forward. She'd never seen him like this before, never. She feared what he might say or do next. 'Come to bed, love. It's the drink talking, Father, take no notice.'

Dan shook her arm impatiently away. With the skill peculiar only to the very drunk, he steadied himself and faced his father with narrowed eyes. 'You told me she wouldn't stick at it. You told me Meg would give up as soon as things got tough. You promised me that I could have Broombank, for me own.'

Joe regarded his son with something very close to pity. What a clod hopper he was. When things didn't quite go his way he got peevish, or turned to drink. Why had he ever imagined that this son might make a good farmer? But he was his eldest and the other one wasn't shaping to it at all, so he had to make the best of it.

For the first time in his life, Joe wished that Dan had some of Meg's skill and half her spunk and common sense. It was true, she was doing well at Broombank, he had to admit that. Despite his better judgement Joe felt a grudging admiration for his daughter. Why had the wrong one been born a boy?

'Happen thee will have it, one day. It's just taking longer than I thought.'

'It won't ever happen. She won't give up and you know it. Meg's as stubborn as you. She'll never let me have Broombank, and you won't let me run Ashlea. All I am is a bloody labourer. You're too damn mean to pay me a living wage, and I can't even afford to keep me own wife and children, not without food from your table.'

Sally Ann was crying now. 'Stop it, Dan. It doesn't matter.'

'Aye, it does matter. It matters to me. I've had enough. I'm a man, aren't I?'

The bloodshot eyes focused with surprising clarity and terrible ferocity upon Joe. 'I have my pride.' He took a step forward and laughed out loud when he saw his father flinch. 'Aye, you might well look nervous. Things are going to change round here. I'm taking no more orders from you.' He jabbed a wavering finger in his father's face. 'I'm going to see our Meg in t'morning, and tip her out of

158

that cosy nook she has, once and for all. I want a place of me own, and mean to get it, one way or another. I'm not ending up bitter and dried up like you.' Swinging to Sally Ann, he clutched her about the shoulders, pulling her to him, turning maudlin now. 'You're a grand lass, Sal. I'll see you don't become his skivvy, like our Meg did. I won't have it, d'you hear?'

'I'm not. I won't,' she protested but Dan shook his head.

'Oh, aye, that's what he does to people, turns them into skivvies and labourers to do his bidding. It don't matter to him what *you* want, only what *he* wants.' Dan wiped the spittle from his lips with the back of his hand. His mind was starting to fog over again and he'd lost track of his thoughts. 'I've had enough,' he said, and slid senseless to the floor.

Which gave Joe the opportunity for the last word, as usual. 'You can both be out first thing in t'morning, if that's the way you feel about it.' Then turning his back in disgust, he went upstairs to bed.

Sally Ann, crying bitter tears, not knowing whether to berate Dan for his folly in losing them a comfortable home, or admire him for finally standing up to his father, pulled off her husband's boots and covered him with the rug from the settle. There was no way she could get him upstairs, so she left him where he was and went to bed.

—

Meg could scarce believe the pain she felt. A great gaping hole was left where once joy had been. She lay sleepless at night, tossing and turning in the great empty bed, her mind and her body crying out for Tam. She thought she would never get over the pain of losing him.

Nothing she had ever felt before could possibly have prepared her for this. It was as if a part of her were missing.

She wrote to him every day and lived for his letters, which were never often enough for her liking. She tried to fill her days with work but she seemed to have lost interest and became listless, without her usual energy. Every morning she had to drag herself downstairs and couldn't face the breakfast Effie tried to make her eat.

'It'll be all right in the end,' Effie consoled her. 'He feels he has to do his bit, that's all. As you have to do yours. When this topsy-turvy world rights itself again, he'll be back.'

Meg's grey eyes turned upon her friend, begging for it to be true. 'I can't cope without him, Effie. There seems no point in anything any more without Tam here beside me. Was I wrong? Should I have married him, even though I couldn't end it properly with Jack?'

Effie's face turned blank. 'Don't get me into that one. I'm a kid, remember. Anyroad, that's your decision. No one else's.'

'I was afraid too, Effie. Afraid that if I married Tam, committed myself to him, it would hurt more if he ever left and didn't come back.' She gave a hard little laugh with no humour in it. 'I can see now that can't be true. With or without a piece of paper, I'm committed. I couldn't possibly hurt more than I do at this moment.'

'Course you're committed, and he is to you. Don't worry. He understands.'

'Does he?' Meg remembered the harsh words between them and wished she could feel as certain as Effie. She glanced about the breakfast table and wondered what right she had to complain. They were all safe and well. Lissa happily playing with the ever patient Rust. Effie healthy and fit, growing into a lovely young woman, reading the papers which recently had been full of what were being dubbed the Baedeker Raids.

From May through into June, while the foliage thickened, the cold earth softened and the spotted coats of the new deer calves could be sometimes glimpsed in Brockbarrow Wood, many of England's most famous historical cities had been under attack. Meg wept to hear of the terrible consequences of these attacks. They were at least safe here.

This morning there was at least the joy of a letter from Charlie. She held the crisp blue envelope in her hand now, savouring the anticipation of opening it.

'Families are trekking out of the cities each night and sleeping in the fields to keep safe,' read Effie. 'I don't blame them. They won't get bombed there.'

Meg glanced at the picture Effie showed her. A weary group of people with smiles on their faces, carrying their entire belongings in parcels, trying to make the best of life. But if you looked closely, you could see their agony all too clearly behind the bravery. Plymouth, Bath, York, so many towns had suffered devastating damage. Whole areas of ancient buildings wiped out.

'Those cities weren't as prepared as London,' Effie said. 'Anyway, they thought the raids were all finished by the end of the blitz. Now it's starting all over again. Do you think we'll bomb Germany again?'

Meg ripped open the envelope, anxious suddenly to read how her brother was.

Charlie's handwriting. She held a part of him in her hand. She smiled at Effie. 'He's all right. We should re-member that however terrible it is to bomb cities, the real tragedy of war is its effect on each and every individual.

War is a personal tragedy and we should never forget that. What matters is Charlie, and all the other Charlies. Every single family like that one in the paper, not just bricks and mortar, stone and slate, however precious.'

There was no address at the top of the single sheet of paper, but Charlie's happy voice came over loud and clear.

'Is he still flying?' Effie quietly asked.

Meg nodded. 'Says he's fine. Doing a second tour, as he said he might.' She started to read aloud.

'He says "Feeling fine. Sue OK but don't get to see her as much as I'd like now she is in the ATS. Well into Second Tour of Ops. The big one is coming up soon. Don't want to miss it."'

'The big one? What does he mean?' Effie looked as troubled as Meg felt.

'I don't know. We must pray for him, Effie. Every night.'

The young girl nodded, blinking furiously. 'Oh, I do, Meg. I do. And Lissa does too, don't you, sweetheart?'

Lissa happily nodded, not understanding, and went back to feeding Rust with toast crusts.

'He'll be all right. Eat your breakfast while it's hot, there's a hard day's work ahead, and I mean to churn some butter this morning.'

Meg folded the letter and tucked it into her overall pocket. One day at a time, that's all you could hope for in this war. Today, Charlie was fine, and Tam hadn't got anywhere near the fighting yet.

—

Meg was busily engaged in checking the feet of one of her sheep later that morning when Jeffrey Ellis called.

'Got foot rot, has she?'

'I don't think so but I'm giving her a dab in the foot-bath, just in case. I think she's only sprained it though.'

Rust lay close by, nose to his toes, keeping a wary eye on the sheep just in case it should take any daft notion of escape into its silly head. Meg finished her task and opened the gate to let her go. The ewe hobbled off at a cracking pace to rejoin a very noisy, anxious lamb. Jeffrey Ellis laughed.

'Someone's been missing Mum.'

She chuckled. 'Lively as bairns they are. I love to watch them. Can I get you a cup of tea?'

She was always ready to spend time with him these days. He'd been good to her, and to Lissa. Jeffrey Ellis had once seemed a lonely, careworn man. Now he was alert, alive again. All due to Lissa, no doubt about it. The child had given him a reason for living. He looked particularly fit and well this morning, showing signs of the handsome man he had once been in spite of the greying hair. 'No thanks, I mustn't stay. I know you're busy.'

'I'm thrang, as my father would say, but all the more ready for a break. Particularly on a lovely bright morning like this.'

The June sun shone fat and yellow as if it were high summer. Somewhere in the distance a cuckoo made its two note song and wood pigeons hooted. A day for lovers, Meg thought, for cherry blossom and weddings. For a moment the keenness of Tam's going pierced her heart so fiercely she had trouble catching her breath. But she must keep her heart and hopes high. He would be back, Effie had said so.

Jeffrey Ellis grinned at her. 'The searches have been done and your mortgage prepared. You only have to go in and sign the papers and it's yours.'

'Oh, it's an omen! This lovely day, a letter from Charlie, and now my mortgage. I shall go right away, this very minute.' She turned to run, then remembering Mr Ellis, leaped up and gave him a swift kiss upon his cheek. 'Bless you,' she said.

Jeffrey Ellis stood and laughed at her excitement. 'Now who's acting like a bairn?' he teased.

Meg dashed into the house to find Effie and tell her she was off into town to see her new bank manager. Then she changed into clean slacks and pulled on a light sweater.

Moments later she was out in the yard again. Rust came straight to her heels. 'No, Rust. Stay here, there's a good boy,' she instructed the dog. He looked most put out, as he always did at being so abandoned. He lay down by the gate so that he could watch her go along the lane, and see her the moment she returned. He could also keep a guard on the house from this position, so no one would come or go that he didn't know about.

Meg watched this with amusement as she pulled out her bike. 'Effie is inside making butter, aided and hindered by Lissa, of course. She'll gladly put the kettle on, if you want that tea,' she told Jeffrey Ellis, feeling guilty at abandoning him too.

'Don't worry about me. I won't stop the good work. But I might pop in and just say hallo.'

A stocky figure loomed into sight on the lane. 'Oh no, what does Dan want? I really have no time this morning for my brother's moans and groans.' Meg grabbed her bicycle and dusted off the seat. 'Tell him I was in a hurry, will you? Apologise for me,' she begged.

'I'll tell him this is the best day of your life.' Meg grinned and was off, pedalling furiously along the lane. Oh, he was right. It was the best, by far. Not counting the times with Tam of course.

Dan called to her, 'Here, Meg, I want to talk to you.'

'Later, Dan. Go and see Effie. She'll make you a mug of tea if you ask nicely. I won't be long.' As she reached the corner of the lane she turned to wave. Dan was glowering with fury but Jeffrey Ellis was still where she had left him, laughing, his hair glinting like silver in the sunshine. Most of all she saw Broombank, its white walls almost beaming with pleasure, windows blinking with delight at the promise of this new future.

When she returned later that day, the paperwork all done, her mortgage secured, and a precious bottle of wine in her cycle basket to celebrate, she found the roof of her lovely home had been lifted off as if by some giant hand and placed, very neatly, in the next field. Half the walls, the ones that had taken the worst of the blast from the bomb carelessly dropped by a passing bomber, had fallen in. Just as Effie was stirring her butter with a rowan twig, to make it turn quickly and protect it from witches.

Chapter 10

It had all begun as a great lark so far as Jack Lawson was concerned. Chasing Italian warships off Italy and sinking the ships which carried enemy troops and supplies, without too many British losses, was right up his street.

But that had been back in March 1941. The feeling that it was some sort of game had ended by the summer of 1942.

By the autumn, enemy submarines and shore-based aircraft started picking off British ships, one by one, like fish in a pond. In no time at all the Med was not a safe place to be and longer routes had to be taken around the Cape and through the Suez Canal to supply reinforcements for the men fighting in the Western desert. Rommel decided Suez was a place he coveted, and as far as Jack was concerned, he could have it.

At the first sign of the enemy it was Jack's task to man the antiaircraft guns while Len, his best mate, fed in the ammunition. They did their best, gave it all they had, firing in what sometimes seemed the forlorn hope of hitting one of those black shapes that swooped and dived, high in the heavens. Sometimes they'd be wet with fear, but mostly they kept their minds safely blank. Do the job and leave the thinking to those in fancy hats, that was the best way.

Then a shower of shells lifted Len from his feet and nailed him to the deck. Jack grabbed the gun, rage burning so fiercely behind his eyes it took three men to wrench him free as he swung the gun round and round, firing indiscriminately, in more danger of killing someone on the ship than hitting an enemy plane.

And so Jack Lawson lost his taste for war.

Was it any wonder, he told himself, that by the end of that year he was less than thrilled to learn he'd been assigned to Special Boat Ops? His task was to row a small rubber boat under cover of darkness, carrying a select group of men whose target was a munitions dump on mainland Italy. That mission changed his entire war, perhaps even his life.

He'd certainly been fleeing for his life ever since.

He never learned what went wrong. The four men didn't come back, simple as that. And when Jack attempted to return to his ship, the pathetic little boat had been shelled out of the water, fortunately before Jack had climbed into it. He'd been blown backwards on to the shore and supposed he should feel lucky to escape with only a broken shoulder even though the pain of it in those first few days had made him almost wish he was dead.

But now he had Lina.

The days that he had spent crawling and dragging himself through rough country were a blur in his mind. He'd probably spent Christmas on his belly somewhere, though he had no recollection of it. Only of the bitter cold, and the ceaseless pain.

He remembered being thankful to find an area of peace and quiet, nursing his injured arm across the stony ground till he came to lush farmland on the edge of a small village.

Somewhere in the distance could be heard the roar of guns, the skies lit with red every night to remind him of it, but here all was quiet.

He saw a row of houses, a few shops, one of them giving off a most enticing aroma of fresh bread. It reminded him how hungry he was and he had made his way round the back of them, hoping for a chance to find some of the delectable stuff. Most of all he recalled his first sight of the barn, huddled in a ramshackle group of wooden buildings. He chose it because it reminded him so much of the one at Broombank, and when he'd seen Meg he'd been sure of it.

Only it wasn't Meg. This girl did not have Meg's golden curls or her bright smile. This girl was dark, olive-skinned, and her lips were wider than Meg's and a paler pink. She did smile occasionally but mostly she looked anxious and hurried.

Most of all he remembered her hands. Soft and comforting, he had wanted to fold himself into those hands and cry like a baby. He hadn't done so, of course. He was a man, wounded but still Able Seaman Lawson. Grown men don't cry, however much they might hurt and feel the need to.

'You are Breetish?' she'd said to him that first day when she'd found him, and the relief of hearing his own language spoken to him so gently by this delectable creature turned his innards to water. Jack recalled with shame how he had emptied the contents of his stomach into the clean hay which she had packed about his battered body for comfort.

But she hadn't seemed to mind. 'Do not fret, you are safe here. Stay quiet.'

For all she was Italian and the enemy, he had believed her. She'd brought her brother, Giovanni, and together over the following weeks they had tended to his wounds, strapped the shoulder up and fed him as if he were a child when moving was too painful to contemplate.

Now, at last, he was beginning to feel half human again. The strappings were off the arm and he was learning to use it again, anxious to repay her kindness and get out of this hot, musty barn. The snows had long gone, spring was turning into summer and the sun looked enticing. He wanted to be out in it, to feel the baking heat on his face.

'Let me do some chores,' he begged her now. When she pulled a face he grasped her hand and pulled her down beside him. She was bewitching when she pouted at him in just that way, one shoulder lifted beguilingly. No man could resist her. 'I'm fit now, and bored silly with staying in this loft. I owe your family some labour if nothing else.'

'My family are happy to help you. We are not fascist, you understand?'

'I understand.'

'All Italians are not in favour of the new regime but we have to be careful, yes?'

'You think I will endanger their lives? I wouldn't dream of it.'

'I know you would not intentionally do so. But it ees so very dangerous. You must stay here, where you are safe. I would have nothing happen to you.'

When he would protest she set soft fingertips against his lips and Jack wanted to crush her to him, and take her then and there in the straw. Instead he smiled and kissed the fingers.

He loved the way she wore her long, glossy black hair in a tumble of curls down her back, and the brightly coloured frocks. They looked as if she'd made them herself out of a selection of others that had been cut up for the purpose, as perhaps they had. Nothing matched, not the sleeves, nor the bodice with the skirt, but the patchwork effect was delightful and the flowing style clung to her body and rippled about her brown legs.

She leaned over him to refill his water pitcher and he had a clear view of her breasts and nipples, enticingly dark.

As if aware of him for the first time she looked directly into his eyes. It was a moment to savour, a moment when words were not needed. An understanding was reached and would, in the fullness of time, be acted upon.

'You may come into the house thees evening for supper,' Lina told him. 'My father, he ees very strict. You will have to be the gentleman. Sì?' Jack gave her a lop-sided smile, one side of his face still bruised and swollen from his abrupt landing on the rocky shore. 'Scout's honour.' She did not understand him and he felt obliged to explain but then she offered one of her rare, shy smiles and as he sat watching the dust motes settle after she had gone, he began to appreciate the extent of his good fortune.

–

Jack spent the long hot summer doing odd jobs for Lina's father. He told himself that he wasn't really a deserter. He would willingly go back, only how could he when his ship had left long since? To wander about an enemy country on his own, looking for more British, would be madness. Besides, he enjoyed working at the bakery. Mr Ruggierri was teaching him how to mix and knead the bread dough.

'You make good baker,' he said in Italian, and Lina laughed as she translated for Jack.

'He looks so Italian, does he not, Papa? With his black curly hair and charming smile.'

At this, Papa frowned and started to scold, sending Lina away. 'Good girl,' he said sternly to Jack, in perfect English, wagging a finger.

Jack smiled and agreed, anxious to keep the old man happy.

Every moment they could they spent together, and Lina started to teach him a little Italian. She was so beautiful, so delightful to watch, the lessons were a joy and the summer passed speedily and pleasantly enough.

–

Kath strode down the street, a trail of GIs in her wake. 'Aw, come on, hon. Have a cigarette.'

'Sorry. Don't smoke.'

'How about chocolate? Everybody likes chocolate. Or I could put my hands on some real perty silk stockings if you like.'

'So long as my legs aren't inside them, that's fine by me.'

She smiled to herself. Verbal and sometimes very nearly physical combat with the American military had become a daily hazard since her posting to HQ three months ago. She'd been in many stations since Bledlow, but this one was proving to be the worst in many ways.

Group Headquarters was a large, redbrick house situated on the edge of a small market town in Cambridgeshire. Whenever Kath walked through the ancient streets she felt a jolt of surprise that people still carried their baskets to market, wheeled babies in prams or rode their bicycle to college in the next town, just as if life was normal.

But step through the blue-painted door and she became a WAAF again with a job to do, swallowed up in a sea of blue and brown uniforms. The latter, of course, worn by the American airmen who, to Kath's way of thinking, were far too full of their own importance.

She ducked now into a tea shop to avoid her latest pursuer and with difficulty found a seat in a corner farthest from the door. She ordered tea and a scone and pulled out her newspaper, hoping that here at least a rather new Corporal might find a few moments of peace.

There was certainly none in HQ. The place buzzed with activity. Teleprinters spewed out their news from the many out-stations in the Group, WAAFs operated switch-boards, plotted weather charts and peered short-sightedly at strange-looking instruments. Middle aged men seemed to be absorbed with pins and flags and sheaves of paper which they wrote upon endlessly and carried back and forth for no apparent purpose.

'Is this seat taken?' Kath looked up to find that today she had happened upon one of the more stubborn type. Not only had this airman miraculously found a seat in an otherwise packed-to-the-door teashop, but it was at her own table. The cheek of the man!

She offered what was meant to be a frosty rebuff. 'I really wouldn't know.'

'Great. Then I'll take it till I'm kicked off of it.' He sat down, ordered tea, and started to pull out a pack of cigarettes.

'I'd rather you didn't smoke, if you don't mind?'

'Oh, sure. No problem.' He slipped them back in his breast pocket. Kath was lonely. She missed the cheery faces of the aircrew coming and going all the time, and their lively banter, though admittedly she did not at all miss having her sleep interrupted by the roar of Merlin engines and aircraft taking off at all hours of the night.

She missed the many friends she'd made on all of the stations. Olive, Rosie, Alice, but most of all she remembered blunt, cheerful, open-hearted Bella who'd started the war with her way back in 1940, three years ago. But most of all she missed Wade, still, after all this time. She'd heard of him from time to time on various postings but they'd never been given the same one, and he had made no effort to contact her. Not that there was any reason why he should.

But she had no wish to be reminded of him now by this cheeky faced GI, looking for a woman, any woman with two arms, two legs, and everything in the right place in between.

Much to the amusement of the other customers he smilingly continued his conversational battery as if they were old buddies. 'Hey, how about you and me taking in the dance on Saturday night, honey, up at the station? You'll just love it. I bet you're a real sharp little mover.'

'I don't think so.' Kath offered him her best drop-dead-Corporal stare. It didn't work.

'Why not, for heaven's sake? What else is there to do around here? Unless you're fixed up already? I've no wish to tread on anyone else's toes.'

I'd just love to step on yours, Kath thought. She drank her tea, rather more quickly than she'd intended, and stood up. 'Thanks, but no thanks, if you get my drift.' Turning on her heels she walked out.

Maybe it's the loneliness that makes me feel so sour and hard, she thought. Or all the neglected things that she'd meant to do one day but had constantly pushed from her mind. Like write to Meg. There were some things best not thought about at all. What she had done to her friend was one of them. Nothing could ever be the same between them again, deep in her heart she knew that, and regretted it more than she could say. Perhaps that's why she hadn't written.

Then there were her parents. I suppose they don't even know if I'm still alive, she thought. Strange feeling, and another source of guilt.

Somehow it was as if the optimum moment had passed. As each week, month and year had slid by, sometimes whirled by in a welter of work and sleepless nights, the unresolved decisions seemed harder to make. Now, in the summer of 1943, a simple letter to her family would prove to be a major incident. One she could well do without.

What was the point, anyway? Getting to know and like people was a waste of time. You only lost them in the end. Meg, even her parents, must have grown used to her absence by now. So what did it matter?

Except that she had a daughter somewhere, whom she ached to see.

—

'There is a war on, you know.'

Kath arrived back at HQ to be told to pack a bag and drive a Commander Thompson to Lincoln, and could she get a move on? 'I wish I had a pound for every time I'd heard that remark,' she muttered. 'It is my day off. I was planning on going to a matinee this afternoon.'

'Not now it isn't. Get a move on, Corporal.' Having delivered his bombshell, the jumped-up little sergeant went to harass someone else while Kath stumped off to her room with every sign of ill grace though secretly pleased to be on the move again. She hated having nothing to do. Nevertheless a moan was expected, the point needed to be made.

'It's a madhouse. Thank heaven I don't have to stay in HQ longer than it takes to collect my passengers,' she wrote that night in her regular letter to Bella.

'I spend most of my time driving the top brass to some meeting or other in camps all over East Anglia. I've slept in more strange beds than any decent woman should in one lifetime.'

Though Kath decided not to risk mentioning it in the letter, it was hard not to be aware of an air of expectancy about the place. Everyone had the feeling that there was to be some great push soon to finish off the war. Tension was high and tempers often short. No one quite liked to talk about it too much, in case they spoke out of line. But the Second Front was definitely being planned. All these meetings she'd driven to must have some purpose, for goodness' sake. Everyone knew it. But then Bella could read between the lines.

Kath chewed on the end of her pen for some time then added a postscript. 'Have you heard anything of Commander Wades on lately?' She didn't know why she felt the compulsion to ask. He too had moved on long since, but every now and again Kath couldn't resist putting it in her letter. Bella would reply that no, she hadn't seen him in an age, and that would be that. When her friend's reply came a couple of weeks later, Kath ripped it open at once, eager for news, for the imagined sound of a friendly voice.

She flicked through the usual jokey stories and mishaps of WAAF life and then was brought to a stunning halt.

'Hey, what do you think, old sport? I'm getting married. Yep, got the divorce from old po-face easy as pie and am doing "The Deed" on Saturday. He's called Alan and he's a dear. Wish me luck.'

Doing '*The Deed*'. Getting married? Kath could hardly believe it. And I won't be there. Damn. It hurt, more than she cared to admit, not to be invited. But weddings were often in a rush these days, and transport was always difficult. Would Bella leave the WAAF now, or carry on?

She turned the paper over and saw the postscript. 'Funny you should ask about old Wadeson. He called in to see me once when he was visiting Bledlow. Asked after you. Where you were stationed and so on. Did he contact you? Glad to hear you are enjoying your work. Will write again when more time. Love Bella.'

To her shame, the letter made Kath feel more lonely than ever. Bella, frustratingly, hadn't said when Wade had called. But no, he had not contacted her, not in all of the last three years. Why she even expected him to was beyond reason. No doubt he flirted with all the new young WAAFs. But try as she might, it was hard to put him out of her mind.

On Saturday morning Kath was bargaining over the price of a pair of new shoes at a market stall when the same GI turned up again, persistent as a bug in bed. Which is where he'd like to be, Kath thought, unable to quench a smile at his cheek.

'Hallo again. How ya doin'?'

Kath very nearly told him to go and take a very long walk off a very short pier but the memory of Bella's letter was still strong in her mind. Great big cheerful Bella, who had once sworn that she had given up men for good, was getting married.

When she stopped to think about it, several of the other girls she'd come to know in recent months had also done 'The Deed'. Not only was there no likelihood of herself following suit but, Kath thought morosely, at very nearly twenty-four years of age she was ashamed to say she didn't even have a fella, let alone a whiff of orange blossom. Drat the war. Drat Ewan Wadeson.

'Is that offer still on?' she asked suddenly, laughing at the shocked surprise on the GI's face.

'Sure thing.'

'See you there about eight?'

'Wow! Okay, lady, you're on.'

Kath was aware of his eyes following her all the way down the Market Street. Oh lordy, what had she done now?

–

The five-piece band was really not at all bad, but the dancing was something else again. Lots of girls in bright red lipstick and curled hair dancing cheek to cheek with the American airmen and soldiers. 'It's called smooching.'

'Really?' Kath had no wish to try it. In fact she was beginning to regret accepting this GI's offer of a date at all. She longed suddenly to be back in her room at HQ with a good book.

'The other is the jitterbug. Have you ever tried it?'

'Don't even consider rolling me across your shoulders in that way,' Kath warned, and he moved his gum from his mouth, stuck it on the door post, and grinned at her.

'Why not? It's fun.'

'In a tight blue WAAF skirt it could be hysterical.' Not to mention the regulation knickers.

'What did you expect? The waltz?'

Kath gave a thin smile. Maybe she had, but nothing on earth would have her admit as much. 'Is there a way to do this jive without quite going overboard?'

'Sure thing. Come on, I'll show you.'

And he did. Brad, as he introduced himself, was an expert. To be fair, Kath soon found she was enjoying herself. The music quite chased the blues away. But Brad wasn't Wade. She'd make this the first and last date. By the way he clung to her, she'd best find a crowd to go home with.

At the interval, when the band took a rest, Brad went in search of ice cream while Kath sat and fanned herself in a corner. She was so busily engaged in trying to overhear a most interesting argument going on between a GI and an ATS girl right behind her that she didn't see the man approach until he was standing right in front of her.

'Kath Ellis, isn't it?'

Then she gave a loud squeal, bringing everyone's head swivelling in her direction.

'Dear lordy, *Charlie*! *I* don't believe it. How are you? What are you doing here? Where have you been? Oh, Charlie let me look at you?' He was laughing and hugging her and swinging her round and trying to answer her questions, all at the same time. Breathless with laughter, they both fell back on to the chair, Kath on his lap, since there was only the one.

'I'm stationed near here,' he told her. 'What about you?'

'HQ. Driving the top brass to hush-hush talks.'

'A WAAF?' He held out her arms to examine her properly. 'Who'd have thought it? This is a far cry from haytiming in Westmorland. Wait till I tell Meg.'

The smile died from Kath's eyes.

'Oh, I haven't told her or anyone about my being a WAAF. Where I am, or anything.'

Charlie regarded her with Meg's look-alike eyes, then ran a hand through the pale gold hair that still fell forward on to his brow. 'I knew there was some sort of problem, and that she's been anxious about you. But I didn't know what.'

'It isn't important.'

Charlie gave a disbelieving smile. 'It must be for you two to fall out. Are you going to tell me about it?'

She shrugged her shoulders with airy indifference. 'Meg is better off without me. Let's leave it at that, shall we?'

'About Meg…'

They were interrupted by Brad returning with two dishes of ice cream and the usual broad grin. The latter swiftly faded when he found 'his girl' sitting on another guy's lap, particularly since he hadn't even reached first base.

'Hey, what gives?'

Kath scarcely glanced at him. 'Sorry, Brad, this is Charlie, a very old and dear friend of mine.'

'So I see.'

Charlie set Kath on her feet and put a hand on Brad's beefy shoulder. 'What Kath says is right. We go back a long way.'

'And I bought the goddam' tickets.' A stubborn unpleasantness was now coming into the other man's eyes and Charlie held up a placating hand.

'Hey. Look, mate, I don't want any trouble.'

'Well, you sure as hell got it.' Brad flung the ice cream aside and hit Charlie smack in the jaw. Charlie went sprawling across the dance floor, sending couples flying, girls screaming.

In a frighteningly short space of time a pair of MPs appeared, fighting their way through the melee of arms and legs to march both Charlie and Brad away.

'I'll call you later,' Charlie shouted as Kath stood, dazed and helpless, watching them go. 'I need to talk to you.'

'Forget it, airman. You won't be calling anyone for a long time.'

A few days later Kath found a note from him in her pigeon hole. 'Survived the glasshouse. Want to see you. Can you get away Friday? Fourish. The Bluebell Caff?'

Kath was at a table by three-forty-five. She'd always liked Charlie. He'd seemed chockful of enthusiasm and plans as a boy, and just the same now by all appearances. But she was also anxious suddenly to hear all the news of Broombank and Meg. To know that her parents were well. She allowed her thoughts to go no further than that.

The tiny doorbell tinkled and in he walked, broad-shouldered and cheerful as ever, with the kind of easy swagger she'd grown used to seeing on aircrew. But as he came towards her she recognised that some of the cheeriness was no more than bravado. She'd seen that too, in any number of faces going off on ops. A certain stillness, a haunting quality in the eyes, the skin tight and the mouth drawn in. Later, when the crew returned after a successful mission, they would be relaxed and noisy, laughing and boisterous.

He took the seat opposite her. She'd no intention of fussing him, that wouldn't do at all. If he wanted to talk about it, he would. They ordered tea and two sticky buns, which were an improvement on the 'wads' they got at HQ.

'Where are you stationed?'

He told her. An out-station no more than a mile or two down the road. 'You'll come and see me? I have a bit of time free sometimes, in the late afternoon and evenings.'

'No ops these days?'

Charlie shook his head. 'I've done two tours, one with Stirlings, one with Lancasters. That's enough.' His face lit up for a moment. 'W for Whisky. We were the cream.'

Kath laughed. 'And don't you know it!'

He grinned. 'Why not? It was a good feeling. We were the survivors after all.'

Silence for a moment as they both thought of the less lucky ones who did not survive, so many young friends lost.

'When the invasion starts, will you be with them?'

'Who knows? The Americans are having a terrible time of it. Finding daylight raids not such a good idea. But I've done my bit. Time to stand down.'

'So you're flying a desk now?'

'No chance. I'm no paper shoveller.' The enthusiasm was back in his face and Kath saw with a start how young he was. No more than twenty-two, after all. 'They've got me on a course in aeronautical engineering, which is great. There'll be a good future in aviation after the war and I mean to be involved in it.'

'Building aircraft?'

'Why not?'

'Good for you.'

Silence fell again, awkward and strained, and a terrible fear was born inside of her. If he wasn't worried about ops, then what was it that tightened his jaw in that dreadful fashion?

'What is it, Charlie?' she asked, suddenly afraid. 'Tell me what's wrong.'

Chapter 11

'We'll be closing soon, dear. Will you be wanting any more tea?'

'What? Oh, sorry.' Kath's cup stood cold and untouched while she sat stunned, unable to take in all that Charlie was telling her. 'Meg's all right, you say?'

'Oh, yes. And your father. He didn't go in the house apparently, though he was about to, for a cup of tea. Then when Dan arrived he changed his mind and took Lissa for a walk instead.'

Kath held her breath. 'Lissa?'

Charlie met her gaze evenly. 'Meg got a little girl from an orphanage in Liverpool. Lovely little thing called Melissa, but we all call her Lissa for short. Seems to suit better.'

He didn't know.

Kath cleared her throat, her mouth having gone suddenly dry. She raised her hand to the waitress. 'Perhaps I do need a fresh pot after all. This one is stone cold.'

'That's all right, dear. I'll fetch you one.' The waitress hurried off. She'd seen that white-faced look a lot lately. Why folk always chose to tell their bad news over a pot of tea was quite beyond her. Waste of a good brew, it was.

'So Meg is back home with Father and it's not going down too well,' Charlie continued. 'Losing Broombank has knocked her flat. Feels she's right back where she started. Not quite true, of course, because she still has the land. Though she lost a lot of the stock she'd built up.'

'And Dan… was he killed?'

Charlie nodded. 'Outright. Effie too.' He blinked and swallowed a mouthful of cold tea. 'Everyone loved Effie. She was an evacuee. Came up to Westmorland because it was a safe area. Loads came at the beginning of the war but most went right back home again within days. Effie found she loved it. Meant to stay for life. She loved Meg. Like a mother to her, Meg was.'

'How dreadfully sad.'

There seemed nothing else to say for a long time after that. The waitress brought a fresh pot and cups, whisking away the old ones with comforting clucks of her tongue. Charlie and Kath sat and sipped the soothing liquid, deep in their own thoughts for some time.

'You'll go and see her?' Charlie said, anxiety in his voice. 'She could do with a friend right now.'

Kath kept her eyes down. 'I'm not sure she'd want to see me.'

'I don't believe that. You two were the best of friends. Inseparable.'

'So we were. Once. Things change.' Seeing the questions in his eyes, she shook her head. 'Don't ask, Charlie. It's complicated.'

'And none of my business?'

'I didn't say that.'

He smiled. 'You didn't need to. OK, I'm not one for pushing my nose in where it's not wanted, but don't let this thing, whatever it is, go on too long. Soonest healed, soonest mended. Isn't that what they say?'

Kath tried to smile but it came out wrong, twisted somehow. Her head teemed with questions. All about what Meg was doing living at Broombank. Perhaps Lanky had died. He was an old man. But how did Tam O'Cleary come to be there? Most of all she wanted to ask about Lissa. What did she look like? What colour were her eyes? Was she well? Did she seem happy? Did she laugh a lot? So many questions they all scrambled together in her throat, and none of it came out.

She stood up. 'I have to go.'

Charlie walked with her up the street. At the corner where their ways parted he put a hand on hers. 'I know this has been a shock to you. But maybe we can talk again later, about ordinary things?'

Kath nodded, and turned a bright smile upon him. 'That would be lovely. What about the farm? Ashlea? Now Dan isn't there to...' Charlie shuffled his feet, looking uncomfortable for a moment. 'I can't live Dan's life for him. He's gone. Father will have to find some other solution for Ashlea. I don't want it, never have. I'm an uncle now, did you know?'

Kath punched him playfully in the chest. 'Good for you. How many?'

'Two boys, so that should keep Father happy.'

'Not thought about it yourself then?' she asked, and as she saw the bright young face darken a shade, wished the words unsaid.

'I'm married.'

Kath gasped and hugged him. 'Why didn't you say? Congratulations.'

He shrugged, giving a half laugh. 'She's called Sue, and in the ATS. We kept it secret because we didn't want her moved. Only they did move her. To Scotland, would you believe? Haven't seen her in six months. There's talk her lot might go overseas. God knows where. In the thick of it she'd be then.'

'Oh God, I'm so sorry. Still, it might never happen. She might be lucky and get another posting. It happens all the time.'

'Bloody war.'

He left her soon after that, swinging up the street whistling, determined to be strong, as they all were. But sometimes she wondered. What was the point?

—

One evening that September Jack heard that Italy had surrendered. Never with any real heart for the war, Lina's neighbours celebrated as if they had won it.

'Eet is good, yes? Now you will be safe,' she murmured, flinging her arms about Jack's neck in the excitement of the moment.

Mama Ruggierri advised caution. The country was still overrun with soldiers, she said. 'The Germans will not give up. The Germans have not surrendered.'

At the end of September they heard that the American Fifth Army had broken through the German lines on the Salerno Mountains, and entered the Plain of Naples but there would be no speedy end to the war in Italy. Winter was coming on again and German patrols were holding their own.

Papa Ruggierri liked to explain to his guest what he learned from his customers as they bought their bread in his shop. Lina quickly translated, her dark eyes wide with fear.

'The Germans are quickly taking over some of the Italian prisoner-of-war camps. They are searching houses and barns, picking people up and taking them to Moos-burg in Bavaria, and to camps in Czechoslovakia and Germany. We should make plans to get Jack away.'

'Soon,' she protested. 'Not yet, Papa, Mama. Soon.' And the old couple sighed together, looking anxious.

It became even more important after that to keep Jack well hidden, and he began to worry about the danger he put these good people in. But the thought of leaving filled him with dismay.

He had come to love this area, the cypress trees, the warm musky scents of oleander and pine, the sight of a lizard basking in the hot sunshine. He didn't want to leave. Not ever.

One evening Lina came to where he was sleeping in the loft, begging him to hurry, to wake up, dragging him to his feet. Jack's heart jumped with terror. Was this the end? Had they discovered him?

'*Tedeschi*, *tedeschi*, Germans, Germans. It is a patrol of soldiers, wanting food, I think. Quick, quick.' She pushed him, loudly protesting, out into the yard and under a dung heap, piling the fortunately dry material over his head.

'You must make no sound. If they hear you they will kill you.' She kissed him briefly, and left him to his fate.

While the Germans tucked into a delicious supper and laughed and joked with the Ruggierri family, Jack lay like stone beneath the straw-caked manure, thinking of England and Broombank, Meg and Kath. And of Lina and her family.

'Buongiorno, Jack.'

Impossible as it seemed he must have fallen asleep for here it was morning and Lina and Giovanni were laugh-ingly tossing aside the stinking straw.

'I think perhaps a bath, sì?'

Now Jack was laughing. He was still alive and a beautiful girl was smiling down at him. The German soldiers had moved on and he had survived. Life at this time consisted of such sweet pleasures.

Britain must be winning if Italy had surrendered. He only had to keep quiet a short while longer and he would be safe.

–

Jack sat naked in the stingingly cold river while Giovanni helped him scrub himself clean. Little more than sixteen, he nevertheless was not short of the famous Latin charm and Jack supposed the village girls fell at his feet for a smile or a kiss. He said as much and the boy blushed and laughed.

'You like my sister, yes?'

Jack gave a non-committal shrug but something in his expression must have given him away for the boy continued in a hoarse whisper:

'Then you must get her away from here. Take her with you when you leave. My family, they are kind to you, but they mean to marry her to the butcher. He has had two wives already and is fat as a sow.'

'Pig.'

'Sì.'

This information troubled Jack more than he would have expected. He had put all thought of leaving from his mind. Why should he consider it when he was content here? He had no wish at all to return to the killing. Whenever he gazed upon the surrounding blue-grey mountains, daunting and alien, a chill would settle about his heart at the prospect of crossing them, into the unknown.

'Why would you marry this butcher if you don't love him?' Jack asked one morning when Lina brought him breakfast. The fresh scent of coffee and rolls made the juices run in his mouth, but his appetite for good food paled beside his delight at seeing Lina each day. He waited always in anguish until she came, worrying that something might have happened to her in the night.

'He has asked for me and young men are in short supply in thees village. They have all gone to the war. Carlo, he has money, and a kind heart.'

'But you don't love him.' Jack broke off a piece of bread and held it out to her. Lina pursed her lips and caught the bread between her pretty white teeth.

'No, but I think he will not let me go hungry.' She laughed but Jack did not. He looked into those velvet dark eyes and recognised the glaze of sadness in them...

'You haven't thought it through properly,' he told her. 'No woman can marry a man she doesn't love. If I were Italian I'd offer for you myself.'

Startled eyes opened wide. 'What you say, Jack?'

His head was soaring. He knew well enough what he was saying and he didn't care. He took Lina in his arms and cradled her, as if she were made of some precious material and he was afraid to tarnish her. 'You know what I'm saying. You feel it too.' His voice was gruff with emotion.

'Oh, Jack. You are so preetty.'

Her lips were warm, trusting, and Jack was hard put to control his need. 'I want you, Lina. How I want you. I will speak with your family. Ask them if I might come into supper tonight.'

'Oh, but...'

'You must ask them, Lina.' He kissed her again, his hand smoothing the length of her silky thigh, wanting to remove the pretty patchwork dress.

But when she came to him that evening it was all too evident that she had been crying.

'I am sorry, but my family they not want you in the house again.'

'Why? What did they say?'

Lina sat down upon the straw, her skirt sagging between her knees, the heart-shaped face a picture of disaster and despair. 'They wish for you to leave. They mean you no harm, you understand? You can stay no longer. It is too dangerous, they say. They have others to theenk of, my grandmother, my brothers, my sisters...'

Jack interrupted before she felt duty bound to recite the entire family to him. 'I get the picture. I do understand.' The thought of losing her brought an odd tightness to his chest. He didn't want to leave Lina. The thought of never seeing her again appalled him. Dear God, was this what he had spent a lifetime avoiding? *Was this love?*

She was talking again, giving him instructions. 'I will bring you food, and a map that I will draw for you, to point the way.'

A map? Point the way to where? 'Through the mountains, do you mean?'

'Sì. It is the only way to go.' She was crying again, turning from him, scrambling to her feet in the straw.

'Lina.' He grasped her hand, pulled her down beside him. She was warm and fluid in his arms, smelling of sunshine and sweet hay. The patched dress slipping easily from her shoulders, the breasts almost leaping to be caressed. No more words were spoken. None were necessary. They clung to each other, biting, tasting, loving, needing. Knowing that death might come at any moment made the coupling doubly sweet.

He plunged his fingers into the mass of her glossy curls and held her to him while he kissed her throat, her arms, her lips, her breast, as if he could not get enough of her. Only when he had spent himself, shuddering inside her, did he lie unmoving, unwilling to end this amazing moment of fulfilment and love.

It was then that he heard the sound outside. 'The soldiers, they are back!' Lina cried, scrambling to her feet and quickly adjusting her dress.

The loft doors burst open and Jack knew that this time there would be no escape. Surprisingly, his last thought, before they took him, was of Meg. If he'd stayed at Broombank to marry her, he wouldn't be in this mess.

Chapter 12

1943

Meg sat in her chair by the empty hearth.

It was where she always sat. From the moment she finished milking the cows and doing her few morning chores, to the moment when she could thankfully return to her bed, she sat in this chair.

What else was there to do?

She'd moved back into Ashlea because there was nowhere else to go. But there seemed little point in anything. She could still smell the acrid smoke, the scorched air, still hear the terrible silence. Still see the flames devouring her home, clinging to the walls and running over the grass towards Effie's garden. Meg flinched, as she always did at this point.

A hand touched her shoulder and she jumped. 'Would you like a cup of tea?' Sally Ann. Dear Sally Ann had lost her husband and then her baby, and all she ever thought about was whether Meg wanted a cup of tea or a bite of something to eat. She was constantly complaining about the weight that had dropped off her. 'You must eat.'

'Why? What would it matter if she didn't?'

There was nothing for her at Broombank now. In the long year since it had happened Meg had never been back but she could imagine how it looked. A broken-down building with tarpaulin where once the roof had been. The great inglenook fireplace with its shining andirons that Lanky had so loved still flanking the living room but giving off no warmth now. Grass would already be starting to grow between the cracks. The new kitchen stove she'd bought with such pride a twisted lump of rusted metal. And the old scullery and dairy flattened beneath a pile of rubble. It had taken near a day to find Effie and pull her out.

She still had the rowan twig and butter churn in her hand.

Not even the sheep remained. The bomb blast had sent them running, crazy with fear, probably back to the safety of their old heaf. Meg didn't know and didn't greatly care. She had done nothing about getting them back. What was the point? It was people who mattered, not land nor sheep. Who was there left to work for, or with?

'Come on now,' said Sally Ann, urging Meg from her chair. 'Come up to the table. I've got a nice bit of fish to tempt you today. Here, take Daniel while I carry a tray up to Father.'

Father. Still suffering from the stroke he'd had when he heard that his son had died in the blast. Nevertheless Joe Turner was a survivor. He sat in his bed at the top of the house, half his body paralysed but issuing orders as ferociously ever. Still a bully. Why did only the good die?

Tears filled Meg's eyes. She hadn't the energy to hate him any more. She felt only pity for this half existence that drove him to the abyss of despair. To be dependent upon two women for his every need was, for Joe Turner, worse than death.

But this was war. They had to accept terrible things in wartime. Oh, but it was hard. So very hard.

'It's Will Davies.'

Meg, eyes closed, pretended not to have heard.

'Will Davies,' Sally Ann said again. 'He's at the door. He'd like a quick word.'

Meg opened her eyes and brought them into focus. Lissa was busy setting out her tea things, pouring out imaginary cups of tea for Nick and Daniel to sip politely. She was telling them, in her bossy way, how to hold the cup with the saucer neatly poised beneath. Effie had taught Lissa her own hard-won etiquette, and the child had never forgotten. There was a lot that she hadn't forgotten. Things that woke her screaming in the middle of the night. She still asked for Effie, wanting to know where she was and when they would be going home. It broke Meg's heart every time.

But at least Lissa was alive. Every day Meg thanked the good Lord, and Jeffrey Ellis, for saving her lovely child. Nowadays Meg never left her side, not even for a moment. It wasn't safe.

'Tell him to come in.'

Will Davies stood before her, cap in hand, fidgeting his booted feet, clearing his throat.

'Sit down, Will,' said Sally Ann cheerily. 'I've got the kettle on. And I've a carrot cake made we can cut into.'

'Don't bother about me, lass. What I have to say won't take more than a minute.'

'Take the weight off your feet while you do it then,' Sally Ann smiled. 'Go on with you.'

Will cleared his throat again. 'I was wondering, Meg, what you wanted doing about your gimmers.'

She stared at him, uncomprehending.

'You'll recall as how your sheep – well – they were a bit startled like and…'

'I know,' she cut in, sparing him, and herself, the agony of reminiscence.

Will took a deep breath of relief at her response. Worried him it did, to see her so blank and shut off from the world. Did no good at all. Like it or not, life had to go on. He only wished they could stir some life into Meg. 'You'll know that most of those new Swaledales you bought went back where they come from, to their old heaf? When we had our Autumn Meet… not that it were a merry one I should add, as it usually is. Wouldn't have been proper, that, in the circumstances. We found out where they were. So we took the chance to deal with yours, along with the other lost sheep, even though you weren't there.'

'That's very kind of you, Will,' she said dully. 'Only…'

'Oh, it's no trouble. What are neighbours for, after all? I'm sure you'd do the same for me if the boot were on the other foot as it were. I spoke to Joe about it. I hope that was right, since you were, well, not quite yourself at the time.'

Meg nodded and smiled, trying to be polite but not really listening to what he was saying. Her head was aching again and she felt so unutterably weary she wished only for him to say what he had come to say and leave her in peace.

'Nobody wanted to trouble you last backend. What with one thing and another, we thought happen you had enough on your plate. You've been ill for so long… Anyroad, Joe said as how you wouldn't be wanting them back.'

Something seemed to penetrate then. 'Joe? He said what?'

Will tucked his cap in his pocket and sat down at last, relieved that she'd responded at last. 'Said as how you'd had enough of farming and wouldn't want to start all over again. We agreed a price, a fair one, mind, and took your sheep off your hands.'

Meg held up a hand, wanting to stop him, but not able to find the words for a moment or two.

'You took my sheep?'

Will looked perplexed. Perhaps she hadn't quite taken it in. 'We didn't pinch them,' he stressed. 'Paid a fair price. Joe took care of all that like.' He half glanced across at Sally Ann, his old eyes begging for support.

Sally Ann at once stepped forward to rest a hand upon Meg's arm. 'You couldn't expect folk to look after them for ever, Meg, and you weren't up to it. Then there were the mortgage payments to find.'

Meg blinked, struggling to unfog her mind. Mortgage. Of course. Why hadn't she thought of that before? Who had found the monthly payments to the bank? She asked Sally Ann now.

'Joe, of course. Who else?'

Joe. Meg was struggling to her feet. 'Are you telling me that my father has been paying the mortgage on Broombank, my farm, for the last year? And that *he has sold my sheep*?'

'For a good price,' Will cut in, worried now by her response. 'We thought that was what you wanted.'

Meg found that she was trembling. What had she been thinking of to sit here and do nothing for months on end while Joe Turner took over? 'Who is looking after my land?' she asked.

'I've kept me eye on Broombank. You don't have to worry about that.'

'But the ewes are gone?'

'Aye,' Will agreed, nodding and shaking his head sadly all at the same time. 'Those that Joe sold have all lambed again, done well this spring they have. Course, they'll have taken to another heaf now. Wouldn't be worth your while to buy 'em back, even if you wanted to. Not now.'

Meg slumped into her chair again. Will was right. A lamb gave its loyalty to the land on which it was born and spent its first formative year. It was of vital importance on these high fells where a sheep could roam for miles if it chose, with little to stop it. Its homing instinct was its means of survival.

'So I must start again,' she said bleakly, wondering if she had the energy.

'Well, not exactly. That's what I'm trying to tell you, Meg. The lambs born that spring on your own heaf, before the bomb – before – they all came back. Well, they would, wouldn't they? Those gimmers didn't know any place else to go. Question is, do you want to keep them or do you want me to sell them on for you this backend?' He waited for her decision.

For a long time it seemed that she would never speak and then Meg blinked and focused properly upon Will. 'They're not all lost then?'

'Dear me, no. You still have the progeny from your Swaledales, and money for the ones that went back home.'

Meg was staring at him now with the first glimmer of hope in her eyes. It would be almost like starting again, but not quite. She still had a good young flock, Will said so. Then she turned to Sally Ann. 'I owe my father money for the mortgage?'

Sally Ann nodded. 'You can pay him back. When you get on your feet.'

The thought sickened her and yet increased the new determination that was starting to flow through her veins. To many these empty fells must seem hostile and inaccessible, yet if you studied them, lived on them, you learned there was order and sense to the rhythm of life in these remote parts. You learned where the old drover roads and tracks led to, the passes you could cross and those best left alone. You learned from nature. Her new Swaledale lambs had returned to her, as the unexplained instinct bred in them compelled them to do. She had been given something back.

'Our Hetty says if you do decide to carry on like, she'll be glad to help out, look after little Lissa any time. That's if you want her to. Course, Tam said as how you might not want to.'

'Tam?' She was alert in an instant. 'When did you see Tam?'

'Oh, not since he was here on his last leave.'

She'd rather not be reminded. It had been too terrible for words. Joe being as difficult as he could be about Tam's turning up here, as if he had no right. Taking his ill temper out on them all when Meg had quietly insisted that Tam did indeed have that right, as her friend.

Connie had arrived in the middle of it all, complaining nobody had told her about the accident and that she hadn't heard a word from Jack in months. As if Meg had time to worry about him now.

Everyone's patience had been stretched, tempers shortened, and she and Tam had had their worst row yet. He'd accused her of wallowing in self-pity, of not having the guts to carry on.

'Can't you see there's no point in carrying on now?' she'd screamed at him. 'Broombank is gone. It cost Effie her life when she came here to be safe. Dan was killed too. It isn't worth it. No land is worth such sacrifice. No house should matter more than people. You said that yourself. If Mr Ellis, thanks to fate or the hand of God or whatever you believe in, hadn't taken it into his head to take Lissa for a walk that morning, and not let her help with the butter making, she might have been dead too. How could I have borne that?'

'It's not your fault that they're dead,' Tam had gently told her, and Sally Ann had said it too.

But Meg wouldn't listen. She knew better. She'd been obsessed with owning Broombank for years. Because of her first lambing she'd failed to go to Kath when she needed her, had then neglected Lissa and robbed Effie of her childhood. As soon as she held her mortgage papers in her hands, the fates had taken it from her, together with the one person who had loved and trusted her most in all the world. What was that if not a punishment?

How could she live with such a terrible tragedy?

'Father can have it,' she'd said then. 'And good riddance to it.'

Now that it was perhaps too late she was changing her mind. Lissa came to lean against her knee.

'Are we going home, Meg?' she asked, reacting with that uncanny instinct children have to the sensitivity in the atmosphere.

Meg swallowed, and slipping an arm about the child, pulled the sturdy little body close. Three years old and starting to ask questions. Life went on, whether you wanted it to or not. She had Lissa to think about, entirely dependent upon her now.

'Broombank could be put right, given time,' Will said, carefully watching the thought processes in her eyes.

Meg met his shrewd gaze. Then she looked at Sally Ann. Paler, thinner, a deep sadness about her, but still determined to keep going day after day, for the sake of her children.

She thought of her lovely Tam. How she missed him. He got home on leave when he could but it wasn't enough. Meg needed his warmth, his strength with her always. Though they might do nothing but argue these days, she still needed him. When this war was over, what sort of woman did she want him to find? He always said he loved a woman with spirit.

Putting down a hand Meg stroked Rust's floppy ear. He was lying against her foot as usual. She heard him breathe little gusts of pleasure.

'The other two dogs, Tess and Ben, where are they?'

'They're with me,' Will said. 'We thought it best to sell Dan's trail hounds, but knowing your land and sheep as they do, I kept yours. They've been working hard. Good dogs both of them. But with nowhere near enough work to keep them happy. Tess and Ben need you, Meg.'

Rust sat up at sound of these familiar names, one ear cocked so comically that Meg actually laughed out loud, for the first time in months, for all there were tears in her eyes. 'Look at him. Never say die, lad, eh?' The tongue lolled as he grinned at her, alert, expectant, reading her mind, knowing her decision almost before she knew it herself.

'I reckon it's time we all got back to work. First thing in the morning, eh, lad?'

Rust gave one joyful bark, understanding exactly and replying in the only way he knew.

When autumn comes to the high fells there often seems to be a final celebration of colour and long hours of sunshine, like a last waltz before the close of a glorious dance. The wetness of summer had dissolved into a rare brilliance but this year Meg took no heed of the beauty around her. Her mind was entirely on work.

Two POWs had been appointed to Ashlea after the accident, both quite amenable. Brought each day in a truck, they got on with what had to be done without bothering anyone. Karl had lived on a farm in Germany so the work progressed well, and Sally Ann had been glad to have someone else to think about and feed. The War Committee had done Meg's ploughing and every neighbour in the dale had come in to help with the harvest. Now Meg felt as if she'd been away for too long and was glad to be home and working again.

The autumn dip took place and somehow the familiarity of the daily routine began to soothe and heal her wounds. Though there would be no forgetting, Meg was learning to live with the pain. Effie no longer haunted her days and at night she slept the healthy sleep of a tired body after a satisfyingly hard day's work. The relief was profound.

It was a relief, too, to get out of the house, away from the sound of her father's voice calling down the stairs, demanding something or other every five minutes of the day.

'Tell him to wait,' Meg warned Sally Ann as her sister-in-law sat a complaining Daniel in his chair and started up the stairs for the fourth time in as many minutes to do his bidding.

'What else does he have, all on his own up there, not able to move properly? I can't just ignore him.'

Meg watched this performance day after day until she came to a decision.

With the help of Will and Hetty Davies, they cleared space in her mother's parlour and brought down Joe's bed and personal belongings. Then the four of them carried the protesting, grumbling old man and placed him in it.

'There you are,' said Meg, pleased with the result. 'Now Sally Ann won't have to run up and down stairs all the time.'

'It's come to summat when you're a bother to your own family,' mourned Joe.

Meg lifted a warning finger to him. 'Don't try anything on with Sally Ann. She'll up and leave you in two shakes of a lamb's tail if you don't treat her right. She has a family of her own, remember. She doesn't have to stay here and take your bullying. So mind your manners for a change.'

'And thee mind thine, young madam. I suppose you think you can take over the running of Ashlea now that Dan has gone?' Strangely enough Meg had not got so far in her thinking. She was aware the work of Ashlea would be added to her own, but control of it had not crossed her mind.

'Ashlea is yours, Father,' she said quietly. 'Always will be. And after you, Dan's two boys, as he would have wanted. But if there's something particular you want doing, you only have to say.'

'How will I know if thee's done it?'

Meg laughed, though not unkindly. It lit up her face, reminding Joe of the old spunky Meg and for a moment he was glad they were into a battle of words again. He'd missed them. 'You'll just have to trust me, won't you?' she said.

'Tch. I'll be out of this bed in no time, just you see if I'm not.' There was resolution in the faded eyes, and a new expression: fear. Meg saw it and felt her heart stir with pity. Though how could she feel pity for a man whom she did not love? Yet how could she hate him? He was her father and he had lost everything, just as she had.

''Course you will,' she said softly. 'Sally Ann and I will help you do it. I'll talk to the doctor, get some advice. In the meantime you've no need to worry about the farm.'

'Humph, that's all thee knows. I never thought the day would come when I depended upon a woman to run my farm for me.'

'You never can tell what life will throw up next, do you, Father?' she said, and went away smiling.

—

Meg had often walked on her beloved fells this last year, needing the peace to soothe her soul. She had watched the blaze of broom blossom and die away, followed by the bright patchwork of summer flowers. Now the white caps of mushrooms were sprouting all over the fields.

But she'd never come this close to Broombank before.

Its emptiness echoed in her heart, the solitude of the place more marked than ever before. The only sound was of a rustle of dry leaves where a quarrelling shrew warned insects in its high-pitched squeak that it was hunting and they'd best watch out.

But Will Davies was right. Broombank could be saved. The dairy and old scullery could be built up again and the roof restored. How much would it all cost? Did she have the heart to do it? Wouldn't it always remind her of Effie?

The door was not locked and a rush of memories met her as she walked into the living room: of Effie making cabbage soup, drinking cocoa by the fire, soaking in all of Meg's stories. Charlie pounding out tunes on the old piano in the parlour next door. She could hear it all as clearly as if it were happening now.

Anything worth saving had been removed. The lofts and spare rooms at Ashlea were full of boxes and pieces of furniture, stored for safe keeping. Broombank stood a shell, empty of the life and love it had known throughout its long existence. Meg's dreams and plans for it too must surely be dead.

She went to the bedroom she and Tam had shared. All she could hope for now was to get through each day. Do what had to be done, for the sake of her sheep. She couldn't look any further than that.

Unable to bear it she turned away, but something bright caught her eye and she looked down. At her feet, half buried in the dust, she saw it. The Luckpenny that Lanky had given her with the sale of his land. Bending down, she picked it up and held it in the palm of her hand. She could hardly see the coin for the tears swimming in her eyes.

'You didn't bring Effie much luck, did you?' she said, but there was no bitterness in the words. Death was a part of war. It had to be accepted. She'd come to terms with that now. A part of her would always grieve for Effie, but she could go on now.

Her fingers tightened over the penny. It was meant to bring good fortune to the land, and the farm. They were both still there, weren't they? The house was badly damaged but not as badly as she had feared. The young sheep had returned, and her friends and neighbours had stood by her, as they always did. She tucked the penny into her pocket. It would be needed if she really did start again.

Meg left the house, Rust at her heels without needing to be told, and climbed Dundale Knott.

Angry slashes of red cut through a grey, lowering sky as she gazed down upon her former home from high upon the fell. She had felt just that sort of red hot anger within herself this last year. The feeling that she wanted to slash at everything, strike out at the tranquil beauty of the place. Feeling so much pain, it had seemed impossible to go on living. But that was fading now.

'Life is stirring in me again, Effie. I can feel it. Try to understand. I have to go on, for Lissa's sake. For Tam. Are you pleased for me?' Behind her came the sound of the quiet cropping of the grass by her sheep. Above her head, the lonely mew of a curlew, like a sad echo of happier times.

She remembered the day that Charlie's plane had flown over and Effie and Sally Ann had been scared out of their wits. Then they'd celebrated Charlie's engagement with some of Effie's awful beetroot wine, joking and giggling, teasing Tam about going to the dance. The sting of tears came to her eyes at the memory.

Yet despite their fright, they had imagined themselves in no real danger of being bombed. Not here, amongst all this beauty and tranquillity.

Meg brushed the tears angrily from her eyes and got to her feet. The time for crying was done. Best not to dwell on things, that's what Sally Ann said.

As Meg turned to climb higher up the fell, she saw a flicker of movement below. A dark figure broke through the hedge from the lane. Someone was crossing the field, walking towards Broombank. Curious, she stopped to watch. Not looters she hoped. Who dared trespass on her land? What should she do? Send the dogs down to chase whoever it was away, or... Meg stopped, and her eyes fastened disbelievingly on the figure. It couldn't be. It couldn't. It was.

'Tam!'

Then she was running, falling, slipping and tumbling down the fellside at such a rate it was a wonder she didn't go head over heels right to the bottom, Rust bounding excitedly beside her. She was laughing and crying all at the same time and she could hear Tam laughing too. How she loved that sound.

Seconds later she was in his arms, smothering his face with kisses.

'Oh, my darling, my darling.' When she could draw breath she ran her hands over his beloved face, across his shoulders and down his strong arms and back to his face again. 'Let me look at you. Oh, you look so good.' He was a soldier in an American uniform. A stranger. But not a stranger. He was her love.

'You look pretty good yourself,' he said, moss green eyes devouring her as she had so loved them to do in the past. 'I thought never to see you smile again.' His lips were seeking hers, devouring her, needing her, and Meg felt the first shafts of desire like the stirring of new life within her.

'How long have you got?' She wished the words unsaid almost as soon as they were uttered for she didn't want to hear the answer. 'Long enough,' he laughed, holding her from him so that he could study her.

'It's never long enough,' she mourned. 'Why don't they give you a decent leave?'

'I'm lucky to be here at all. Isn't it nearly always cancelled? I've dreamt of nothing else but taking you to bed, Meg Turner, and I mean to do so. I mean to make love to you all night long, till you beg for mercy.'

'Oh, I want you too. I've needed you so much, Tam, so very much. But not at Ashlea. I couldn't bear it, not with Father listening and making acid comments. And Sally Ann all hollow-eyed, remembering.'

Tam smoothed a hand over her cheeks, her chin, down her throat, making her shiver with fresh longing. 'You're looking a bit hollow-eyed yourself, me darlin'. The beauty of the cheek bones was still there, for all the skin looked pale, but stretched tight with tension, the eyes like dark bruises.

'I'm mending, slowly.'

He kissed her again, with poignant tenderness. 'Then where?' he whispered. 'When? I must have you before I go mad.' The touch of his lips on hers, the remembered maleness of him, set her senses whirling, her pulses quickening.

'Is it too cold today?' she asked, teasing him wantonly with her eyes, remembering past days of loving in the bracken.

'For the fells? In October? Aren't you as shameless as ever, Meg Turner?'

'Oh, I am Tam O'Cleary. With you, l am indeed.'

As one they looked towards Broombank, and she shivered. 'I wish I had a home to offer you,' he said.

'You have yourself, my love, and that is all that matters.' She felt his sigh and clung to him, wanting so much to prove with every part of her being, how much she loved him. 'There are always the barns.'

So the barn it was. Warm and dusty, fragrant with hay and old apples, and because of the perversity of fate, untouched by German bombs. As they loved and touched, kissed and became one again, many ghosts were laid. Meg gave no thought to another time, another loving in this very same barn, in another man's arms. Tam was all that mattered now.

–

Connie came again that Christmas of 1943. There seemed something about the festive season that caused her to visit. Even last year, despite their being in mourning and not wanting to celebrate at all, she'd turned up, like a bad penny, Meg thought.

Now she was filled with guilt when Connie announced she'd had official word that Jack was missing.

'Does that mean…?'

It was no good, Meg could not speak the words. She had lost too many people already. Surely not Jack as well.

'No, it means nothing of the sort,' said Connie stoutly, setting down her great tapestry bag and her hat box with a thankful sigh that sounded very much as if she meant to stay for the duration, as perhaps she did. 'A cup of tea would go down a treat. And I'll have a piece of carrot cake, Sally Ann, if there's one going.'

Sally Ann went smilingly to put the kettle on.

'It means, so say the powers-that-be, that he's been taken prisoner. Went on some special boat operation and never returned. Well, he would, wouldn't he? Very special, my Jack. They must have appreciated his worth, mustn't they?'

'I suppose so,' Meg said. Somehow she didn't feel up to more bad news. She didn't love Jack any more, but she would always think of him as a friend. And despite what he had done to her, he was still Lissa's father.

Sally Ann put a comforting arm about the older woman's shoulder. 'I'm so sorry. It's dreadful to lose someone you love.'

Connie scarcely blinked an eyelid as she eased herself away from the embrace. 'A dab of milk and two saccharine for me. Couldn't get a sniff of a cup all the way here.'

Sally Ann obeyed, avoiding Meg's amused glance. 'Go in and see Father, he's in the parlour since his stroke.'

'Is he not up and about yet? Do him no good to sit about feeling sorry for himself.'

Meg shook her head. 'He's got some movement back, but it's limited.'

Connie sniffed her disapproval. 'Self-pity is the killer, not the stroke. Never indulge in it myself. Get on and do what you have to do in life, that's my motto. See you make a proper job of it. We'll have to get him going.'

'Connie, you are probably exactly the tonic he needs,' said Meg, laughing. 'We'll leave him in your capable hands.'

She actually smiled. 'You do that.'

'How's Peter?' Meg asked later as they all sat down to a meal.

'Pork, eh?' Connie's eyes blazed with interest as the plate was set before her. 'Haven't tasted meat for months.'

Not since last Christmas probably, thought Meg.

Connie jabbed in her fork and carried a sizeable chuck straight to her mouth. Moments later she thought to answer the question. 'Didn't I tell you? He was killed in action in '42. I felt sure I must have mentioned it. I could manage another potato, if you've got one going spare.'

So a husband was disposed of, between the meat and the veg.

—

Kath arranged to visit Charlie's station a few weeks after their first meeting and was given the full conducted tour. Not that she really needed one. Same long low Nissen huts, same coke stove belching out evil fumes.

'Nothing changes,' she laughed as they stood in a long queue for the privilege of eating an unidentifiable stew and two slices of dry bread in the Airmen's Mess.

As if to set the seal on those words Kath walked right into the solid presence of an officer and tipped the awful mess of it right down his uniform.

'Oh, I am so sorry. I wasn't looking where I was going.'

'Katherine Ellis, as I live and breathe.'

She stared dumbfounded, her throat closing so tight she could hardly squeeze the words out. 'Wade, what are you doing here?'

'I could ask the same of you.' He glanced behind her at Charlie and sketched a salute to them both in response to Charlie's smartly clicked heels. 'Only I can probably guess. How are you these days?' Kath was frantically trying to clean the mess with a cloth she had grabbed from the table.

She'd forgotten how blue his eyes were. Could he hear her heart beating? He must, it almost drowned their conversation. She kept her head down, her eyes fixed upon her task. 'I'm fine. Thanks. And you? But this jacket is ruined, I'm afraid.'

'That's okay, it'll clean. If I go and change it, you won't run away again, will you?'

'Er, we are in rather a hurry, I think. Charlie is showing me over…' Wanting to say so much, and daring to say nothing.

'Sure. That's okay. Well, good to see you again. Carry on, airman.'

After he had gone, Charlie brought her another plate of stew although Kath had quite lost her appetite. How cool he had sounded, how matter-of-fact. Giving no indication about how he felt. Kath couldn't even tell whether he was pleased to see her or not. Drat those pips on his shoulder.

Charlie was, of course, agog. 'You know old Wadeson?'

'I used to drive him places, that's all.' To a quiet patch of woodland where he could kiss me, she might have said, but didn't.

'He's well liked around here. Decent sort of bloke. Don't you think?'

'Hm.'

'His wife is lovely too.'

Something inside Kath crumpled and died. 'Wife?'

'She came here once, on a visit. Didn't stay long though. She was a real smart lady.'

'I see.' No, she didn't. She didn't see at all. Wade had made no mention of a wife. The rotten cheat! Red hot fury gushed through her veins. What else should she have expected? Men didn't change, did they? The world was full of Jacks. 'Are you going to show me where you are going to be working?' she asked, with brittle brightness.

'Sure thing.' Charlie pushed aside his empty plate and led her outside, along the cinder path to the airfield. 'You've gone quite white, sure you're up to it? You should have eaten the stew, it wasn't that bad.'

'Don't worry about me. I'm up to whatever life can throw at me, Charlie. Lead the way.'

She might have guessed that he would be at her car, waiting for her. Charlie saw him first, leaning against the vehicle, arms folded, as if he'd wait all day if necessary. Charlie stopped.

'I'll say goodbye here, shall I? Don't want to get another sock in the jaw, or another spell in the glasshouse. He's out of my league.' Charlie's eyes told her he thought Wing Commander Wadeson out of her league as well, but he was too polite to say so. Kath wondered why she had the knack of latching on to other women's men. She needn't let it happen. Not again. The next guy she went out with, would be all her own. She wanted exclusive rights. Katherine Ellis was done with sharing.

Reaching up she put her cheek against Charlie's and kissed him. 'Take care.'

'You too.'

'Let me see you again before they post you off to some other Godforsaken place.'

'Yeah. That would be fun.'

'And do me a favour, will you? When you write to Meg, *don't* tell her that you saw me.'

'For God's sake…'

Kath put a hand to his lips. 'I'll try to explain some time, just a little. And I promise I will contact her myself, when the time is right. I do need to, for lots of reasons. But these very special reasons mean it must be me who does it, not you or anyone else. Promise?'

Charlie looked far from happy. 'I suppose I'll have to. Can't I even say that you're alive and well? Meg deserves a bit of good news. Your parents too. What about them?'

Kath blinked away a sudden rush of tears. After a long silence she nodded. 'All right, you can say that you've seen me, that I'm in the WAAF. But don't say where.

No details, not even a hint. I'll take it from there when I've worked some stuff out in my mind. When I'm ready. All right?'

'I don't know what's going on and maybe it's none of my business but so long as you play fair with Meg, that's all right by me.'

'I owe Meg a lot. No one knows that better than me. But our relationship is somewhat confused at present.'

Charlie glanced across at the Jeep. 'I think your commander is getting a bit impatient.'

Kath smiled and wrinkled her nose with a hint of the old mischief. 'Do him good to cool his heels for a bit.' She tugged her jacket into place and straightened her tie. 'Wife indeed.' And turning smartly on her heel, she strolled towards her vehicle, hearing Charlie's soft chuckle as she went.

—

'So, Wing Commander, this is a surprise.'

Kath stood before him, attempting nonchalance while her heartbeat pounded in her ears. She knew she looked good. A neat trim figure in her blue uniform. Hair smartly brushed up beneath her cap, tie knotted in the correct fashion, the buttons on her tunic palely glowing from many hours of polishing.

'Katherine. Life seems to have treated you well.' His eyes moved to the two stripes halfway down her arm.

'Yes,' she said coolly. 'Hard work brings its own rewards they say.' Meg would love me for that, she thought, smiling at the thought. 'Seems to have made you happy.'

Why did he look so uncomfortable? Probably embarrassed by the recollection of their little flirtation, hardly worthy of the title affair. Kath sat on the driver's seat and swung her legs inside, the skirt ricking up slightly as she did so. To her great astonishment Wade groaned.

'That was what did for me in the first place,' he said.

'What?'

'The sight of those lovely long legs swinging in and out of that staff car. Oh boy, Katherine, you're even more beautiful than I remember.'

Unable to help herself, Kath burst out laughing. Wade leaned on the windscreen and grinned at her.

'Did you forget me?' he asked.

'As a matter of fact, I didn't.' She glanced at him from beneath her lashes. 'Why did you never tell me you were married?'

'Who's been talking?'

Kath started the engine.

'Okay, I won't ask. My marriage with Donna was over long since. I should have told you, only I'd every intention of getting a divorce.'

'But she came over here to see you, to try to win you back?'

Wade gave a sceptical smile. 'She's a wily gal. Didn't like the thought of losing all that lovely real estate we own. She came to do a deal personally, where her lawyers had failed.'

'Presumably she succeeded?'

'Sure. I gave her most of what she wanted. After she'd come all that way, how could I refuse? I'd fallen for and lost you by that time and was pretty mixed up. What did property matter? I thought.'

'You're still married to her?'

'Only temporarily. The divorce is going through any time now.'

Kath met his gaze coolly. 'It seems to be a slow business.'

'You can say that again.'

'She may think of other delaying tactics.'

'What's that supposed to mean?'

'That could be her aim, couldn't it? If she keeps the discussions going long enough, the war will be over and you'll be home.' Kath hated the sour note in her own voice but somehow she couldn't seem to help herself. Jack had promised to finish with Meg, but he hadn't, had he? 'Maybe then she can change your mind.'

'She means nothing to me. It's you I want. You know that, honey.' Kath's lips moved into a smile but it didn't reach her eyes. 'Now where have I heard that before? Goodbye, Wade. It was nice knowing you.'

She drove off, leaving him standing alone on the parade ground.

—

Meg was clearing out Joe's old room when the letter from Charlie came. She'd tucked it into her overall pocket at breakfast, thankful just to see his handwriting, proving he was well. She meant to bottom this room properly and give it a thorough cleaning. Then she'd read the letter over her morning tea. Soon it would be Hogg Day again, then the lambing, and she wouldn't have a minute.

'What are you doing?' Sally Ann asked as she discovered Meg, broom in hand, rolling up the bedroom carpet.

Meg giggled. 'Not like me is it? To be so domestic. Partly therapeutic. I need to establish in my mind that I'm staying here, that Ashlea is again my home. For the time being anyway.'

Sally Ann offered a sympathetic smile. 'I can understand it must be difficult for you. Make your mark then. Put some of your own things in here if it makes you feel better.'

'It seems wrong. This house is yours now. Yours and your children's. I'm the outsider, the interloper, and I've no wish to take it from you. I want you to know that.'

'I do. But you know very well that I couldn't manage Ashlea without you. What would I do with a farm?'

Meg gave a wry smile. 'At least you like cows, which was more than Effie did, and she managed.'

Dear Effie.

'So I thought if I stopped living in that cramped little loft bedroom, I might feel as if I belonged.'

'And Tam can share it with you. Good idea.'

Meg flushed. 'Is it so obvious?'

Sally Ann hugged her close. 'You love him. Why don't you marry him? You can't go on feeling guilty about Jack. He might never come home.'

'Don't ask, Sal. It's too complicated. I've got so used to waiting I don't think I'm capable of making a decision any more. When the war is over, we'll sort it all out. For now I would just like Tam with me, and to hell with what Father says.'

Sally Ann shrugged. 'He thinks you're immoral anyway. Come and read your letter. Tea's brewed.'

Meg read it in stunned silence, her whole body tightening into rigid tension. It was not at all what she had been expecting.

Sally Ann, seeing her reaction, paled visibly. 'What is it? What's happened? Not Charlie. Oh no, please, not Charlie.' She pulled Daniel on to her lap as if for protection.

'No, no. Don't panic,' Meg hastily reassured her. 'This isn't bad news.' At least she hoped not. 'This is news about Kath.'

'Kath?'

'Yes. She's all right. In fact, she's more than all right.' Meg started to relax. There was nothing in the letter about Lissa. Not a word to ask how she was even. Perversely, that irritated her for all it brought relief. 'She's a corporal in the WAAF, would you believe? Charlie says he met her in East Anglia and she's fine and well, through he's not sure exactly where she's stationed.'

Sally Ann clapped her hands in delight and Daniel joined in, gurgling with pleasure, thinking it a new game. Lissa and Nicky came rushing into the kitchen to see what all the commotion was about and Lissa, catching sight of the letter, reached out to grab it.

'Me look,' she demanded, and flushing with confusion as if guilty of some crime, as if the child could actually read her life story in it, Meg folded it quickly and tucked it into her pocket. 'No, darling. It's a letter for me, not you.'

'Would you credit it?' Sally Ann was saying. 'After all this time. Why has she never contacted us?'

Meg shook her head, lifting the protesting Lissa on to her knee to hide her own flushed face. 'Who can say?' She had told Sally Ann nothing about Lissa's parentage and did not feel now was the right moment. It had been a secret shared only with Tam and Effie. And Jeffrey Ellis had guessed, of course. Meg felt numb inside, any pleasure she might have felt at her friend's well-being overshadowed by old doubts and new fears.

'With that girl I could believe anything,' Sally Ann said. 'But a WAAF? That doesn't sound like Kath's sort of thing at all.'

'No, it doesn't. Not the Kath I knew. But I suppose everyone comes to terms with reality and responsibilities some time in life, even Katherine Ellis, particularly when there's a war on.'

'Oh, but it is good news,' Sally Ann repeated. 'You must hurry round to see Jeffrey and Rosemary Ellis. They'll want to know right away. I'll finish the room for you.'

'Yes,' said Meg slowly. 'I suppose I'd better.'

'You don't sound too excited about it?' Sally Ann asked, a frown marring her own delight.

Meg swallowed. 'Oh I am. I'm pleased that she's safe and well. Just a bit startled that's all, hearing about her out of the blue.'

'Maybe she'll write herself now.'

'I dare say she will.' And ask for Lissa? Oh, dear Lord, please don't let her do that.

Chapter 13

1944

'Have I got a daddy?' Lissa's great pansy eyes gazed up trustingly into Meg's.

Meg shook out the tea cloth she was holding and hung it carefully on the line to dry, while she gave herself time to think.

'Of course you have a daddy. Everybody has a daddy, sweetheart.'

'Where is my daddy then?'

Today was Lissa's fourth birthday and she had already amply demonstrated she was an individual with a mind of her own. And judging by the firm set of her small, pointed chin, she did not intend to be fobbed off with platitudes on this occasion either.

Lissa's birthdays were growing easier. There had been a time when Meg hadn't wanted to remember that day when she had gone to find Kath in Liverpool and found a web of deceit instead. Betrayal, where she had looked for friendship and love.

In time she had come to accept this. But since the arrival of Charlie's letter she had hardly known a moment's peace. Inside she felt cold with fear.

It was impossible now to wish that she'd never let herself come to love Lissa. She was a child after all, needing love, and Meg hadn't been able to help herself in the end. Only it made the thought of losing her all the more painful. How would she bear it?

'Well,' she began. 'The thing is, it's the war, do you see?' She hunkered down to the child's level and gathered her in her arms. Lissa smelled sweet, of soap from her morning bath and fresh spring air.

'During a war, men must go away to fight. They do this because they feel it is the right way to protect their loved ones. And so your daddy has gone to fight for his King and country, along with all the other daddies.'

'To fight for me?'

Meg swallowed. 'Yes, darling. And for you.'

'Will he come back?'

There seemed little point in lying. Everyone had to be grown up in wartime, even children. 'We hope that he will, one day. But we haven't heard from him in a long while. If he doesn't, it won't be his fault, or yours. Not all the men who go away to fight manage to get back home. Something might stop them – another soldier from another army, another country, or an accident at sea.'

Was it right to be so blunt with her? Meg didn't know. But Lissa was bright and intelligent and it seemed wrong to let her go on in ignorance. As if there would be a fairytale ending.

'Will my mummy come home too when the war is finished?'

'She might. You remember how I explained, Lissa, that we aren't too sure where your mummy is right now?'

'Is she looking for me?'

'No. She knows you are safe with me. That's what she wanted. For me to look after you until…' Meg swallowed and blinked very hard. 'Until she is able to do it herself.'

Lissa considered this very gravely. 'You're not my mummy, are you?'

'No,' Meg answered quietly, gathering her close. 'But I feel as if I am. I'm your second mummy. Not every little girl has two. See how lucky you are.'

'What does my daddy look like?'

This was easy. 'He looks just like you, sweetheart. The same heart-shaped face, the same curly black hair, the same naughty eyes.'

Lissa giggled, and, apparently satisfied with Meg's answers, moved on to other things, as children do. 'Can I go and play with Hetty this afternoon? She promised I could help her make dough babies.'

Meg hugged the child to her breast in an impulse of love as strong and natural as if Lissa really were her very own. She wished, in the intensity of that moment, that she was. Then she could keep her safe, for all time. 'Of course you can. I'll take you after your nap. Don't be a nuisance now.'

'I won't.' Warm hands wrapped tight about Meg's neck. Hot, sticky lips pressed firmly against her cheek. 'I wish you were my first mummy, Meg.'

Meg's heart throbbed in agony but she could find no words to answer.

After a moment Lissa stroked back Meg's hair, very gently, and cocking her little face on one side, smiled at her. 'I do love you best, you see.'

'Do you?'

A fierce nod.

'How much?'

'More than all the world.'

'That's good.'

'I won't have to go if I don't want to, will I?'

'Go where?'

'With my other mummy?'

A short pause. 'No, of course not.'

'That's all right then.'

And as she skipped happily away, Meg bit down hard on her bottom lip, fighting back the tears. Oh, but she didn't want Kath or Jack to come back for Lissa, not ever.

—

'Why won't you marry me?' Wing Commander Wadeson glared despairingly at Kath.

'You've been asking me that question for months now, Wade, and my answer hasn't changed. I can't marry you and I can't tell you why, not just yet.' It had been easy enough to say goodbye to him that day on Charlie's station, quite another to mean it. In no time at all they were right back where they'd started.

'Katherine, honey, I want to understand, really I do. This will be our last day together for heaven alone knows how long. All leave is cancelled until further notice, you know that. As from Monday.'

'I know.' A prickle of worry touched her spine. 'You aren't going on a mission, are you?'

'Now, honey, you know better than to ask. I do what I have to do. The invasion is coming. No doubt about it.'

'Let's not waste time arguing then.'

For a time they didn't. They were in their favourite spot, deep in a wood some miles from the station. The times they could escape to it were rare and therefore all the more precious. Kath found it astonishing that Wade didn't push her into more than she was ready to give. Their lovemaking was exciting but carefully controlled. And although Wade was becoming more and more irresistible, Kath had no wish for things to be otherwise, or to take risks, not just yet.

The Kath of old was quite gone. Not for this Katherine the careless rapture of a moment followed by months of pain and guilt.

So why didn't she marry him, she thought, when it was what she wanted most in all the world? Wade had got his divorce, yet still she held back. Lissa. Why else? She had not yet plucked up the courage to tell him about her child. Bad enough to abandon a daughter, Kath thought. To deny her existence must be abominable.

'I thought we said no more secrets. Sounds like a goddamned excuse to me.'

She sighed. 'Some secrets are hard to reveal. Look, I'm not a girl to be pushed around, Wade, so don't try it. I'm my own person and I'll tell you when I'm good and ready and not before.' She trailed a hand over his chest. 'Anyway, as you would say, what's the big deal? You managed to ignore me this last three years, so why the rush now? And you had a few secrets of your own, remember, a wife no less.'

'I didn't ignore you. I thought it best not to pursue the relationship because of our rank. I got you in trouble once before, honey, I didn't want to risk messing up your life. Hell, but it was hard. I kept asking that friend about you – Bella. I didn't dare ask exactly where you were posted in case I forgot myself and came after you.'

'So what changed your mind?' she asked, guessing the answer.

'It was seeing you again with that guy.'

'Charlie?'

'Yeah. Charlie.' He pulled her into his arms. 'You'd never believe how jealous I felt. It shocked me, I don't mind telling you.'

Kath chuckled. 'That's good. I was wondering what would bring you out of the woodwork?'

'Out of the what?'

'Never mind.'

'I need you, Katherine. I guess I've been pretty patient but hand holding and kisses won't do for me much longer, however passionate. We have something special going for us. Be generous. I adore you, I love you, I want to make you happy. I want you to be my wife. I know it's breaking regulations but no one need know, not till the war's over, which it soon will be.'

Kath softened, kissing him gently. 'I think we have something special too, Wade. But I can't give in, not yet. Maybe one day I'll be able to tell you about my problem. When I've sorted a few things out. Will that satisfy you?'

Wade put his arms about her and gathered her close, as if she were very precious. 'What is it, honey? Tell me. You ain't got a husband tucked away somewheres?'

'No, of course not.' Only a daughter, she wanted to say. A child I had in a seedy institution for wayward girls. One I never held, didn't love, and gave away to the woman I betrayed. For a moment his eyes, his touch, were so gentle and reassuring the story almost poured out. Almost. Would she ever be able to tell him? Kath wondered. He might leave her, once he knew the truth. Then it would all be over, and Kath knew that she couldn't bear the thought of losing him. Oh, what a mess she had made of her life.

'Whatever it is, we can sort it out,' he was saying. 'No crime you may have done in your murky past can be so terrible as to put me off. Aw, Katherine. Come on. Trust me. We can get rid of the problem, whatever it is, honey.'

Get rid of the problem. Was that what Lissa was? A problem to be disposed of? Kath's guilt at ignoring her child during these first precious years of her life was bad enough. Could she abandon her own daughter for ever, or was that one sacrifice she wasn't prepared to make?

–

Connie's matter-of-fact attitude to life and death gave Meg the courage to approach her with her own problem.

'When will we hear for sure, about Jack?' she asked.

Connie's keen eyes regarded her shrewdly. 'Why do you want to know? You don't seem to have been too bothered about where he's been for a long while.'

'I've been thinking of little else these last months.'

Connie's eyes moved to the third finger of Meg's left hand. 'I've noticed that you no longer wear his ring. Haven't worn it for years, have you?'

'It gets in the way of my work.'

'A ring from the man you love? Funny way of showing you care.'

'I do. At least…' Meg stopped to correct herself. 'I did love him. Once.'

'I thought that was the way the land lay.'

Meg fell into shamed silence. After a moment she said, 'I'm not sure that we – that we could carry on, anyway. Things had changed.'

'It's that Irishman, isn't it?'

Meg smiled. 'I can't – won't – deny it. I never meant to love Tam but I do. But Jack and I, our relationship was over before – before Tam and I became friendly.'

'Became lovers, you mean,' said Connie sourly. 'Don't think I'm stupid. I've seen you making up that big bed that was your mother's. Should be ashamed of yourself, you should.'

'Don't say that. I've done my best, really I have. It didn't seem right to tell Jack, to end our engagement when he was so far away, fighting in the war. It seemed heartless and cruel to...'

'Send him a "Dear John" letter?'

'Yes.'

'So you had an affair with someone else instead?' Meg's cheeks flooded with heat. 'That's not fair. Jack had...' She stopped. Why couldn't she say it? Why didn't she tell this narrow-minded, silly woman what her brother had done to her? Meg got up and walked to the door. 'I can't talk about it.'

'I know what you want to say. Why don't you go ahead and say it? That Jack was the father of Katherine Ellis's child.'

Meg stopped and stared at Connie in shock. 'You knew? You knew all along?'

'Let's say I made an intelligent guess. I thought she was yours at first, but then by the way you were behaving, so cold towards her, I realised who the real culprit was. Jack had talked about Katherine quite a bit. About both of you as a matter of fact. I put two and two together.'

Meg was astonished. 'But you never said. Why did you never say?'

'Nothing to do with me. Men will be men, after all. That's the way they are. It's up to the girl to stop them. If she doesn't, then she only has herself to blame.'

'Oh, my God. I don't believe I'm hearing this. You think Jack is innocent?'

'I don't see why he should pay for someone else's lack of morals.'

'You don't believe he's responsible for the child he has created?'

'Why should he be? Don't tell me you would have wanted him to marry Katherine Ellis, make an honest woman of her. I thought you wanted him for yourself, so you could get your hands on Broombank. But then you managed that anyway, didn't you?'

Meg was stunned into silence by this totally selfish attitude, this warped view of the facts.

Connie continued with her venom. 'There must have been something wrong, something lacking on your part for him to go looking for another woman in the first place.'

'I don't believe I'm hearing this.'

'I'm only saying God's truth. A man doesn't stray unless he feels unwanted.'

'That simply isn't true.'

Connie sniffed disapprovingly, then dabbed at her eyes with her hanky. 'That's easy to say now. Now that's he's missing. Possibly even dead.'

Meg could think of nothing to say in the face of this show of uncharacteristic grief. It was as if she were the guilty one, not Jack, or Kath.

It certainly helped to ease her own sense of guilt for not having told either Jack or Connie that Melissa was a part of their own family. Connie had known all along and blamed everyone but her own selfish, foolish brother.

'The ring he gave me is upstairs, in my room,' Meg coolly told her. 'I'll go and fetch it for you. When Jack comes back, as I'm sure he will, I'll explain to him about

Tam and me. I agree that I should have told him before. I wish I had now. Before it was too late.'

'Too late?'

'Now it seems that my own life is on hold. I can do nothing. So long as Jack is missing, for whatever reason, I feel tied to him, trapped by my own soft heart, my strong sense of loyalty. If I couldn't tell him when he seemed far away, stationed down south, how can I marry Tam, as he wants me to, while Jack is a prisoner somewhere? That would be even worse.'

Connie gave a little grunt of satisfaction as if pleased that Meg found herself in this dilemma.

'Things don't always go as you would like in this world,' she said sanctimoniously. 'If you do finish with our Jack, what about Lissa? His daughter, mind? And what about your precious Broombank? Have you thought about that? You'd leave him homeless too, would you?'

—

The invasion of Europe began in early June 1944. The weather was far from perfect with rough seas and too much wind. The Turner family, as did everyone else, listened constantly to the BBC for any scrap of news, good or bad. Bulletins were frustratingly brief. But everyone grew skilled at reading between the lines. No news was very definitely good news in time of war.

'The bridgeheads are being held,' Joe announced. 'It's going to succeed. This is what we've been waiting for. We'll push them back, see if we don't.'

'There's no question,' Connie agreed stoutly. 'It mustn't fail. I never tolerate failure. Come on now, Joe, time for your exercises.'

'What a woman,' he said, gratification evident in his voice. 'Worse than a little Hitler she is. Get up. Do this. Do that. Stretch. Pull. Lift. Never stops going on at me, she doesn't.'

'And look at the good it's doing you. You can get out of bed on your own now,' she said.

'Aye,' Joe agreed. 'I'll be giving that daughter of mine the run around yet.'

As summer continued, the combined armies managed to make real progress on French soil, winning more and more territory into allied hands. At the end of August Paris was liberated, shortly followed by Brussels. But the jubilation was soon dulled with the failure to seize the last of a series of bridges at Arnhem, by which the Allies were to advance into Germany and finish off the war.

–

A wet and windy summer turned into a depressing autumn where the allies seemed bogged down either by bad weather or German resistance. The thought of a sixth year of war turned Kath's earlier exhilaration into fear and despair. Fear that even in these closing days of war, she could lose Wade, just when she'd realised how much she needed him.

She knew that he was itching to be up there, in the skies, taking part in it all. Being grounded had never quite appealed, however vital his role in operations.

But she had one piece of good news. In September she heard that she'd been posted back to Bledlow. She couldn't wait to see Bella again who'd been lucky enough to spend her entire war in the same place.

Nothing had changed. She found her old friend huddled over the belching stove, writing letters. She looked up in delighted surprise. 'Kath, you old layabout. Let you out of HQ to come and do some real work, have they?'

Kath laughed. 'Am I glad to see you.'

When the joyful reunion was over, cocoa was made and they settled down to a long catching up of news. A buoyant feeling of hope prevailed, that soon they would see an end to the agony of it all.

'At least we're making progress now,' Kath said. 'Pushing the Germans back where they belong.'

'Aircrew always seem to be ready for off or coming back exhausted,' Bella agreed. 'Every night to Berlin and Nuremburg. Scared rigid most of the time, they are. It's a long way across France and Germany to Berlin.'

'It's plain enough what they're after. Not that we can say. Careless talk costs lives and all that. So long as they help our invading armies to advance unhindered, that's what counts.'

'Losses are heavy though,' Bella said quietly. 'You can see desperation in their eyes sometimes. Makes my heart bleed. I hope it's all worth it.'

'It will be.'

'It'd help if the weather would be a bit kinder. If it isn't the rain or the wind, it's the fog. Thank God my man is reasonably safe. Works on the ground crew at the next air field. Handy, you know.' She grinned. 'Though it can get a bit dangerous when a plane comes back with its bombs still on board. Unsung hero, I tell him he is,' said Bella, with her usual dry humour. 'What about your commander? Don't say he isn't, because it stands out a mile what's going on between you two.'

'Nothing is going on.'

Bella looked shocked. 'Then it's time it was.'

'He wants to marry me, that's all.'

'That's all? Then why don't you, girl? Jump to it, straight into bed.'

Kath laughed. 'You make it sound so simple.'

'It is. You pull back the sheets and…'

'Stop it, Bella. There are complications.'

'Tell me.'

'Thanks, but no thanks. I'd best tell him first.'

'Fair enough. Get on with it then. Live for today. Who knows what tomorrow might bring? Everyone knows he's crazy about you. Asked after every letter you ever wrote me, till he got posted too, so get on with it.'

'Oh, Bella. I wish it were that easy. Maybe I'll tell him tonight. What about old Mule, is she still here?'

As if on cue, WAAF Officer Mullin walked in. Face as sour as ever, she ran a swift eye over Kath's neatly dressed figure. Not a sign of untidiness. No scarlet lipstick on the sculpted lines of her wide lips. Hair grown longer but pinned up, well off the collar. Nothing at all to find fault with. Kath could almost feel her disappointment.

'I see we are to have the pleasure of your company again.' The eyes fastened upon the two stripes. 'Corporal.'

'Nice to see you too, Officer Mullin.'

And then, as if it pained her to have to say it, 'There's a telephone call for you. The Wing Commander, I believe. Asked for you to ring him back.'

'Oh, thanks.' Kath waited until the woman had gone then looked askance at Bella.

'What's with her? Why didn't she come down on me like a ton of the proverbial bricks?'

'There's more to worry about now than whether two different ranks get together. Go and talk to lover boy. Get that ring on your finger.'

Kath had butterflies in her stomach long before she got through to him. It was often like that these days.

'Sorry, hon,' he said. 'Can't see you tonight. We have some Mosquitoes ready to go out here and we're one experienced flier short. It's a bit foggy so I can't ask just anyone.'

'A bit foggy? It's like a pea souper out there. No one should be going out, let alone you.'

'Sure, the weather is too bad for the Lancasters to take off but Mosquitoes are smaller, lighter. And our boys need whatever air cover they can get right now, at whatever cost.'

'But not you, Wade! It's months, years, since you flew.'

'It's okay. Like riding a bicycle. You never forget.' Suddenly Kath wanted to tell him, wanted to pour it all out, there and then. 'Wade, I need to talk to you.'

'Sure, honey. I'd love to talk to you too. But tomorrow, when I get back. Take care.'

A click on the line told her he had gone. Dear God, let it not be for good.

─

Joe stood by Meg's side, leaning on the rail by the auction ring. It was the first time he had been out since his stroke and his presence had caused a stir. Even so he'd been surprised by the obvious respect shown by the farmers to his daughter. Not simply a doffing of caps or inclining of the head towards a pretty young woman but they stopped to talk to her about farming matters. One or two even asked her advice. Joe could hardly believe it.

Only last week he'd offered to deal with the buying for her when she'd gone looking for some new gimmer lambs to replace her lost Swaledales, but she'd only laughed and told him to stay at home.

He'd insisted on coming to today's auction. He wanted to see what she was up to. So here he was watching his own daughter come into the ring with her own sheep. Broombank sheep.

'Why do you still call them that?' Joe had wanted to know. 'Broombank has gone.'

'Because that's what they are, and always will be. Only the house has been damaged, not the land, nor the sheep. I know I owe you money for paying my mortgage all those months, for which I am truly grateful, but it's still mine.'

Joe had thought for a moment that she was going to embarrass him by kissing him before all his colleagues, but she'd contented herself with a smile. 'I'll pay you back. You'll get every penny, don't worry.'

'I'm not,' he told her.

'And we'll get the interest agreed in writing, shall we? So there's no doubt what the final sum will be.'

'Right enough,' he'd said, too bemused to argue. What else could he do? She'd rumbled him. Joe looked thoughtful now as he listened to the auctioneer singing the praises of her stock. She'd learned a thing or two, this lass of his.

'You couldn't find a finer bunch of Swaledales anywhere in the district,' chanted the auctioneer, and Joe listened to the rapid bidding in open astonishment.

When Meg returned she was exultant, unable to keep the pride from her voice. 'They're fine sheep, aren't they? See that speckled faced one? She's had twins two years running. And the greyer one beside her is so greedy you hardly need a dog to fetch her in. Rattle a bucket and she'll follow you right into your own kitchen.' Meg chuckled, not noticing how Joe stared at her, wide-eyed.

'You sound as if you know them all?'

She looked at him then, a smile of embarrassment on her lovely lips that showed she was a woman still. 'Wicked, isn't it? Don't be sentimental, that's what you told me, so I've tried not to be. I was sad to see the Herdwicks go but the Swales have a broader frame, and bigger lambs. Make more money in the long run. Don't you agree?'

Joe had never considered anything so risky as a radical change of stock in all his life, but he didn't say so. He was too bemused by what was happening before his eyes. He could not deny what he had seen. Meg had done it, for all she was a girl. Broombank sheep had sold for a good price, the top price achieved at this auction mart all day. Should have won a prize, the auctioneer said. Perhaps Miss Turner had best try entering her stock for the County Show next time it was on.

Flushed with pleasure at her achievement, Meg went home that day with a fat pocket. And Joe with a pocketful of thoughts.

–

That night was the longest of Kath's life. She had ample time to wish many things were different. To wish she had never played dangerous games with Jack. It had seemed so unimportant at the time, a way of proving how close they were, that they could get away with the fun of sex without worrying about the love that should go with it.

And it was time to question her own motives at abandoning Melissa. How young she had been, how selfish. So wrapped up in her own needs she hadn't given a thought to the child. Then there had been the awful feeling of inadequacy. Greenlawns had been good at nourishing that feeling in everyone. They hadn't even let her hold her own baby at birth. No wonder she had felt nothing for her.

Now that she had found love it looked as if she might lose it. Was that to be her punishment?

Oh, dear God, let Wade come back this night, then I can spend my life loving him. If he still wants me, that is, when he learns what a cold-hearted, selfish young woman I really am.

Oh, Melissa. Can you ever forgive me? Is it too late for us to try again?

–

Kath and Bella sat with the other girls not on duty by the window, waiting for dawn, for the sound of six aircraft overhead.

'How could they take off when visibility was practically nil? And to carry a bomb of that size slung underneath the fuselage has got to be some madman's idea of a joke.' Kath's mind had relayed every possible catastrophe. The tiny Mosquitoes had been shot out of the sky a dozen times in her dreams as she struggled to sleep. Now that she was awake the pictures in her head were even more dramatic. 'And if anyone says there's a war on, I'll hit them.'

Not a soul spoke. Everyone knew that these kind of missions were common. They took place nightly, nearly always in less than ideal weather conditions, and to undisclosed destinations. What made it different was the fact that Kath knew one of the pilots intimately. There wasn't a girl present who hadn't gone through the same torment.

And then they heard them.

'There's one,' Bella said, jumping up. 'And another, and another.' They counted them in, an achingly long pause before the last. 'They're all there!' Whoops of joy and hugs and kisses all round.

Kath didn't hesitate, not even to grab her heavy coat. She sped out of the door and headed for the spot she knew Wade must pass when he returned to his quarters.

Waiting for him seemed to take an age. Oh, do come, my darling. I have so much to tell you. That I love you for one thing.

Then she saw the flames on the airfield, flaring up into the sky, offering a beacon of light for any enemy aircraft to follow. She started to run towards it. Hands held her back and she was screaming his name. 'Don't let it be Wade. Please don't let it him.'

'We don't want it to be anyone,' a hard voice said, and Kath sank to her knees in shame, for it was true. Why should anyone else have to die in this terrible war? Hadn't the fates had enough? She fastened her hand to her mouth to stop the sobs, watching as dark figures ran, calling instructions, desperately trying to put out the blaze as one Mosquito burned to the ground.

'Hey, what's this?' He was there. Unbelievably, beside her, holding out his arms for her to run into them.

'Oh, my darling, darling Wade. I do love you, I do. And I will marry you. There's so much I want to tell you.'

Chapter 14

1945

Lissa wriggled her hand free from Meg's as they walked across the school yard. She did not wish to look like a baby. Her new shoes clip-clopped very satisfactorily and over her coat she carried a Dorothy bag with two wrapped biscuits inside, for her morning break. Hetty had knitted the bag for her out of some old blue wool.

It was a new year, she would be five less than three months from now, and this was to be her first day at school. Deep in her tummy was a knot of excitement. Apprehension too, had Lissa been able to put a name to such an emotion, but not for a moment would she show it.

'I'll be all right now,' she told Meg as they both watched Miss Shaw come out into the playground and clang the school bell.

'I think I'm more nervous than you, sweetheart,' Meg said, bending down to kiss her. 'How will I get through the day without you? How will I manage all the chores?'

Lissa giggled, secure in her knowledge of being loved, she could afford to be generous. 'I can help you after I finish this afternoon. You will come to fetch me, won't you, Meg?'

Meg nodded, very seriously. 'I will be here on the dot of three thirty. Now you be a good girl and do what the teacher tells you.'

Miss Shaw came up. 'Hello, Melissa. Are you ready to come in?'

Lissa agreed that she was. 'You're not going to call me by that silly name, are you?' she asked, liking things to be straight from the start.

Miss Shaw hid a smile. 'Lissa then, if you prefer it. Say bye-bye to Meg. Then we'll go inside and sing some songs, shall we?'

Lissa was given a peg with the picture of a cat above it, but she could already read her name so she thought that a bit babyish. Someone, she couldn't quite remember who, had told her that it was very important to know such things before you started school, so she'd made a point of learning it. Lissa didn't like surprises. Or big bangs. And she was glad it was a cat on her hook, and not an aeroplane. She didn't like aeroplanes either.

She needed no help to unlace her shoes and put on her plimsolls. Meg had taught her how to do that, and made her a pretty bag with her name in daisy stitch to keep them in. She was ready for school and meant to enjoy it. She smiled at everyone, brisk with a new importance as she went into the warm classroom, secure in the knowledge that she was welcome here. Half the children present were already her friends from Sunday School. If they liked school and could do the work, then so could she.

–

How different from dear Effie's first day. Just a skinny little evacuee feeling as if she didn't belong, poor Effie had been wracked with nerves, not even able to read her own name. Meg couldn't help but remember that day as she walked back down the lane. The thorn hedges were heavy with snow and beneath a stand of beech a small flock of bramblings were foraging. She took little notice of their antics this morning but thrust her hands deep in her pockets and walked on, printing fresh tracks in the snow as her mind turned inwards. If Lissa was more ready for school than Effie had been, then the thanks, in no small part, were due to Effie herself.

'I should have taken her right to the door that day,' Meg said aloud, her words echoing in what seemed now to be a very empty world. 'Instead of being so concerned with the land and the sheep.'

She'd been so determined to prove to her father that she was capable of running a farm of her own that for a time nothing else had mattered. People had seemed unimportant besides the overpowering nature of her obsession, and the enormous challenges she faced. Some had even represented a threat. Her father for one, and Dan. After the betrayal of her two best friends, she hadn't been able to trust or care about anyone for a quite a while.

As a result she had almost lost Lissa's love.

Now she knew different. Now she understood that people were every bit as important as her ambitions. More so. People mattered most in life. Tam and Lissa were her life. What use was Broombank without them?

Meg felt a huge pride in her heart taking Lissa to school today, and an odd sort of loneliness. She supposed every mother must feel the same way on her child's first day at school. The day that stretched ahead of her seemed suddenly empty, although there was plenty of work to be done. Most mothers, of course, were real mothers, and often had other children at home. Meg wondered if she would ever have a child of her own, one who didn't actually belong to someone else. The question had never troubled her before. Now, for some reason, it did. She wanted a child, Tam's child, so badly in that moment, it was a physical pain.

Everything I have is borrowed. The land, which I can only guard for future generations. Broombank, which was destroyed before it became truly mine to keep. And Lissa. Even Tam is only a lover and not a husband, so might still leave.

But thanks to Lanky's Luckpenny, most of her sheep were safe. She should be grateful for that.

Meg told herself that she mustn't grow morbid, just because the war still rumbled on. It was a crisp, January day. The sun was shining on lavender pale mountains and the snow squeaked cleanly beneath her booted feet. The kind of day that made you feel good to be alive. And she wasn't the naïve young girl she had once been. She was a woman, strong and independent. She could cope with anything now. Almost.

Best of all, Tam was home on leave. She could at least be glad of that. She'd left him deep in conversation at the breakfast table with Joe. It was odd that those two talked so much these days. They even once took a walk together up to Brockbarrow wood. Could Joe be softening in his old age? He still missed Dan, perhaps that was it. He was enjoying having another man around.

'Whatever is it you talk about so keenly?' Meg asked Tam as they lay together in the big bed that night.

'He's worried over Ashlea. Can't persuade Mr Ellis to sell it to him at a fair price. Joe wants it for the two youngsters one day and Jeffrey Ellis seems to have plans of his own.'

'Lissa?'

'That's what I'm thinking too.'

'Oh, dear God. You haven't told Father you suspect that, have you?'

'Is it daft I am? Do you want me to ruin the child's life? No, indeed. But I wish Jeffrey wouldn't do it. It will only cause trouble in the future.'

Meg snuggled down beside him. 'Then let's leave it till the future to worry over it. Who knows what might happen by then?' Whatever her differences with her father in the past, it was good to see him making such a good recovery. He still walked with a stick and slurred his words a little but he got out and about most days, visiting friends or the auction mart. He'd even taken up his moneylending business again. Almost like old times. Except that he wasn't permitted yet to work on the farm.

She had to hand it to Connie for achieving such miracles. He'd even made no protest when Sally Ann started inviting the POWs into the kitchen to eat. It was a changing world, that was certain. But then they'd all been moved by the upsetting stories of lines of refugees seen moving through France and Italy this winter. Perhaps even Joe had seen the cruelty in objecting to the presence of a pair of young men whose own war was over.

'The war will end soon,' they all kept saying. But even if the Germans were being pushed back, there was still the war in the east, still that awful uncertainty, for all it only seemed a matter of time.

Joe cheered when they heard of Hitler's suicide at the end of April and finally, on 8 May, came the announcement they had been waiting for. Victory in Europe at last. VE Day, as it came to be known.

Sally Ann and Meg went wild, cheering so much that Rust started barking and couldn't stop, the two older children looked bewildered, and little Daniel burst into tears.

That evening they left the children with Joe and Connie and went down into Kendal with Hetty and Will Davies to join in with the celebrations. The streets were crowded with people, flags and bunting hung from every building, and with no blackout, lights blazed from every window.

'It's like Christmas and birthdays and Fair days all rolled into one. Isn't it marvellous?' Meg cried.

There was dancing in the Abbot Hall Park and at midnight hordes of people collected outside Kendal Town Hall, laughing and singing. The celebrations were somewhat quiet and orderly, tempered by the knowledge of those who had died and weren't here to share in the victory.

It was well into the early hours by the time they arrived back at Ashlea but Sally Ann had made a decision. 'Tomorrow we shall declare a holiday and have the best party ever. We'll invite our dearest friends and neighbours, empty our cupboards and eat till we burst.'

–

Hetty and Will Davies came, always delighted to fuss over the children, particularly Lissa.

'I've bought her a clockwork clown that bangs a drum. I hope you don't mind? Only, she's the grandchild I never had,' Hetty whispered, flushing brightly with embarrassment.

Meg hugged her. 'And you are the grandmother she loves as her own. I don't know how I would have managed to bring her up without you.' Jeffrey and Rosemary Ellis came too, because they were invited and Mr Ellis would not permit his wife to be so rude as to decline. Not on this special day.

'We've only popped in for a moment,' said Rosemary, tartly. 'We can't stop long as we are due at the Taylors for dinner at eight.'

They sat and sipped tea on the sofa and Rosemary studiously refused to glance in Lissa's direction.

'Uncle Jeffrey,' the little girl cried, climbing up on to his knee and almost knocking the china cup out of his hands in her demand for attention. 'See what Hetty has brought me.'

'You are a very spoiled little girl,' said Rosemary in her most starchy voice.

'I seem to remember another little girl, equally spoiled,' said Jeffrey dryly.

Meg withdrew to the kitchen, not wishing to be involved in this little drama. If Rosemary wasn't interested in Lissa, it didn't matter one bit. Lissa had more than enough people to love and care for her.

'Oh, but it is lovely to think the war is over,' she burst out, seeing Sally Ann recklessly slicing carrot cake and doling out tinned peaches she'd hoarded for over six long years. Would they be fit to eat? Meg wondered, and didn't care, she'd eat them anyway. Rust sat and watched the operation, just in case she should make a mess of it and drop a piece inadvertently on the floor.

'I shall be glad when we find some currants again. I'm sick of carrot cake. You pour the punch,'

Sally Ann instructed. 'It's homemade and pretty tame stuff but all we have.'

Meg grinned. 'It can't be nearly so bad as Effie's beet-root wine. Do you remember that? And Charlie's first leave when we all sang songs and got very drunk?' Tears sprang to her eyes. Effie. If only she had lived to share this precious day with them. But that was the way of war. It took no note of its victims. At least I had the privilege of knowing you, Effie love.

'We can start planning our future now,' Sally Ann said gently. 'Where will we all be a year from now, do you think? Five years.'

In Meg's skirt pocket was a letter. It had come that morning. She could tell from the handwriting that it was from Kath, and it didn't take a genius to guess it would concern Lissa. This was the first news she'd had of her since Charlie's letter two years back. She remembered telling Mr and Mrs Ellis about it at the time, seeing the light of excitement in Jeffrey's eyes, the tightening of Rosemary's lips.

'We might hear from her soon then?' Jeffrey had said. But they hadn't. Until now.

Where would Lissa be a year from now? Meg thought. Five years? Her heart shrivelled a little inside. Before the day was over she had to find the courage to open the letter. To read Kath's decision.

'Some of us have planned our futures already,' Joe announced, puffing out his chest. And then to Meg's great astonishment, he turned and winked outrageously at Connie, who stood patiently by his side.

'What is this then?' Jeffrey Ellis jovially teased. 'Secrets?'

'Not any more. Connie has done me the honour of agreeing to become my wife,' Joe announced, very properly, and there was a small shocked silence, then everyone started to talk at once, and laugh and slap him on the back.

'Good for you.'

'Congratulations.'

'Well done.'

Meg found herself hugging her father and wishing him every happiness. And to her own surprise realised that she meant it. 'I hope you will be very happy, both of you,' she said, dutifully kissing Connie on the cheek.

If only Tam was here, she thought suddenly, the aching need for him so strong that she had to turn away and pretend to busy herself with pouring more punch so that she didn't make a complete fool of herself. He would be home soon, they all would. Charlie and his young bride. Kath. And Jack?

Mr Ellis made a toast. 'To absent friends and loved ones. May they return to us soon.' He half glanced at his wife but Rosemary only sipped at the bland punch with pursed lips, almost as if it might poison her.

It was a day of happiness. Songs were sung, jokes told, reminiscences exchanged. Nothing was permitted to spoil it. After the Ellises left, the other ladies sat and drank tea while the men swopped war stories and the children stayed up far too late.

After a while Meg crept up to her room to read her letter. '*Darling Meg,*' it began, and she gave a grunt of disbelief. How could Kath so address her, just as if nothing had happened, nothing had changed between them? She smoothed out the paper and prepared herself for the worst.

The words spun and blurred before her eyes so that she was forced to close them for a moment to bring her jangled emotions back under control.

> *I know you will be delighted for me when I tell you that Wade and I got married last Saturday. We still have some months to do before we are demobbed but hope to be out late next year. It is our plan to go to Canada since Wade has a home and family there. I'll write again with a date.*
>
> *I would like to see Melissa. How is she? I know it must have been difficult for you but we can talk about what I owe you later. Perhaps it would be best if we took her out occasionally, when we are finally demobbed, to let her get to know us a bit first. Look forward to seeing you again.*
>
> *All my love, as ever, Kath*

Meg sat rigid on her bed and read the letter again. She read it three times before the contents had finally been assimilated into her brain.

Kath was coming for Lissa.

And for the first time a small knot of burning anger lit deep within. Owe? What I owe you. How dare she suggest that Meg should be paid for loving and caring for Lissa? The insult of it was humiliating, as if you could buy love. And the calm assumption that Kath could call and collect Lissa, like a doll, and take her out for a walk. Well, Lissa wasn't a doll, Meg thought rebelliously. She was a living, breathing person with a mind of her own.

Yet Kath was the child's mother. She had the right to take her if she wanted.

Folding the letter with trembling fingers, Meg put it into her handkerchief box. She didn't want Lissa to find it. Not until she'd had time to prepare her.

But how did you prepare a five-year-old to meet a mummy she has never seen? A stranger who is coming to take her to a faraway country?

How did Meg begin to prepare herself for the shock of losing this beloved child? She lay down upon the bed, every muscle, every limb shaking. She mustn't cry. She mustn't let anyone, Lissa most of all, see that she had been crying.

'Oh, Tam. Please come home soon. I need you.'

–

A day or two later Meg called upon Kath's parents. Rosemary received her in the kitchen. No cosy fireside chairs in the drawing room on this occasion. There was a coolness between them these days, all signs of their original friendship quite gone.

Meg laid the letter out on the table. 'I thought you might wish to see this.'

Rosemary glanced fiercely at the letter, without touching it, then turned away to reach for the kettle. Jeffrey walked in at that moment, picked it up and took it to his chair at the head of the table to read it in silence.

'I wondered if you would want to see her, when she comes?' Meg said.

'Why would we?' Rosemary said, filling the kettle with a fast jet of water. 'She hasn't troubled to keep in touch all these years.'

Meg swallowed. Whatever her personal quarrel with Kath, this she knew to be unfair. 'Did you give her reason to think such contact would be welcomed?'

Rosemary sniffed disdainfully. 'She made her choice years ago. And she chose not to come home. Best to leave it at that.'

Meg met Jeffrey's bleak gaze. 'You could make things change, if you wanted to. Put the past behind you, as we all must with many things that have happened during this war. You could welcome your daughter home.' She made no mention of Lissa. Meg could not have borne to hear Lissa criticised simply for existing.

Rosemary set the kettle carefully on the solid fuel cooker and started to set out blue and white kitchen cups and saucers. 'Katherine brought shame upon us all with her dreadful behaviour. For a time I could not bear to go out, to look my friends in the face. I have no wish to go through all of that again.'

'Have you heard from her?'

Rosemary looked uncomfortable and Jeffrey glanced at his wife in surprise. 'You have, haven't you?'

'There was a letter, last year. And another a day or two ago. I burned them both unread. It's for the best,' she cried, when she saw her husband's devastated expression.

'Oh, Rosemary. How could you do such a thing?'

'She intends to go overseas, to Canada,' Meg said. 'You might never see her again. Don't you care?'

Rosemary tightened her lips in the familiar way and began to pleat and unpleat her fingers. 'It's best not to open up old wounds.'

'Perhaps so,' said Jeffrey cautiously, seeing how agitated his wife was becoming. 'Let things lie, for the moment.'

'She says she wants Lissa.' Meg made the announcement, unable to hold back her fears any longer.

They both stared at her, the one with compassion, the other uncomprehending of her distress.

Jeffrey Ellis reached out and squeezed Meg's hand. 'She is the child's mother. I suppose she has that right.'

'*No!* She doesn't. Lissa is my child now. I have brought her up. I was the one who nursed her when she was sick. I was the one she came to for love and understanding, the one who taught her to read, fed her, bathed her, took her to school that first day. She is *mine!*' Only the sound of the humming kettle coming to the boil could be heard in the small kitchen.

Jeffrey Ellis clasped his hands in his lap and stared down at them in misery. 'There's nothing I can do, Meg. Much as I would like to, I can't help you with this one.'

She ran from the room.

The following months were the longest in Meg's life. Waiting for another letter from Kath. Waiting for Tam to come home. Waiting to hear if Jack was alive. Always waiting.

Fortunately they were busy with the clipping and harvesting, and her tired body made sure that she slept.

The war with Japan ended in August 1945, but then a long winter crawled by before Tam came home on his last leave in March of the following year. Meg fell into his arms with relief. The joy of having him with her was enough to banish all other concerns from her mind, at least for a while. 'When will you be demobbed?'

'In just a few weeks,' he promised, kissing her.

'Then I shan't ever let you go away again.'

'I shan't ever want to.' They lay together in the big bed in her parents old panelled room, and if they slept at all that night Meg had no recollection of it. It felt so good to be held in his arms again. She loved to taste the sweetness of his lips and relish the scent of his skin against her own. All their past quarrels seemed silly now. She couldn't think of anything that she would let come between them. Not ever again.

Joe and Connie's wedding took place at the little dale church on a perfect spring day. The sun shone, bees droned and the song thrush sang its heart out. The woodlands that enfolded the tiny church flowed with gentian and silver pools of bluebells and garlic flower.

They should by rights be working of course. But for today all was celebration. A respite of much needed joy.

Charlie had come home on leave with his own young wife, Sue, looking flushed and excited over the discovery that she was pregnant. Meg held Charlie tight in her arms till the tears rolled over her cheeks and dampened the collar on her new dress. 'There were times when I never thought we'd see this day,' she said, rummaging for her handkerchief up her sleeve.

'Oh, fickle-hearted woman. I never doubted it,' boasted Charlie, but his eyes and the strength of his hug told a different story. 'I'll be demobbed soon,' he said, but then, casting a glance at the keenly attentive Joe, drew in a deep breath.

'Might as well own up to it now, Father. I won't be coming back to Ashlea. I've got a job lined up in the aircraft industry. A good one too.'

Meg held her breath as she waited for Joe's response.

'Aye, just as well. I don't reckon your sister would welcome you back here. Place is crowded enough already and you know how she likes to be in charge.'

They all laughed then, releasing the tension. Perhaps the war had taught Joe something too. Or Sally Ann had asserted a greater influence upon him over the years than even he realised.

His daughter-in-law came to kiss him, the only one who dared do so without fear of being rebuffed.

The wedding went off smoothly. The bride and groom looked suitably happy. Lissa, prettily dressed as a flower girl in lemon seersucker, carried a basket of buttercups and daisies made up by Hetty, as was the bride's posy of yellow iris and sweet-scented orchids. Nick and little Daniel were page boys, though not without some protest at the bow ties.

The happy couple were planning a prolonged stay in Connie's house at Grange-Over-Sands, by way of honeymoon and convalescence for Joe. They were being taken by taxi to the station, at Charlie's expense, as a treat.

'We've got our minds set on a nice little bungalow by the sea,' Joe said.

'Bungalow?' Meg's eyes widened. 'You're not thinking of retiring, are you. Father?'

'Aye, I thought happen I might. Doc MacClaren seems to think it a good idea. It's a touch warmer down Grange way and it suits Connie better.' She folded her hands possessively upon his arm. 'Your father isn't as young as he was, Meg, and that stroke was a bit of a shock to him.'

'Yes, I can see that it was,' Meg agreed, finding the thought of Joe Turner retired hard to assimilate.

'I thought we'd take a place with a bit of ground. Just enough for a dozen sheep,' he explained, and everyone laughed at Connie's shocked expression. 'Sheep?'

'Aye. To keep lively like.'

'That's more like it, lad,' said Will Davies. 'Farmers never retire. Not properly.'

'Well,' said Connie, but in a tone that meant she was prepared to concede defeat on that one.

'Thee can manage the farm without me, I suppose?' Joe said dryly to Meg. 'I seem to remember you wanted me out of the way all along.'

'That's not true. I just wanted my own bit of independence. A place in life of my own,' she protested.

'Aye, well, I reckon you've got it.'

Had she? Right now it didn't seem as if she had anything of her own. The home that she'd struggled so hard to buy had been bombed. Old loyalties and ties with the past prevented her from marrying the man she loved. And her lovely Lissa was to be taken from her by the end of the year. Not exactly what she'd had in mind when she'd pleaded for an independent life all those years ago.

Everyone stood and cheered as Connie climbed into the taxi, tossing scraps of confetti into the wind.

Joe came to Meg where she stood quietly, in the porch of Ashlea, before going to join his bride. 'We'll be off then,' he said.

'Bye, Father. Be happy.'

Joe cleared his throat. 'We've had our differences in the past, you and I.'

Meg couldn't help but smile. 'You could say so.'

'Aye, well, sometimes a lass has to be kept in place. It's just that you were harder to keep to it than most.'

'A chip off the old block maybe?'

'Aye, happen so.' He turned to go then seemed to hesitate. 'Broombank is yours and always will be. I'll acknowledge I didn't win that one.'

Meg tried to look happy about that.

'But Ashlea is for Dan's boys. I haven't persuaded Jeffrey Ellis to sell me the freehold yet, but he will when I've had time to work on him. You have to appreciate that.'

Meg met his gaze steadily. 'I've already said as much, haven't I?'

'I just wanted it understood.'

'It is.'

'That chap of thine wanted me to lend you money for the rebuilding. I told him no. I need it for me own retirement. I'm not made of brass.'

Meg froze. 'Tam had no right to do that.'

'Aye, well, he happen thought you wouldn't have the guts to ask me theeself.'

'It's not a question of guts. I don't need your money, Father. You helped me with the mortgage payments when I was ill, for which I am truly grateful. But I've nearly paid you all that back now, so I'll manage on my own, thanks very much. As for Broombank, I intend to take the problem to the War Committee. It's not my fault a German plane unloaded its bombs on my house by accident. So it's not my place to put the roof back. The Government can do it.'

'Pigs might fly!'

Meg straightened her back and a light came into her eyes, one that Joe couldn't help but admire. 'Oh, they'll do it all right.'

He gave a shout of laughter. 'Mebbe they will when they come face to face with your stubbornness. Happen I were wrong, all them years ago. Happen you're the best son I've ever had.'

Meg gasped and took an instinctive step towards him but he turned quickly and climbed into the taxi, waving to his family and friends as it drove away.

'Did you hear what he said?' Meg asked Sally Ann. 'Did you hear?'

Sally Ann laughed as she linked an arm in Meg's. 'Perhaps he's seen the truth at last.'

1946

Chapter 15

Meg and Tam had separated the lambs from their mothers and the ewes were now being pushed through the dipping trough. The clean warm water was well laced with the necessary chemicals to kill the keds and mites that would damage and possibly kill the sheep if left to fester and grow undisturbed.

It was an unpleasant operation, disliked by shepherd and sheep alike, particularly on a hot August day like this.

Tam pushed them through one at a time while Meg held each head under water with a bristleless brush for a few moments, whilst trying to keep the sheep's mouth closed to stop it swallowing the stuff.

'What a way to spend my leave. How many sheep do you have now?' Tam asked as they stopped for a breather and Meg grinned.

'Not counting Ashlea sheep which I'm also taking care of at the moment, near five hundred.'

Tam gaped at her. 'And I thought you were a poor woman.'

'I would be without you,' she said. 'It's been hard building up the flock but I never thought for a moment that I wouldn't do it. One day, sooner than you think, I mean to have twice that. That will be a day to celebrate, eh?'

'Looks like everything is going right for you at last.'

'In some respects,' she murmured.

'I'm proud of you, Meg. You've done what you set out to do. To own the finest flock in the district. It humbles a mere man to see your success.'

She looked at him in surprise then gave a shout of laughter and struck at him with the brush in playful disbelief. 'You were never humbled in your life, Tam O'Cleary, and certainly not by a woman. What blarney you do talk.' And grinning broadly he pulled her to him.

'Sure and I'd take you here and now on this damn hillside were it not for the fact that you stink to high heaven.'

'Get off with you.' Content with each other, catching glances and smiles as they worked, they put the next sheep through the deep pool and chuckled with sympathy as it stood on the side afterwards, miserably dripping and shaking itself while the surplus dip ran back into the trough.

'You'd think yourself too grand to wed a poor Irishman now, I suppose?' Tam called across to her.

Meg lost her grip on the poor sheep she was holding so that it very nearly escaped a proper ducking, until she bethought herself and recaptured it.

'You choose your moments to ask,' she said. 'How romantic, to be proposed to over a sheep-dipping trough.'

'When are you not with your precious sheep?'

'There have been other times when you've had my undivided attention. Perhaps you would care to repeat your offer then.'

'Huh. Take it or leave it now, Meg Turner. I'm not a man to beg.'

'I never thought you would ask me again,' she said quietly, suddenly nervous in case he didn't mean it. 'After me refusing you once already.'

'If you don't know a good thing when it's offered, the more fool you. But then, as I said, you'll be thinking yourself too grand perhaps, for the likes of me.'

'Do you want to be dipped in this pool, Thomas O'Cleary?'

Tam backed away. 'Indeed I don't.'

Meg put back her head and called out in a clear, ringing voice: 'Carry my words, wind, to anyone who cares to listen. I love this man, Tam O'Cleary, and he is to be my man for all time.' She looked at him then, at the broad strength of his shoulders as he casually lifted a sheep and tossed it into the water, at the warmth in his soft green eyes, the curl of his smiling mouth. Oh, how she loved him. 'All mine. To have and to hold from this day forth. Is that right, Tam?'

'That's right, my lovely.'

The following Saturday, when Meg went out to do the morning milking she found Jack sitting on the doorstep.

—

A wind was gathering the black clouds over Bowfell to Fairfield, like an impatient farmer with his flock. The chill feel of a storm in the air echoed in the beating of Meg's heart.

'Jack?'

He was sitting with his head resting on folded arms, raised his head, blinked, and focused sleep-dulled eyes upon her. 'Where have you been?' he complained. 'I've been waiting here for hours.'

She was taken aback for the moment. 'It's only six o'clock in the morning. Why didn't you come in? The door was unlocked.'

'I didn't want to risk a blasting from that father of yours.'

Meg held open the door. 'He isn't here as a matter of fact. Come in, Jack. I'll make you a mug of tea, you look half frozen.'

He was dressed in an ill-fitting suit, a soft trilby hat on his head. It sat oddly with the way he picked up a battered suitcase and rolled, sailor fashion, into the house. Meg could feel her heart pumping as she moved between kettle and teapot, mugs and milk. Her mind felt frozen, unable to focus upon a single sensible thought. What could she say to him?

When she had settled him in a chair by the fire with a hot mug of tea cradled in his hands, she stood back and smiled at him, in what she hoped was a welcoming manner. 'It's good to see you looking so well.' It wasn't true. He looked pinched and thin, skin pale almost to the point of yellowness. The once handsome features had slipped somehow, sunk inwards to a gaunt mockery of their former beauty. The glossy black curls had lost their shine and even the violet eyes looked paler, without their usual lustre. 'Did you have a hard war, Jack?'

His glance seared her, condemned her as a well-meaning, silly female who knew nothing at all about it. Meg cringed at the bitterness in that gaze. He didn't answer her question.

'What happened to Broombank? I went up there first.'

She sat on the edge of her seat, aware that the cows needed to be milked, the hens let out. She could hear their noisy cackle already, yet did not like to desert him the moment he'd arrived. 'It was bombed. A stray bomb some German pilot let drop, probably on his return home from the West coast.'

'Anyone killed?'

She told him about Dan and Effie. He looked at her blankly and made no comment, offered no condolences. 'So that put paid to the idea of your owning Broombank.'

Meg stood up. She had a desperate need for fresh air. 'Will you excuse me a moment? I have to do the milking. Sally Ann will be down shortly and she'll start on breakfast. But I must...'

His smile was more of a smirk. 'It's all right. I well remember how you always put the animals first.'

'That's the way it has to be,' she said, with commendable serenity, and left him.

–

Meg found she was shaking when she got outside and had to lean against the dry stone wall, pulling in deep breaths before she could bring herself to walk a step.

After she had let out the hens it was a relief to hide herself in the byre and feel at one with the lowing warmth of the cows. Jack had clearly had a hard time of it and she must be patient. It was no good thrusting all her own problems upon him the moment he walked through the door. She must tread with care.

It proved to be easier said than done. Jack was not in the mood to make concessions, and he had little time for anyone else's war but his own.

'You don't know what it was like, being shot at, bombed, taken prisoner. Safe as houses you were, up here,' he said, choosing to ignore the inappropriate choice of phrase in view of their tragic loss.

Meg agreed that they'd had an easy war, apart from the loss of Effie and Dan, and Broombank.

'We've worked hard though,' she said, feeling irritated by his high-handedness, as if they'd been enjoying themselves on some long party all these years. 'But then women have had to pull their weight with all the men away fighting. Some even built tanks and aeroplanes. That's good, isn't it, to see women taking a full part? If this war does nothing else, I hope it will win us equal pay and health welfare for ourselves and our children. Education for all. These things are important to fight for too. As for us, well, we ran a farm. Produced food for people to eat. And proud to do it.'

'You can stop all of that now I'm home. You can sell Broombank, give up Ashlea too if there's no one to take it on, and go back to being a proper woman.'

Meg felt her hackles rise. This was not the time for a political argument yet she could not resist standing up for herself. 'I never stopped being a proper woman and I've no intention of throwing away everything I've built up. Why would I? What would I do?'

Jack glared at her. 'So Broombank is still more important to you than me?'

She sighed and got up to go. 'We have to talk, Jack. But perhaps now is not the time. Later, when you are well enough.'

But somehow the right moment never presented itself. He made one visit to Kendal to look for work, at Meg's suggestion. But when he failed to find employment, he said it wasn't worth trying again because of all the other returning soldiers.

'This town is too small. We need to get away. All I want is a quiet life. A bit of peace, and a wife to look after me. Is that too much to ask?'

Meg said nothing. Perhaps when Tam came in she would find it easier to broach the subject.

—

The moment Tam walked into the kitchen, the air positively crackled with tension.

'Glory be,' he said, in his quiet, lilting voice. 'So this must be Jack.'

'And you must be an Irish conchie.'

Tam's ready smile froze. 'It's not how I'm normally thought of, as a matter of fact.'

Sally Ann, setting out the warmed plates for breakfast, clucked her tongue at Jack as if he were a naughty child. 'Tam fought on the side of the Americans, Jack, you've no call to make such accusations.'

The once handsome lips curled into a sneer. 'The Americans? Then he's had a pretty short war, and an easy one.'

Meg, coming through the door in time to capture the taut atmosphere, took off her coat and shook the raindrops from it. 'Would you believe it's raining again? When does it ever stop? Oh, scrambled eggs, lovely.' She smiled brightly at everyone as though there were nothing untoward in the two men standing facing each other as if about to embark upon mortal combat. Sally Ann fussed the children into place at the table, hoping they wouldn't notice.

The meal was a sample of the climate they were to endure over the coming days. Whatever was said to Jack he disagreed with it. Whatever opinion you offered, it was the wrong one.

The children irritated him by standing and staring at him, as children will, and every day he asked if there were any letters for him. When he was told there was nothing, he slumped in the chair and sulked for the rest of the day. Perhaps he's hoping for the offer of a job, Meg thought sadly.

They tried to be understanding but it was difficult. If Sally Ann mentioned a friend or neighbour whose son or nephew had not returned, he quickly capped it with a story of an entire household being lost.

Mostly he said nothing, only sat and stared into the fire, his legs thrust out, one side of his mouth lifted into a sour curl of displeasure. After a few days of this Tam took Meg for a walk.

'We have to talk,' he said, marching her off before she had time to protest.

They walked up towards Whinstone Gill. The beck gushed beside them, as it had done on that day six years ago when Kath had tried to warn Meg to leave Jack well alone, and she had refused to listen. An icy froth of water was racing down from the mountain tarns above, which were no more than melted glaciers from a past age and about as cold, Meg thought, as her own feelings towards Jack.

'Why can't I feel sorry for him?' she asked. 'Why don't I feel compassion for what he has obviously endured?'

'He fills me with rage just sitting slumped in that chair, swamped in his own self-pity, expecting you to wait on him hand, foot and finger. Can he not see how hard you have worked? Can't he see that you have suffered losses too?'

And might yet lose Lissa, Meg added to herself. She had received no more letters from Kath on the subject so had tried to put it from her mind, not even mentioning it to Tam. But the thought had set off another worry.

'I should tell him, I suppose, about Lissa. But how? What do you think his reaction will be?'

Tam gave a snort of derision. 'If you want the truth, entirely selfish. The pity of it is, he doesn't give a toss for anything or anyone but himself. Probably never has. The sooner you ask him to leave the better.'

Meg stopped and grasped Tam's arm. 'He's hurting, can't you see? So much he can't even bear to talk about it. We should try to get him to unload the pain then he'll start to heal. It does no good to bottle it up inside. It certainly will do no good at all to throw him out. Where would he go? He has no home now that Broombank has gone.'

Tam growled with exasperation. 'He wouldn't have had a home even if Broombank was still standing. Lanky left it to you, not to Jack. You and him are finished, old history. Aren't you?' Tam's face became suddenly very still. 'You have told him about us? You have given him back his ring?'

She stared at the stones on the path at her feet, kicked one and watched as it rolled along the path to fall with a plop into the beck and be swallowed up by the gushing water. 'Not yet. There hasn't quite been the right moment.' She shivered.

Tam whirled about, putting his hand to his head in despair. 'Right moment? For God's sake, so that's why you creep to my bed like a guilty creature? Don't you see that you make it worse the longer you leave it? You must tell him. Explain that things have changed.'

'I will, I will, Tam. As soon as he seems well enough to take it in. Can't you see how ill he looks? He barely touches his food.'

'He's been a prisoner of war, his stomach has shrunk. But he hasn't been a prisoner all that long, and not in the worst type of concentration camp. He'll survive. Tell him. About us at least. I'm not sure about Lissa.' He grasped Meg's shoulders and gently shook her. 'You have to be fair with the man, and with us.'

Tears stood proud in her grey eyes. 'I know you're right. It's just so difficult to face a man with the fact that he has nothing left. Leave me alone with him this evening and I'll do the deed then. Now kiss me, Tam, please, to make me feel better.'

The moment supper was finished Jack got up and announced he was going out for a walk.

'Oh, where are you going? Up to the tarn? I'll come with you,' Meg said. 'I need to talk to you.'

'No.' He glanced desperately about him, like a ferret caught in a trap. 'Not now, Meg. Not yet.' And he was gone. Much later, she heard him come in. It was about two o'clock in the morning and judging by the noise he made, he was drunk.

–

'Who is that man, Meg?' Lissa asked one morning as they walked to school. 'Why has he come to live with us?'

Meg swallowed. She couldn't tell the child the truth, she couldn't say, 'He's your father.' Not just like that. Jack looked so awful. Nothing like the handsome, swaggering rogue he had once been. He had taken to going out every evening and coming home rolling drunk. Where he got the drink from she did not know, nor care to ask. His mornings were spent in bed and his afternoons in a sullen sprawl by the fire so Meg still hadn't had the much-needed talk with him. Tam was right though, as each day slipped by, the decision to do so became harder to make. So she said nothing to Lissa. No child deserved to have a drunkard foisted upon her as a father.

'He was a sailor in the war. He's staying with us because he has nowhere else to go just at present and he needs time to rest.' He could go to Connie, Meg's inner voice said. She had suggested it at breakfast only this morning and Jack had turned on her in a spitting rage.

'Want to be rid of me, do you?' he'd shouted, making Rust growl and Lissa flinch at his harsh tone. 'My own girl wants me out of the house. The woman who has promised to wait for me for ever. Only you can never trust a woman, can you?'

That had been the moment she should have seized, should have told him that she was no longer his girl, could no longer wait for a man she didn't love. But he'd dropped back in to the chair, put his head into his hands and sobbed like a child. How could she, after that?

'Get that dog out of here. I can't stand the way it glares at me.'

So Meg had despatched Rust to the barn and given Lissa a reassuring cuddle before getting her ready for school.

'Will the sailor go when he's found a house of his own?' she persisted. She liked to have things tidily sorted in her mind. 'He isn't very happy, is he?' She wondered why Meg let him stay. It was all very puzzling.

'He's hurting inside. We must try to be kind to him, try to understand. We don't know what he may have suffered

267

during the war.' Meg smiled at Lissa. 'Here we are. Is it country dancing today?'

Lissa's small face lit up. 'No, Miss Shaw is going to teach us how to make potato prints. Won't that be good?'

Meg laughed. 'Oh, I remember enjoying that. So lovely and messy.' They had reached the playground and she leaned down to kiss Lissa. Two small arms clung about her neck and soft lips returned the kiss.

'I love you, Meg.'

'I love you too, darling.'

'How much?'

'More than all the world.'

'That's all right then,' Lissa said, and as Meg watched her skip away, small bottom wriggling importantly, an almost unbearable tightness stretched across her heart.

–

'Jack, we have to talk. I know things are not quite what you expected. Will you walk on the fells with me so we can be private?' He sat moodily staring into the fire, not answering, the square jaw showing a four-day stubble and the violet eyes shot with red. 'You can't keep all this pain inside you. We need to talk it out.'

A short grunt of impatience was his only response but Meg was determined. Something had to be done and she might never find the courage again. She glanced across at Sally Ann who made encouraging signs. On the pegged rug at Jack's feet, Daniel zoomed up and down with an empty packet of soap flakes cut and stuck into the shape of a car. He was making loud noises in his piping, toddler's voice.

'We'll get no peace here,' she laughed, and tugged gently at his sleeve.

It took some persuasion but at last she got Jack to put on his coat. Out in the yard Rust got up to follow, as he usually did.

'No, boy. You stay here.' He looked affronted but obeyed, lying down again with a sigh of hurt resignation.

They walked up to Brockbarrow Wood. It was here that she had first let him kiss her. How young she had been then, how foolish. It seemed like a lifetime ago. She still remembered the satin smooth bark against her skin, the sound of lapping water, the scent of spring in the air. Such an innocent she had been. Naïve. She had thought the signs of sexual desire on his part were the evidence of love. Now that she had Tam's love, she knew better. She had learned many things over the years. How to survive was one.

Jack sat beneath the same tree and leaned back against it while she sat on the grass some distance away. He was silent. How to begin?

'We can't go on like this, Jack.'

'Too much of a nuisance to you, I suppose.'

'It's not that. You know you are welcome to stay as long as you like, at least… until you find your feet.'

'And how do I do that? Where do I start?' Tears suddenly filled his eyes and a wash of sympathy flooded through her.

'Why don't you tell me about whatever is paining you? I'm sure you'll feel better for it.'

Very slowly, the story began. She heard how his best friend, Len, had been killed. How Jack had to row a small boat to the mainland of Italy, and how he was the only one to survive the operation.

At first she made a few sympathetic noises but then lapsed into silence as he told her about finding the village, and the bakery. Of Lina saving his life and how they became lovers.

'I never meant it to happen,' he said, staring bleakly out over the hump of the fells, tracing the lines of dry stone wall that traversed them while he thought of Italian mountains, biting hunger and soft, pouting lips. 'It was the war. Where she is now I've no idea. Probably married to the damn butcher. Or dead. The Germans would find her as they found me.'

He said very little about the camp the German soldiers took him to, except to say that they were fed scanty rations and their captors took every pleasure in making life difficult for them. He obviously didn't want to talk about it and Meg didn't ask.

'Even after the war ended it seemed to take ages for us to get home.'

'Have you tried to contact her?'

'I wrote once or twice while I was in the camp and then again when I was in hospital in England. She's never replied.'

Meg couldn't find a word of comfort to offer. All these years she had suffered agonies of guilt for finding she had come to love Tam. She had backed away from ending their engagement by means of a heartless letter and all the time Jack had been making love to another girl. Probably not the first one he had enjoyed during the six years away.

'I suppose you want me to go now?' He gazed at her out of those terrible eyes, the bruises beneath black and awesome. 'Though God knows where. Certainly not to Connie. She would only lecture me all day long.'

'I suppose we're related in an odd sort of way, now she's married Joe.'

Jack gave a bitter laugh. 'Nothing on earth would induce me to go and live with your father.' The eyes lit up for a second with a touch of their old wicked humour. 'Life plays funny tricks, eh? Who would have believed it? My sister and your father.'

Meg smiled too, and, looking at her, Jack saw that the young girl with her hair tied up with string was gone. In her place was a lovely young woman, her curly hair framing a face so enchanting that for a moment he was seized with regret at what he had lost.

He leaned across and tilted her chin with sensitive fingers. 'Can you forgive me? You know what I thought about as the Germans dragged me over those Italian mountains? You. You and these mountains here. You wouldn't believe how I longed for them, the wind in my face, the sound of the rushing beck. All I want now, Meg, is a quiet life. I've lost my taste for adventuring, and for other women. I want a fresh start. How about it? Is it too late, do you think?'

There was an eagerness, a desperate pleading in his voice. As if she were his last hope, his only hope for the future. Meg swallowed. 'It's not that easy. I've changed too, Jack. Everything has changed.'

He stared at her. 'It's that Irishman, isn't it?'

She closed her eyes for a moment then plunged into her explanation. 'Tam has asked me to marry him, and I've said yes.' There, she had told him. She opened her eyes and smiled sadly at Jack. 'I'm sorry, but I can't marry you now. There's nothing left between us. I love Tam.'

Jack's face clenched with tight anger. The thought of some Yank moving in on his girl while he was sweating in a miserable POW camp was enough to wipe all the guilt from his own mind. 'Didn't take him long, did it? He's been living here nearly six years, Sally Ann told me.'

'There were circumstances which made it necessary. I was on my own after your father – after Lanky died. I couldn't manage a big farm like Broombank without help.'

'Very cosy.'

'Don't, Jack. There was a war on. Now it's over. It's too late for recriminations.' All Meg's courage to deal with the other, more delicate matter of Lissa and how she came to be here, seemed to have deserted her.

'So what am I supposed to do now?' Jack coldly asked. 'You have my house, my land. Another man is sleeping with my girl. What do I get? A few crumbs from your table? A crust to see me on my way?'

'Oh, Jack, that isn't fair. You have no reason to be so bitter. I could have written to you long since and confessed about Tam but...'

'Why didn't you?'

'It didn't seem right, not while you were away fighting. I kept hoping you'd come home on leave. But you never did. That wasn't my fault. I tried to be fair. Which is more than you were with me.' She had to say it. She had to get it out, now or never. 'I know about you and Kath.'

There was a long, awful silence, then Jack scrambled to his feet, a snarl of disgust on his face. 'I see. You're going to fling that at me too, are you? I know what you're at. You're wanting to switch all the blame on to me.' He prodded his own chest. 'I'm the one who went away to fight the bloody war. I'm the one left with nothing. No home, no job, one demob suit and a few quid in my pocket.

'All right, so Kath and me had a bit of a fling. What of it? We were young, and you were far too serious too soon, and too damned naïve. So I sought a bit of comfort.

Is that a crime? While you, Miss Goody-Two Shoes, live the life of Riley with a man you're not even married to. I remember when you were begging for me to marry you. So don't try to put the blame on me.'

Meg got to her feet to face him properly. 'I don't blame either of us. I loved you once, Jack, you know I did. But things have changed, that's all I'm saying.'

He pushed his face close to hers and flecks of his spittle hit her face. 'They've changed all right. You've got exactly what you've been angling for all along. Every damn thing that I own. You're just like your father. You're Joe Turner all over again.'

Meg was trembling with dismay and anguish. This wasn't how she'd meant the conversation to go. 'That's not true, not fair. I didn't set out to steal Broombank from you. It was Lanky's idea, not mine. You're only talking like this because you're angry and upset.'

'I've good cause to be.'

She drew in a deep, shaking breath, determined to finish the task, now she had started. 'I've paid a fair price for Broombank. A local bank gave me a mortgage and your share has been put into an account in your name. You're all right financially.'

'A few hundred quid?'

'It'll set you up in business somewhere. Buy you a house, whatever you want. I can see that I've hurt you and I'm sorry for that. You're welcome to stay, just as long as it takes for you to feel well again. But that's all. I have my own life to lead now, Jack.'

'And it doesn't include me.'

'No. I'm afraid it doesn't.'

He hadn't taken his eyes from her face through all of this long explanation. 'Damned if I don't still want you!

You're a fine woman, Meg Turner. I'd forgotten just how lovely you are when your dander is up.' One hand snaked around her back and he pulled her to him, holding her fast in his arms when she tried to resist. His kiss was brutal. Unforgiving, possessive and cruelly demanding. When it was done he grinned at her. 'I wouldn't mind trying to light your spark again.'

Meg pushed him away and started to run back down to the house to find Tam standing just below them on the path. He had obviously seen everything.

She ran down to him and grasped his arms to look up into his face. 'It's all right. I've told him.'

Tam didn't speak for a long moment, nor look at her. His eyes were fixed on Jack. 'Good,' he said. 'Let's hope he was listening.'

Chapter 16

As winter approached and the weather turned cold the tensions in Ashlea mounted. Jack made no further effort to look for employment though he continued to waste his demob money on drink.

'Be careful or you'll have nothing left,' Meg warned.

'There's plenty in the bank, or so you tell me.'

'But that's for your future. It's time you found a job, Jack, and a place of your own.'

'What sort of a future can I hope for now? I feel too ill to work. I need a drink to help me sleep.' Outside, a bitter, north-east wind howled, the windows rattling and whining behind the shutters. How could she throw him out?

Tam kept on asking about their wedding. 'Are you going to fix a date?'

'Soon,' she would say. 'Soon.'

'What is that supposed to mean?'

'What I say,' said Meg in exasperation. There was nothing she would have liked better than to buy a pretty frock and marry Tam. But she daren't relax yet, not for a minute. She felt close to breaking point. Her loyalties to the two men, who avoided each other like the plague, were stretched beyond endurance.

'Maybe it'll be me that leaves,' growled Tam, and slammed out of the house, as he so often did these days.

Still she kept the worry about Lissa to herself, not wanting to discuss it with anyone, even Tam. As if by not talking about it she could pretend that the problem did not exist, ever her failing. Yet every day she dreaded the postman bringing a letter from Kath. It would come soon, Meg knew it. Then she must make a choice. Either she must let Lissa go with her mother, or she would fight to keep her with everything she had.

One day Meg escaped down into Kendal to see the bank manager and check on her finances. She'd go mad if she didn't think of something else besides Jack's problems. Whatever happened over Lissa, it was important that she make every effort to restore their home.

She checked that Jack's money was safely waiting for him, then she paid visits to the War Committee, the Town Council, and her accountant. She even treated herself to tea and scones in a little shop in the Shambles. When she arrived back home later that afternoon she was tired from her exertions but elated.

'The Government have agreed to put back my roof and repair the kitchen and dairy,' she announced, and Sally Ann cheered while Tam lifted her off her feet and swung her round in a hug of delight.

'Well done.'

'No listen, there's more.' Meg was bubbling over with excitement. 'I saw my accountant and he was very impressed with us. We've actually gone into profit this year. Father is paid off. So we are free of debt. What do you think of that?'

Now even the three children caught her excitement and started to dance about and yell, though they couldn't have said quite why. Rust bounded lopsidedly with them, barking delightedly, while the three adults looked on, laughing.

'Would you believe it? Joe has arranged for all decisions about Ashlea to be made by me until such time as he returns from Grange-Over-Sands, or Sally Ann marries again and the boys get a new father.'

Sally Ann flushed dark red. 'Who said anything about marriage? I couldn't. I haven't even given it a thought.'

'One day you will. As Father says, you're too young to live life all on your own, Sal.' Meg kissed her plump cheek. 'And too pretty. But until Broombank is restored, and it won't be a quick job, perhaps we can carry on as we are? It's a bit of a squash, but would you mind?'

'Would I mind? I'd mind if you walked out and left me. How could I run this farm on me own? Anyway, I need your company, Meg. It'd be wicked lonely without you. I'll do the cooking and look after the children, and gladly take on the Saturday market which I know you're not too keen on.'

'That's settled then. Tam and me can look after the animals and the land.'

'A perfect partnership.'

'We'll still need more labour,' Tam said. 'The POWs will be going home soon. Next March, I heard.'

'Broombank will be nowhere near finished by then. We'll worry about that later. Oh, and the bank manager is very happy to make us a loan, if we need it, to do any interior repairs when the building work is done.'

Tam folded his arms and regarded her with open admiration. 'There's no stopping you once you get going, is there?'

Jack, listening to all of this from the corner, smiled sourly. 'Broombank is everything. Sell her soul for it, she would.'

'It would be wiser, I'm thinking, for you to hold your tongue,' Tam said quietly.

'Didn't she tell you that she gave her virginity for that farm?' Jack smirked. 'To me.'

Meg gasped, all colour running from her face. 'How can you say such a thing?'

'You need that filthy tongue of yours clipped out, and I might just be the man to do it.' Tam leapt forward and Meg had to wrench at his arm, to stop him from planting a fist right in Jack's face.

'Leave it, Tam. It really doesn't matter.'

But Tam grasped hold of Jack's collar and hauled him to his feet. 'Apologise for that remark. Don't think you can throw your weight about here. Meg has had to learn to fight for a lot of things these last five or six years. She's not the pushover she might once have been and she can certainly handle worms like you these days. So can I.'

'You have some use then?'

'And what is that supposed to mean?'

Tam was turning white, then red, with anger. Meg felt his whole body tense as again she held fast to his arm, trying to urge him into calm. 'Don't, Tam, don't let him get to you.'

Jack's laugh was deeply unpleasant. 'Seems to me you've got a cushy number here. You can sleep with Meg, live in her house and enjoy her success with no effort on your part whatsoever. Isn't that always the way of it for you Irish? There's a name for men like you, if I could only think what it is. Just as there's a name for women like her.'

'Damn you, Lawson. You can say what you like about me, but I'll not have you besmirch Meg's name. If it weren't for the children having to watch, I'd tear you limb from limb and throw you out of the window to the dogs.'

Jack gave a sardonic laugh. 'You and whose army?'

'No, Tam,' Meg screamed, when he jerked forward, fists clenched.

'Tell him to shut his mouth then or I'll do it for him.' Snatching himself free from her, he strode out of the house. The door rocked on its hinges behind him.

—

Two days later Tam came in and announced that he'd been offered a job.

'To them that hath,' muttered Jack, and Tam glared at him.

Meg paled visibly. 'What are you talking about? You've got a job already. Here with me.'

'I'm thinking mebbe it's time I did something on me own.'

'Where? What is this job?' She was trying to work out how it was her life was suddenly falling apart, just when she'd thought everything was going smoothly at last.

'Lord Carnsworth is looking for someone to see to his horses. He has a team he uses in the trotting races. It'd suit me down to the ground, don't you think?'

It would. There was no doubt that Tam was good with horses. Oh, but how could he desert her like this? Just when she was about to rebuild Broombank. And they could start to rebuild their own life, just as soon as they'd sorted Jack out. 'You're not going to do it though, are you? How would I manage without you?'

Tam gave her an odd look, most unlike himself. 'You managed when I was in the army.'

'That was different. I had no choice.'

'I wouldn't leave you in a mess. I'd give you what time I could until you found a replacement.'

Meg glanced at the interested faces all about her. 'Do you think we could discuss this somewhere else?'

She put on her coat and walked outside. Tam followed.

—

In the dimness of the dusty barn he faced her, and Meg shivered at the remoteness of his expression.

'Why are you not pleased for me?' he asked.

'How can I be? I can't grasp why you're doing this.'

'Maybe because I want to.'

'It's because of what Jack said, isn't it? You hate it because he accused you of living on me, of being a parasite.'

'I don't recall him using that word exactly, but yes, that was what he meant, I dare say. Mebbe he had a point. Broombank is yours. The sheep are yours. I help, but as I've said before, I'm only the hired man.'

'You are my future husband.'

'The emphasis being on the word future, it seems,' he said softly.

Meg had the grace to blush. Then she moved to him and put her arms about him. 'Perhaps I was wrong about waiting for Jack to find a job. We could get married next week if you like. Isn't it possible to get a special licence?'

Tam's eyebrows rose. 'So what's brought this on?'

'I love you.' She leaned against him, put her arms about his neck. 'I have always loved you, and I don't want to lose you. It's just that things have been so confused, so difficult.'

'When are you going to send him away?'

'I beg your pardon?'

'You heard me.'

Meg swallowed. 'He's hurting. Jack feels he has fought a war for six years and come back to nothing. He needs time. Surely you can understand how he feels?'

'That's important, is it? How Jack feels? Jack's sensitive nature. Jack's needs. Why do they always seem to come first? What about *my* needs? What about us?'

Meg had never seen him so cold, so angry. She put her hands to his face, smoothing his cheeks, his lips, his throat, but he twitched away from her.

'Will I tell you something, Meg Turner? You're a difficult woman to pin down. What time you don't spend on your sheep and planning the rebuilding of your farm, you spend worrying over Jack, all mixed up with your own guilt. Though why you should feel guilty is beyond me. Lanky left the farm to you, fair and square. Isn't it time you stopped crucifying yourself for that? What do you owe Jack? Nothing, I'm thinking, after the way he treated you.'

'I can't turn him out to walk the streets, can I?'

'He has a sister.'

'He won't go to her. Particularly now she's married to Joe. He never could cope with my father. I wondered if perhaps I could give him a bit of land. I could spare thirty or forty acres to give him a start. And he could get permission to build a house on it, in time.'

Tam had become very still. 'And where would he live in the meantime?'

'He could rent a cottage somewhere nearby.'

'So he'd live on our doorstep? For ever?' Tam turned away from her in disgust and it cut straight to the heart

281

of her that he seemed so against everything she suggested. 'Sure and it goes without saying, Meg Turner, that I don't want that little toad living anywhere near us.'

A surge of anger went through her at Tam's reaction. 'You are so obstinate. Just as selfish as he is. Why will you not see anyone else's point of view?' She tossed back her curls with a defiant sweep of the hand. Why wouldn't he understand how she needed to do this? For Lanky. And for Lissa. She said as much now.

'Have you told him yet, about Lissa?'

'No. I keep thinking that it's Kath's responsibility, not mine. I have to consider Lissa too.'

'Good,' said Tam crisply. 'At least you're thinking sensibly about that.' His expression softened slightly. 'What about Kath. When is she coming? Has she written again?'

Meg swallowed. 'No firm date yet.'

'Why didn't you tell me? Why did I have to hear about her letter from Sally Ann?'

'Sally Ann knows nothing about Lissa.'

'I'm aware of that. She just told me how surprised you were to get a letter from Kath and how you went to her parents and they didn't want to know. Are secrets such a good idea, Meg? Isn't it time you stopped saving everyone's feelings and brought it all out into the open? Doesn't Lissa deserve that much?'

'I don't want to think about it. I keep hoping Kath won't come.' She lifted her chin a notch. 'But if she does, I mean to put my case for keeping Lissa. She is six years old and should have some say in her life.'

'Good for you.'

'And I will tell Lissa, I promise.'

'When?'

Meg glanced about her, as if cornered. 'Soon.' Tam reached for her then, a smile in his eyes. 'See that you do.' But if he had been having second thoughts about taking this new job, Meg's next words soon stopped them.

'There's something else. I think it would be best, less embarrassing, while Jack is staying with us, if we occupied separate rooms. Would you mind?'

Tam's green eyes narrowed, sparkling like shards of ice. He released her then, and his hands fell to his sides in a gesture of despair. 'You're telling me you no longer want me in your bed?'

Meg felt a stirring of disquiet but stubbornly kept to her request. 'I'm saying that for the moment at least, our privacy is gone, and I can't cope with that. It won't be for long, just till we work out a way of getting him started some place else. I can't bear the thought of Jack at the other side of the wall, listening to us. You do understand, don't you?' Her cheeks were a hot pink but Tam's were frozen white.

'Yes, I understand perfectly. You'll fight for the land and Broombank. You'll fight for Lissa. But will you fight for me?' He shook his head, slowly, from side to side.

'Damn you, Tam O'Cleary.' She was near to tears and hated herself for this show of weakness. 'That's not true and you know it.'

He made a disbelieving grunt deep in his throat. 'That's exactly the way it is, Meg Turner. I hate to sound melodramatic, since you'll only accuse me of more Irish blarney, but it's long past time I said it. It's him or me. Plain and simple. Either he leaves or I do.'

'You're right. That would be melodramatic. Certainly very silly.' She turned to go. 'If you want your supper you'd best be quick about it. It'll be stone cold by now.'

'Have I not made myself clear?'

'Abundantly,' she said. 'But I don't answer to threats.'

'I'll not wed you while your former lover is living in your house. Is that plain enough for you?'

'*Tam!*'

'It's the truth, is it not? If you don't want me in your bed, then it seems to me that mebbe you don't want me in your life at all. It's as simple as that.'

'No, it's not.'

'It is to me.'

'Go then, if that's what you want,' she said, anger making her reckless as tears brimmed. And she stalked off, head high, back to the house. Tam did not follow her.

Meg moved his things into the small loft room she had used as a girl, and lay alone, unsleeping, in the big bed that night. In the morning, she found that he had packed his bag and gone. As it turned out it was only to the lodge house on Lord Carnsworth's estate a few miles up the road, but it might as well have been a million miles.

—

Christmas 1946 was quiet and dull. Sally Ann, Meg and the children, still with Jack present, spent it alone. Joe was too ill to travel but, it seemed, had quite taken to life in Grange-Over-Sand, and for the time being at least meant to stay.

Meg had seen little of Tam in recent months. Busy settling in to his new job, she caught tantalising glimpses of him taking the horses out as she walked Lissa to and from school. He would nod to her from a distance as if they were strangers. She begged Sally Ann to take on this task so that she need never be taunted by the sight of him, so near and yet so far. Heavily disapproving, her sister-in-law agreed.

'I hate to say it but I would even welcome Connie right now,' Meg confessed as the two women sat together on New Year's Day alone by the fire. Jack was out, drinking as usual, and the children were tucked up in bed, hopefully asleep.

'The children enjoyed it. Did you see their faces when they found oranges in their stockings for the first time ever?'

'You perform miracles, Sal, you really do. Sometimes I wonder what we won the war for. Things have seemed to be tougher than ever this year. The rationing goes worse, even bread now.'

'It'll get better soon.'

'And look at us. What a pair we are. It seems ironic that Ashlea has become almost an all female household when once it was very much male, with women kept very firmly in their place. Sad in a way. Is this how we are doomed to spend our lives, Sal? As women with children and no men?'

Sally Ann gazed shrewdly at Meg. 'You could get Tam back tomorrow if you really wanted.'

'By turning Jack out in the snow? I couldn't be so heartless. I'm disappointed in Tam.' Her voice broke. 'I thought he'd more patience, more compassion, and more love for me.'

Sally Ann gazed morosely into her sherry glass and sighed. 'More patience? He's waited near six years for you. What can you expect? He's jealous.'

'He's behaving foolishly. How can that be love?'

'He still works on your land every day, after he's finished with the horses. What's that if not love?'

Meg shook her head, feeling bleak and empty inside, almost taking pleasure in hurting herself as much as possible. 'It won't last, I know it won't. Once the spring comes, before lambing starts, I'll have to find someone else to replace him.'

'There's something else, I can tell. I've sensed an edginess in you for weeks, and it's gone worse over Christmas. It's not like you to be so gloomy. Come on, Meg, what is it? What else is troubling you?'

Meg set her sherry glass carefully on the mantelpiece and drew in a shaky breath. 'Perfectly simple, actually. As well as losing Tam, I'm going to lose Lissa. There was a letter in Kath's Christmas card. She'll be here soon, in the New Year.'

'Kath? What has Kath to do with Lissa?' Finally, at last, Meg told her the secret, all of it. She emptied her heart while Sally Ann sat open-mouthed.

'Oh, my God.' Sally Ann was on her feet, wrapping her arms about Meg, and despite a very decided determination not to cry, her tears were flowing fast. 'Why didn't you tell me before? Does Tam know?'

Meg nodded, struggling to find a handkerchief to stop the flow. 'Tam and Effie were both there when I brought Lissa home. He's always known. But Lissa doesn't and I still have to find the courage to tell her. And how can I, with Jack behaving the way he is? Oh, it's all too terrible for words. What am I to do, Sal? What am I to do?'

Chapter 17

1947

Katherine Ellis drew up to Ashlea in a smart little Morris on the first day of February. She had given due notice of her arrival, asking to take Lissa out for the day, and Meg had been ready hours too soon, so tense was she about the forthcoming meeting. The bitterly cold morning had dragged by in an agony of suspense, Meg unable to settle to anything. How would she feel about facing Kath again? What would she say about Jack and the betrayal? What would Kath say? And how would Lissa react?

The night before, Meg had sat Lissa upon her lap and explained to her, as simply and honestly as she could, who Kath was. She decided to make no mention of Jack at this stage.

'Didn't I tell you that your mother would come for you one day?'

Lissa had said nothing for a long time. Almost seven years old now, her baby chubbiness was being replaced by a schoolgirl legginess that would one day blossom into beauty. Her black curls were kept cropped short and though these and the pansy eyes were all Jack, there was much in her that Kath would recognise as her own.

'Will she love me?' It was a most reasonable question and Meg answered it promptly.

'Of course she will love you. How could she fail to love you? You don't want me to tell her how naughty you really are, do you?' Meg teased but Lissa didn't giggle in response, as she usually did. She turned and looked at Meg with her direct gaze so like Kath's own.

'More than all the world?'

Meg swallowed. After a moment's panicking thought, she let her shoulders sag with resignation. 'That's not a fair question, Lissa, and you know it. Come on, let's go upstairs and choose which dress you are going to wear tomorrow. Shall it be the blue or the pink from your extensive wardrobe?'

Lissa had been unusually quiet as Meg tucked her into bed that night and was equally so now as they both stood, hand in hand, listening to the high heels clicking over the slate slabs of the yard. Suddenly making a decision, Meg turned to Sally Ann.

'Take Lissa and the other children upstairs. I'd like to speak to her first on my own.'

When Sally Ann had gone, Meg drew in a shaky breath and opened the door.

Had she not been so concerned for her own feelings, she might have seen evidence of Kath's own nervousness. In the way she picked at the tan kid gloves, or flicked unseen dust from her warm swagger coat with its smart fur collar. But Meg's head was filled with panic and her eyes saw only a beautiful, carefully composed woman standing on her doorstep, like a threat. True there was some evidence of change. The wide, smiling lips did not sport the usual scarlet lipstick, and the hair was mouse brown beneath a leaf green beret, though that was still tilted provocatively to one side.

The one-time friends stood and assessed one another as the long years between fell away. It seemed only yesterday that they had stood, awkward and unspeaking, on Lime Street Station, the baby thrust into Meg's arms as Kath ran from her life.

'Hello, Meg. How are you?' In the ensuing silence she answered her own question, as had ever been her style. 'You look well.'

Meg held open the door for Kath to step inside.

She took a few steps into the room, glancing about her. 'It's just the same as I remember it. Where's Tam? I thought you said in your letter that he was working here.'

Meg cleared her throat, though emotion still blocked it. 'He is. He was. He's out at the moment.' Her voice tailed off into misery. I still pray nightly that he will return, her mind continued silently.

Kath turned on her in surprise, reading much more into Meg's expression than she was intended to see but tactfully not commenting upon it. 'Have you seen Jack?'

'Yes. He arrived some months ago. Looking pretty sick.'

'He's still here?'

'He has nowhere else to go.'

'So you, soft hearted little fool that you are, let him in. Darling Meg, if I was too selfish, then you were always far too generous. Mix us together and we might make one good one, two sides of one coin. Unfortunately it doesn't work that way. Let Jack go. He's no good.' She was shaking her head at Meg, her eyes sad but very certain. 'You know all that, deep in your heart. And it's not the first time I've said it.'

Meg felt a surge of resentment that Kath should walk into her house and immediately start issuing advice.

Perhaps she hadn't changed so much after all. 'Would you like a cup of tea?'

'I could murder a strong whisky but I'll settle for tea if that's all you've got.'

Meg looked startled for a moment, then let out a burst of laughter. 'My, you have changed. Gin and tonic was always your tipple.'

They sat together over the tea, not speaking for a long time. The log fire crackled and the grandfather clock ticked away the minutes, while both remained locked in their own private thoughts.

Meg couldn't quite frame the words that tumbled about in her brain. Why did you do it? What was it about our friendship that permitted you to hurt me so cruelly? She stayed silent.

It was Kath who finally spoke. 'Is she here?'

'Yes. She's upstairs, with Sal.'

'I heard about Dan, and your friend Effie. I'm sorry.'

'Thanks.'

'It was a sod, this war, wasn't it? Thank God it's over at last. I suppose I was lucky. Didn't lose anyone I loved. Though right at the end a Mosquito burned to a crisp on landing and Wade only just got out in time. One of the ground crew who helped him wasn't so lucky.'

She was talking for the sake of it. They both knew it. This wasn't the moment for swapping war stories.

'She doesn't like being called Melissa,' Meg said. 'I'm to tell you that. And she doesn't care for cheese. It brings her out in a rash.'

Kath stared at Meg, her gaze haunted but she made no comment.

Meg continued to speak now, very quietly and methodically, as if she had worked it all out. 'Sometimes, at night, she wakes up and cries. She has only a half memory of the bomb landing on Broombank but it has affected her. I still send prayers of thanks that she was out walking with your father at the time. But she still hears the sound of the plane sometimes, sees the bright light, the terrible flames that brought death. But then at other times when she wakes it might just be a tummy upset or worry over a mental arithmetic test at school.' Meg smiled. 'Sums aren't her strong point.'

'I understand what you're trying to tell me,' Kath said softly. 'I know that if I take her with me, I shall have a lot to learn.'

Meg swallowed. It had to be said, and now was as good a time as any. She straightened her spine and looked Kath straight in the eye. 'I have brought her up as if she were my own child. I love her as if she were. But Lissa is six, very nearly seven, and she wants to have a say in her own destiny. If she goes with you to Canada, it has to be her decision, not yours. I'm aware of your rights as her natural mother, but if you try to force her, to exercise those rights, then I shall fight you to the highest court in the land, even if it costs me every last penny I have.' Meg stopped to draw breath. There, she had said it. Tam would be proud of her. She was proud of herself, for all her heart was pumping like a traction engine.

Kath simply stared at her, unblinking. 'I would like to see her now.'

—

Meg sat all day in the same place. She chose a corner of the dry stone wall that ran from the back of the house to the barn. From here she would get the first glimpse of the car returning up the lane without being seen herself. It had been the longest day in her life so far. She couldn't eat, she couldn't talk, she couldn't even think.

Nothingness seemed to fill her mind and she wanted to go on feeling nothing, being nothing. It was less painful that way. The alternative, to consider what her life would be like without Lissa, without Tam, was too terrible for words.

Now that she was faced with losing everything she wondered at her own lack of ability to make a decision. She was decisive enough with the land, with the sheep. Why so vulnerable when it came to her personal life?

She looked at her beloved land, how it had been lifted and tipped sideways as if by some playful giant's hand, causing rocks bigger than a house to slide and roll and settle in dangerous heaps. Her life felt like that, as if it were slipping out of control.

In her hand she held Lanky's Luckpenny. Usually she kept it safe, on her dressing table in her room. Today she had felt the need of it by her. It was all foolish superstition, of course. She knew that. But somehow it helped. As if Lanky were still here with her when she needed a friend, wishing her well.

At long last the little car came into view, bumping up the stony track into the farmyard. It pulled to a halt at the door and Lissa was out in a second, scampering towards Meg, her small face alight with excitement. Meg's heart shot through with pain. Did this joy mean that the day had gone well?

'What do you think, Meg, we saw some horses.'

'Did you, darling? Where was that?' Meg pulled stiff lips into a smile.

'We went to Appleby, to watch the harness racing. It was so exciting. Kath says I could perhaps have a pony of my own one day, when I'm old enough to look after it properly.' The cheeks were flushed pink, a quiver with delight. 'Wouldn't that be lovely, to have a pony of my own? Wade has plenty of horses in Canada, Kath says. He's a lawyer but wants to have a whole farm of them. Wouldn't that be grand?'

Meg was unable to speak for fear of it coming out all croaky. Kath came to join them. 'I wasn't trying to bribe her,' she said. 'She could keep the pony here, if she wanted to. It would simply be a gift.'

'Here?' If she stays, Meg thought. If she isn't enticed away to Canada by stories of riches, and horses in plenty. Meg responded to Kath's warmth with coolness. 'I'm sure Tam could find her a pony when the time was right.'

'I suppose he could.' Kath's face looked suddenly haunted and she turned away, to gaze out over the mountains, and there was a new rigidity to the figure, a stiffness about the mouth that hadn't been there before. Meg turned to Lissa. 'Go inside, sweetheart. I think Sally Ann has your tea ready. I'll be in later.'

'Bye, Kath,' said Lissa. 'Wait till I tell Nick where I've been today. He'll be *green* with jealousy.' And she ran off, filled with eagerness to tell her tale.

When the kitchen door clanged shut, Meg faced Kath. 'Well? How did it go? You seem to have made a good impression.'

'Very well. She is a delightful child, Meg. You should be proud of her.'

'I am.'

'Do you mind if we walk a bit, away from the kitchen window? Show me your sheep, or whatever you are doing with Broombank. I've heard enough about them today.'

Meg tried a chuckle but it came out sounding forced and unnatural. 'I can believe it. Lissa loves the farm and is proving to be a great help already.' Everything she said sounded as if she were trying to make a point. One that Kath did not fail to miss.

'She loves the lambs best, she told me.'

'Yes.'

They walked for a while and Meg started to tell Kath, hesitantly at first, of her efforts to make a go of the farm. She told of how she had struggled with her first lambing season, helped by Effie, the loyalty of Rust, at this very moment with his nose at her heel, as usual.

She spoke of the obstinacy of the bank in refusing at first to give her a mortgage. 'Your father put in a word for me there. You'll be going to see him before you leave?'

'I – I hadn't decided.'

'I think you should. Your mother is as intransigent as ever, but your father... Well, he'd really like to see you, Kath. In all these years he's never said a word against you, not once. And treading a path between you and your mother has not been easy for him.'

Kath laughed. 'I can well believe it.' She stared down for a moment, at her smart shining town shoes, unsuitable for stony sheep trods. 'All right, I'll call in. I'd like to see how they are.'

They reached the bend in the road where a stile into the field led down to Whinstone Gill and Kath gave a sad little smile. 'Do you remember that day when you found me sunbathing? Jack was hiding in the bushes. Rust realised it but you didn't.'

'I didn't see because I didn't want to see. There are no shades over my eyes now. I hope I'm not quite so easy to take advantage of these days.'

'And I hope that I am not so selfish. I've certainly been at the receiving end of some malice myself in recent years.' Kath glanced at Meg's face. 'I hope you don't bear me any. I would like us to remain friends.'

There was a small, strained silence before Meg spoke. 'You betrayed me. Both of you. But I've put the pain behind me. All that matters to me now is Lissa. She is the one good thing that has come out of all this. Lissa comes first in everything.'

A figure loomed suddenly on the path, lurching around the corner towards them.

'Well, if it isn't Madam Ellis herself.'

'Jack.'

'Not in uniform? Pity. It suited you. Same old Katherine back again. Done up to the nines as usual.'

'No.' Kath shook her head. 'Not quite the same old Katherine. The war has changed even me. I've learned to deal more considerately with other people's feelings these days. How about you? It doesn't seem to have done you much good.'

Meg stood silent for a moment, wondering how best to cope with this reunion for which she had waited for so long.

'Shall we go back for tea?' she suggested, kicking herself for sounding so mundane. 'Or a glass of sherry perhaps?'

Both ignored her. Meg still hadn't faced Jack with the truth about Lissa, or told him why Kath had come today. She worried over what would happen when he found out. Was it right to want so desperately to protect Lissa that she was prepared to do anything, even cheat Jack out of his rights? Or was it cowardice?

Kath was gazing at him with an expression close to contempt on her beautiful face. 'I'm surprised you've let this idiot back into the house, Meg. Haven't you learned your lesson yet?'

Startled by this unexpected attack, Meg opened her mouth to protest then closed it again. It was too uncomfortably close to the truth to deny.

'Who are you calling an idiot?'

Kath's eyes glazed with frost. 'You like having women fawning over you, don't you? You enjoyed having both of us on a string, the tantalising pleasure of having two women want you. For a time it was fun. I'll admit that. I was young and selfish enough to go along with it. But let me bring you up to date. Jack Lawson, I've grown up since then. I've seen the raw side of life, and you know what? I've learned it hurts when someone rides rough shod over you. It's not so much fate that affects our lives, but other people. I hope I've learned to be less selfish. I've certainly survived, without you, without my parents, without help from anyone. Very much, I suspect, as Meg too has learned to survive, working this farm through all weathers.

'Times have changed. When I look at you now, I wonder what I ever saw in you. I feel mighty relieved that I escaped. Who knows what could have happened if I hadn't been forced, by circumstance shall we say, to go away and make a new future for myself.'

She went to Meg and took her hands between her own. 'We vowed to be friends, the three of us, for all time. I know how we both hurt you, and I'm sorry for it. If I could go back and change things, I would, Meg. I've wished that so many times over the years.'

'It's Meg's fault all this happened,' Jack burst in. 'Panting for me she was. Desperate to be loved. But all she really cared about was that damned farm.'

Kath swung round upon him. 'With a father like she had, she needed love, and what was so wrong with that? Did you have to take advantage of that fact so cruelly? You didn't need to give her a ring and fool her into thinking it was going to be orange blossom and roses all the way. If you'd been fair and honest with her she could have made her own choice.'

'Stop it.' Meg's voice was quiet, but very strong. 'Stop it, the pair of you. I've had enough of your squabbling. Do you take me for a complete fool? If I made mistakes in the past I've had plenty of time to regret them, as we all have.

'When your father left this land to me, Jack, he gave me a Luckpenny to go with it. Always give something back, he said, if you want to prosper. Well, I followed that advice and the Luckpenny did bring me success and good fortune, gained through care and hard work. It didn't save Broombank from the bomb but I know that if I put effort into it, I can build again. You have to give to receive, to make your own luck. It's true of land, of sheep, and most of all, of people.

'Perhaps I did fail you, Jack, by too often putting my interest in the farm first. It was a mistake I've repeated since, before the learning of it sank in. One I don't intend to make again. Ever. But this doesn't simply concern we three any more. There is a fourth party involved. Whose feelings are far more important than mine.'

'What fourth party?' Jack asked, in scathing tones. 'That bloody Irishman, I suppose.'

A long, telling silence in which both women looked into each other's eyes and for a moment they were girls again, sharing secrets. Despite their differences a message passed between them, an understanding. Kath smiled. There was such serenity in that smile that Meg caught her breath. It was going to be all right. She knew it.

'And if she does love the Irishman, what of it?' Kath said. 'I for one would applaud that. Tam is a fine man. Exactly what Meg needs and deserves. I hope you will both be very happy.' She leaned forward and kissed Meg on the cheek. She smelled of some expensive French perfume and the thought flashed through Meg's mind how typical it was of Kath to marry money.

Jack turned away. 'Huh. I'm not staying here to listen to such soppy talk. It's all right for some, those who've had an easy war. I don't have to listen to you, you interfering bitch. I'm going for a walk.'

'You mean a drink.' Meg froze him with the unexpected harshness in her tone.

'What if I do? A man can please himself what he does with his time, I suppose.'

'Not in my house he can't. But I can please myself what I do with my life, my home, and my child.' Meg drew in a deep breath. 'You can pack your bags, Jack Lawson. You've had ample time to sort yourself out. All you do is sit about and feel sorry for yourself. You won't find work sulking at my fireside.'

'What did you say?'

'You heard. You might have had a tough war. So have many others. We've all suffered in our own way. Now it's time to start again. This came for you this morning.' She handed him a letter. 'It's from a Lina Ruggierri.'

'Lina? My Lina?' Meg was astonished, and moved despite herself, to see the drunkenness fall from him and how eagerly he ripped open the envelope.

'It's addressed to me because I wrote to her in Italy. She was taken prisoner, like you, but is home again now. And it seems she wants you. So you can go to her. You have the money to start again in a new country if you've a mind to. Rebuild your life, Jack, as my father has, as Rust here had to do once.' The dog perked up its ears at the sound of its name but did not get up from where it lay, patiently waiting for her. 'As we all have to do.'

'I will,' Jack said, looking somewhat shamefaced at last. 'I'm grateful, Meg, for your finding her. I don't really deserve this.'

She smiled at him then. 'No, you don't. Go on. What are you waiting for? Haven't you some packing to do?'

'I have that.' And he turned on his heel and hurried away down the lane.

Kath shook her head in amazement. 'Still the same generous Meg.'

'I hope I'll always be that. As for you, Katherine Ellis, just remember you're not having Lissa. Not now, not ever. She is a part of me now, a part of this land, and will remain so. She has no wish to leave and I don't intend to make her. Now all of that is quite settled, perhaps we could go and try a slice of Sally Ann's cake. It has fruit in it today, I believe.'

—

Meg was struggling through thick snow up Dundale Knott. It would have taxed a man, let alone a woman. But there was no alternative.

The snow had been piling up for weeks till it was level with the height of the wooden gate that led into what once had been a lane. They'd had to tunnel through it to get out of the house.

The arctic winter of 1947 was proving to be the worst in living memory, beating all previous records. Meg hadn't seen a soul reach her farm in weeks. Britain had ground to a halt as snow piled in fourteen foot drifts across roads and rail tracks. Power stations and factories had closed down from lack of fuel.

If only Tam were here. The snow had started soon after Kath's visit and she hadn't seen him since. It was as if he had rid his life of her. But how could she rid hers of him when she loved him so? An impossible prospect that filled her with a gnawing misery far worse than the bitter cold.

The roof was back on Broombank, so the property was at last properly protected from the worst of the weather. Once spring came the builders would start work on the kitchen and the dairy. She had not yet moved back in, anxious though she was to be near her animals. Ashlea was marginally warmer and she preferred to stay with Sally Ann and the three children, living largely by candlelight, eating their way through a rapidly emptying larder. Seven long, cold weeks when the only way to keep warm much of the time was for them all to sleep together in one big bed.

Here on the fellside were her sheep, stuck fast in the drifts, and she must get to them. The most hated and difficult part of a shepherd's life but it must be done. At her side, struggling with equal difficulty but steadfast loyalty, were Tess and Ben, and of course her lovely Rust.

He lolloped to a halt, wagged his tail furiously and started to bark. 'What have you found, boy?'

A telling hump of snow. Meg stopped too, to gain her breath. She must be mad. No French perfume for her, she thought, wanting to laugh at the very idea, despite the cold.

Yet she would choose no other life. She'd wanted to prove something in that long ago April when she had been young, not simply to Joe but to herself too. And she had surely succeeded.

Despite all the difficulties, all the problems she'd faced, despite the knowledge that it would take some time to restore Broombank, and her flock of sheep to what they would have been if the bomb had not dropped, she would have it no other way. She could survive. Meg knew that now. But she'd paid a price. She had lost Tam through her stubbornness and misguided loyalty. One day Lissa might visit Canada to see her mother and the proposed horse ranch. She might like it and decide to stay. Nothing in life was certain.

For now Meg could only do her best, concentrate on the lambing which had started with a vengeance. There was no one but herself to care for them and many depending upon her now that Joe and Dan were gone. She'd lost too many lambs already so must give them her undivided attention as the nightmare of the snow continued relentlessly.

Sally Ann, and the children too, had been forced to work day after day, for as long as there was light, carrying hay and ash croppings up on sleds to those sheep who were barely coping, carrying down on the same sleds those that weren't. They'd spent days bringing as many sheep as they could find into the intake fields but it was an impossible task. There were too many and their efforts seemed inadequate by comparison. Too easily one could disappear in moments beneath a drift of snow when the helm wind tore across the fells, or the blizzards raged in a storm the like of which no man had seen in a century or more.

'Come on, dig. It'll be dark soon,' Meg told her dogs. 'We must hurry.' They understood her perfectly and dug with their front paws as furiously as she dug with her shovel. 'Wait. I can feel her.' Meg thrust her hands down in to the icy cold and caught hold of sodden wool. She started to pull. Nothing moved.

'And what is it you think you are doing, woman? You'll never do it that way. Is it mad you are?'

Meg fell forward into the snow, getting half buried in it herself, so shocked was she by the voice coming unexpectedly out of nowhere.

Tam's face was grinning down at her. 'What is it this time you'd be wanting me to rescue for you? If it's not a dog, then it's your whole flock of sheep. Is that the way of it?'

She sat up and started to dust the icy snow off herself, for he would make no move to help her, she knew that. She loved that in him, the way he never deprived her of her independence. But perhaps he was no more than a mirage, a snow sickness. She'd been on her own in this awful whiteness so long she could be hallucinating.

'Well, are you going to sit there all day or must I do the work all by meself? Dear Lord, can you not be safe to leave for a moment?'

'It was more than a moment,' she said, finding her voice at last. 'Where the hell were you when I needed you?'

Tam acknowledged the criticism with a wry smile. 'In Ireland, buying horses. And if you don't show a bit more gratitude, I'll wish that I'd stayed.'

Meg grinned at him, feeling suddenly light headed.

'Start digging here, below the sheep. Then we can pull her forward,' Tam instructed.

It took nearly an hour to clear the drift from around the two animals, huddled together, frozen to the wall against which they had run to shelter.

'Take care. Don't alarm them, they're in shock,' Meg warned. 'Come along, my beauties. Be brave, take a few steps.'

'They can't. They're stuck fast.' Tam glanced backwards down the slope. 'Once they do move, they might panic, blinded by the snow. And if we lose them, they'll go right down the scree and end up buried for ever at the bottom.'

'I know it.'

'Get your crook round that one's neck.'

Meg struggled to do so. They were fine sheep, traumatised, as so many she had found, by the freezing cold.

'Has he gone then?'

She didn't ask who he meant. 'Oh yes. Back to Italy. To Lina. I found her for him.'

'Ah. That was clever of you.'

'One has to take the initiative sometimes, I believe, to rid oneself of a problem.'

'Indeed one does. Here she comes, catch her.' One ewe had broken free and started to slide towards them. The wool tore from one side of her body, and remained stuck fast to the wall. But she was free and happily allowed them to pack her on to the sled. The second ewe had feet so raw, drops of blood scattered over the snow.

'She'll be all right,' Meg said. 'I'll make her some boots till they heal.'

'My God, Meg, stubborn and soft-hearted as you are, I do love you.'

'I love you, Tam. Don't leave me again, not ever. If you do, I'll… Oh, I don't know what I'd do.'

Tam grinned. 'Then it's a good job the question won't ever arise. Because I hate to see you lost for words, Meg Turner. Or can I soon start calling you O'Cleary?'

'Oh, yes please. Just as soon as you can get me on a sled and carry me into town.' Then he kissed her, the freezing prickles of his stubble scraping her chin raw, and she loved that too.

'What about Lissa?'

'She's staying here with us. Is that all right with you, Tam?'

'My darling girl. Anything is all right by me, so long as I have you.'

Meg wriggled from his grasp, a smile so wide upon her face it made her look like a happy child. 'Me and my sheep, don't forget.'

Tam reached for the rope to guide the sled. 'As if I could.'